I0762297

Extension

by

Melody Kepler

This is a work of fiction. Names, characters, businesses, places, events, locales, and incidents are either the products of the author's imagination or used in a fictitious manner. Any resemblance to actual persons, living or dead, or actual events is purely coincidental.

ISBN-13 Hardcover: 978-1-7347130-2-2

ISBN-13 Paperback: 978-1-7347130-3-9

E-book ISBN: 978-1-7347130-1-5

First edition: April 2020

Author website: www.keplerpstudios.com

Cover Created by Judah Lamey at www.GlintofMischief.com

For my children.
You helped me grow through the challenges of life and gave me something to fight for.

And gratitude to AJ.
For being a motivator by showing passion and interest in this story. Discussing it with me and allowing yourself to be my soundboard for ideas.

Ayathesti - 1

Is this really the new identity of my life? Savior of our species? I don't know if my heart can take it. The walls of the Zeyo fade back into focus as my thoughts quiet under the pounding of my heart, and the low murmur of the atmosphere grows to full volume around me.

"Aya!"

The glass near my mouth fogs with my sigh when a shrill, twangy voice pierces the hum of conversation in the local lounge. A shiver crawls up my spine in the instant I realize I'm about to drown in the entirety of today's gossip.

Nineveh approaches the bar where I sit. "Did you hear about Tiamet?" With a graceful swoop, she slides a wooden stool from under the bar and sits atop the velvety scarlet cushion.

Thinking only of The Council's decision, which will change every aspect of my life, I'm slow to answer with an unenthusiastic "What?"

After placing the strap of her bag on a hook underneath the glassy granite counter, she looks at me with beaming eyes. "They selected him to lead the expedition!" She pinches her glossed strawberry lips together in a smile, her shoulders shaking with a suppressed giggle.

Though her comment evokes a proper stiffness through my entire body, I maintain my feigned disinterest on the subject. "Expedition?" I ask, staring at my glass on the countertop, arms folded against the padded edge, my voice hoarse from lack of use throughout the day.

I've had a thing for Tiamet ever since we attended The Academy of Science Advancement, or TASA, if you will. The thought of working closely with him turns my stomach over itself, threatening to tie in knots.

Nineveh swats at the air, rolling her juniper eyes. "Oh, stop it! You know . . . the expedition! On that planet to find an indigenous race to breed with!"

With a nod and a smile toward the bartender, I prop my glass between my fingertips. Another round. I wouldn't say I'm a regular at the lounge, but I frequent enough for them to know my usual drink. My gaze sweeps across the mirror behind the bar, illuminated by amber lights embedded into the glass shelves where various bottles rest. To my left is the entrance, hidden behind a wall that separates the lavatory hallway from everything else. Just left of that is a pony wall separating the entrance from the crushed velvet sofas around a low glass table. Single-light chandeliers dangle over the wooden tables, whose surfaces showcase natural curves in the grain.

The same dark marble as the bar counter is infused into them, following these patterns like a black river carving its way through an underground cavern. The ceiling showcases a dark finish, garnished with tiny white lights to mimic the night sky. The same amber lights in the bar shelves wrap around the room to tie everything together.

"I'm thrilled you're privy to all this rather useless information, Nineveh, but we won't *actually* breed with them…" I don't mean to sound condescending, but the uncertainty of how to drive the conversation away from Tiamet gets the better of me.

Nineveh folds her arms, wrinkling her freckled nose. "Come on! I know deep down you're thrilled." Her bubbly demeanor is constantly teetering over a line between being amusing and irritating.

"I didn't know they would select him as director, but I had my suspicions he would be going." After lifting a new glass to eye level, I observe the light refraction of the caramel fluid inside before pressing the rim to my lips, letting it slip through them.

"You don't sound very excited," she says with a look of disapproval.

I raise my eyebrows as a silent request to know when she'd ever seen me excited.

She grips my arm and shakes it gently. "I was certain you'd jump at the news since you're going too."

I hold back a grin and roll my eyes. It must be all she can do to keep from jumping up and down herself.

"You're going too?" Tiamet's voice rings in my ears from behind as he approaches. My heart rattles to a stop at his question. He places himself diagonally from Nineveh and me, leaning against his hands on the edge of the countertop.

"Not by choice," I snap, building my defensive walls higher. "I am completely against creating a hybrid race for this." With another sip, my fingertips collect the condensation from the outside of the glass before I rest it in my hands against the counter's glassy surface.

Discomfort closes in when Nineveh pulls her stool closer to mine, the sweet smell of plums and roses infiltrating my senses. "Oh, come on, Aya! We get to save our planet and do none of the heavy lifting."

"How cool is that? We will be heroes!" Tiamet places his hands on his hips in a heroic pose, looking toward the ceiling.

I roll my eyes. *Why won't anybody around me listen?* "You're acting like it's some big joke," I mumble.

"Come now, Aya, don't be like that. At least explain to your friends why you're so against it." Tiamet nods, motioning a hand to Nineveh and the other toward himself. "We've heard your argument presented at council, but I can tell there's something more." He hides a chuckle in his voice, in that teasing manner I never seem to be in the mood to tolerate.

"It's no laughing matter. It's cruel. Case closed." It takes all my strength to avoid looking at him, but as he leans his forearm against the bar, pulling a stool underneath him, I can't help but glance. His wide palm is balled into a loose fist, sending his arm into a flex.

He's got that look in his eye—the one where he knows he can get a rise out of me. "Well, you act as if you don't even want us to surv—"

"Of course I want us to survive!" I hiss through my teeth. "To think otherwise is idiotic . . . But creating a new race to do our dirty work? Are we too good to get our hands in the mud and collect the gold ourselves?" I slam my glass on the countertop. "Creating a sentient being for enslavement to fit our agenda is wrong, and I'm not convinced The Council has exhausted all other options before going this route! Their creationist, entitled outlook on the entire ordeal makes me sick." I slowly breathe out. *Calm down. I've got to calm down.*

Tiamet closes his eyes, shaking his head. "Ayathesti, they won't be intelligent enough to know the difference. Besides, we'll just let them be once we have what we need, so they're not exactly 'slaves.' They're just . . . temporarily contracted . . . involuntarily."

I glare at the droplets of liquid pooling on the counter's surface.

Nineveh's eyes grow wide, and she puts a gentle hand on my shoulder. "Bring it in Aya! Obviously, he's *kidding*!" I catch her glare at Tiamet as he sits there, propped against the counter with a sly smile pasted on his lips. *It's like he gets some thrill at the ease of getting under my skin.*

I take a deep breath. "No, no. It's a good thing to discuss if we're working together. Having a similar target outcome will help everyone in the long run," I say to them, but the words are more for me. *Maybe I can eventually convince myself of this truth.*

"So . . . let's elaborate then," Tiamet says. The bartender sets a tall glass in front of him. In return, he offers the man a smile and a nod before bringing it to his lips.

"It's simple, really. I don't find it beneficial to our intellectual progress to create a species for one reason alone." I lift my gaze to him while placing a napkin over the droplets on the counter. "Imagine if it were you, Tiamet, working one day, happy and stupid as you are, and out of nowhere—you develop a new neural connection and notice something is off. What are we doing? Why are we doing it? Maybe I'm the only one with any of this intelligence we all keep talking about . . . or at least the only one with enough to anticipate that these beings getting smarter, instead of staying mindless, is inevitable."

I like Tiamet, but his teasing can go too far with little effort. I don't know if I'll ever understand his fascination with it. Is that just me, though? Am I one of those sensitive people everyone jokes about? Our eye contact holds while I attempt to hide the tremble in my chest. I rub my eyes, offering a temporary relief from the weight of the late night and conversation. *If he thinks pushing in on my boundaries will make me open up, he is mistaken.*

A strong, gentle hand lands on my shoulder, making me catch my breath.

"Don't worry, Aya. If anyone can make this work, it's you." Tiamet's hushed voice is inviting, like a soft blanket wanting to engulf my entire soul and extinguish the flame of problems in my chest. My heart pounds so loud I'm certain he can hear it. I hold my breath until the warmth of his fingertips slips away. After gaining my composure, I peer over my shoulder to watch him mingle with another group.

"He's right, you know. I mean . . . he's a complete ego maniac, and not worth your time if I'm being honest, but just now, I think I may have seen a glimpse of what you like about him." Nineveh always seems to make sense of my emotions before I can, with little comments like this. Maybe she's just more observant than me.

"What do you mean 'what I like about him'?" I empty my glass and tip it toward the bartender before looking at her.

"Ohh, sweetie. You can't fake it with me. It's so obvious you have a crush on him. It's actually rather painful to watch." Nineveh giggles as I glance over my shoulder again. "See! Your expression goes soft, and you blush every time you look at him!"

I jerk my eyes to her. "Get off! I do not." Desperate to keep my eyes from wandering back to Tiamet, I examine Nineveh's red hair. *How do those curls stay in such perfect form throughout the entirety of every day?*

"You can deny it until the sun explodes, but that won't help you feel any better about it." She crosses her ankles and pops a mint into her mouth.

"I don't want to 'feel better' about it. Besides . . . fantasies are always better than the real thing." My tone mellows as my gaze drifts back to Tiamet.

"Well then, I won't sit here and watch you torture yourself. To be frank, Aya? You need to get him one-on-one and tell him how you feel! You'll be more content either knowing he feels the same or, in the off chance he doesn't, you can let go and move on." After grabbing her bag from the hook under the counter, she flings the strap over her shoulder and stands from her chair. "Go talk to him! Then get yourself some rest. I'll see you tomorrow!" She turns and walks away, the click clack of her heels fading as she exits.

I come out of my trance and look at the increased emptiness of the room. It's as though the last four hours passed by in a moment. *Was I lost in a zombie-like state the whole time?* After taking care of my bill, I push myself to stand, hands sliding on the smooth surface of the bar, before I make my way to the exit. I push the swinging doors open, revealing a dark starry night overhead with street lights letting off their dim purple haze.

A gentle breeze brushes over me with ease, eroding the weight of the earlier conversation away. Focusing on putting one foot in front of the other, I smile at the memory of Tiamet's hand on my shoulder, his voice echoing in my head, making my heart race and my lungs heavy.

While I turn the corner, away from the Zeyo, a shimmering bright-green light pans from one side of the sky to the other. The sand-faced homes lining the street cast strange shadows as their basic, uniform cubed shapes dance under the waving light above.

My heart swells with gratitude at my luck in witnessing such a rare event. *Could it really be late enough for me to see the elusive aurora?* Streams of light wisp around the stars in a tango. The slow movements, beautiful and mesmerizing, captivate me and pull me to sway with them in the breeze.

I don't know how much time passes while I stand there dancing with the sky, but by the time I'm home, I'm ready to collapse. Tomorrow marks the real start to an extensive journey. The Council has already selected the destination, the planet to save our own: a planet we call Earth.

Tiamet - 2

Stars glisten against the dark sky as I sit on a park bench, gazing up at them. The generators powering down for the night let the beetle chatter and rustling grass in the field be heard. A breeze catches the furry purple tree tufts in a dance and creates soft music against the opening of the gold generation diffusers.

"Which one do you think it is?" Latif sits next to me, face cocked upward.

"We could probably look in the right direction and still never see it. The star is pretty faint."

"Interesting that one of the faint stars in our sky hosts the planet with the key for our survival."

"We've known for a long time that there were more planets like ours." I chuckle.

Latif looks at me and sneers, "You know what I mean, smart ass," he says, laughing.

"Yeah, yeah. I know what you mean. There are a lot of flecks up there. We're lucky they found this one so close to us. Any further and we'd be extinct for sure."

Latif sighs, "I feel so helpless."

I look at him. "What are you on about? You're part of the creation team!"

"Yeah, I know, but I'm not really contributing to any of it." I scoff. "It's true, man," he insists.

"You listen to your boss too much."

"No—I mean, yeah, she's bossy as hell." He chuckles. "But that's not what I meant."

"What then?"

"I think my pop may be getting to me. I could be more effective working in a councilor's office."

"Yikes . . . Maybe he *is* getting to you. Last we talked, you were really set on avoiding his path at all costs."

"Well, maybe working under Ayathesti has a little to do with it."

"Working for her, you mean? She's no taller than you." I smirk when Latif snorts with laughter. "Well, if you're passionate about what you do, you'll never wonder."

He looks at me. "You really believe that?"

"Without a doubt."

"Do you like what you do?"

I look back at the sky, transfixed. "I never saw myself in a leadership position, even though I've always wanted to help people. The best way I knew how to was by understanding them. After reading the mission objective, I thought maybe being in a leadership role would make that easier."

"Aren't you worried about failure?" I lightly punch his arm. He rubs the spot before clasping his hands together. "Okay, maybe not failure but . . . failure. Is there a better word for it?"

"Of course I've considered things not going as expected."

"Yeah, that."

"No, I'm not worried. I have my expectations set, and if they don't come to pass, then I'll move forward with the present circumstances."

"Shit, man, that's deep. How did you get that mindset?"

"Mom. She was so sick some days but acting like nothing was wrong. We learned to enjoy the good times, living in the present, only working through bad situations as they came along. Worry breeds more worry, and that's no way to live. Trust me."

Latif leans forward, resting his elbows on his knees,

and picks a few strands of grass, sending a tangy smell wafting through the air.

"Listen, if your only reason for not following The Council path is worrying you won't meet your father's expectations, then you should readjust your mindset." I pinch my nose to rid it of the tickle from the grass scent. "If you don't want to do it because of disinterest, then make that choice and stick with it. Wandering around through life day by day, stuck in limbo, unsure where you're headed, is worse than making a choice and finding later that it landed you somewhere you don't want to be."

Green light illuminates the field around us, setting the vegetation to a vibrancy it hasn't seen in years. I look up to see the Aurora traveling through the sky. My heart races and I smack Latif on the shoulder. He looks up, jaw dropping open.

"Dude." He gasps.

"The ancestors are pleased with our probability for success."

"Isn't that just an old bedtime story?" He twists the grass between his fingers till it breaks.

"It's really just caused by electrons getting through the magnetosphere and interacting with the atmosphere." I lean back on the bench and gaze up at the sky. "But since our magnetic field has been weakening each year, I like to think Mom is around, helping it communicate with me at this exact moment. Seeing as it usually only shows up every few thousand years . . . the timing is too perfect."

"You and your mom, man." Latif chuckles.

"Lose someone you care about and then talk to me about not wishing they were around."

"I plan on being distanced enough from everyone that I don't have to care about them."

I shake my head and sigh.

"What?"

"Nothing, my young friend. You just have a lot to learn." I stand and pat him on the shoulder. "Your answers on what to do with your pop and possible future on The Council will come. Just be patient, and focus on the present moment."

He mumbles something inaudible as I walk back toward the perimeter of the park and navigate the roadways home.

Ayathesti - 3

A sliver of light pierces through the stained glass window I made, landing on my eyes. I roll over to my back and squint while the room comes into focus. The golden chiffon that drapes over the canopy poles of my bed illuminate the ceiling in a tangerine sunrise. Different colored shapes project onto the wall, crawling along like clouds blowing in a subtle breeze.

My feet chill when I place them on the glassy floor, sending a shiver through me to start my everyday motions. I click a button next to my bed to start a fresh brew of oojo and make my way into the lav. I ignore the mirror until I release the tickle in my abdomen. After picking a few stray hairs from my comb, I run it through my long onyx locks, which I then twist into the usual bun and clip into place.

Do I always look this tired? I think to myself when I meet my own eyes in the mirror. I bite my lower lip and scrunch my nose upward. *Nothing like a little facial exercise to loosen up my neutral expression.*

A hiss echoes off the bare walls as I rub my hands together below a chrome faucet, a mist of water cleansing them. Using the moisture, I brush them over my hair, pulling the shorter loose ends into a curl around my finger. Raising an eyebrow and flashing a small side smile, I try out the new look. With a nod, my thoughts wander to Tiamet. *If we're working closer, maybe I should make a small effort? But not too much, otherwise it'll be obvious.*

When I walk into the kitchen, I'm reintroduced to a dimmed cave-like feel as I make my way to the front window.

I press a button to unravel the shutters covering it, and the dim ambiance drowns in sunshine.

By the sink, I reach for a short glass nestled under a nozzle sticking from the wall. Steam wafts into the air as I remove the cup from the counter. A plate containing my breakfast levitates over the countertop behind me. In a rehearsed grace, I turn around and slip my hand under it and walk to my table tucked under the window. Here is where I get that final moment of peace before starting my long days.

I touch my finger to the corner of a white paper on the table and fold it in half toward me. It flickers on before locking in place. *Right, fix the newspaper.* I make the mental note and sip my oojo tea.

Images appear on the screen. There it is, screaming for attention on the home page of every news post available to the Mujai people: COUNCIL'S MISSION TO SAVE THE WORLD. An article explaining The Extension Project. I skip past the uninteresting read.

Being selected as the lead geneticist for the project, I'm already aware of what the expectations are. Sliding my finger across the top of the paper, I scroll through articles until stopping at the small stories. These are my calm before the storm. The proof that doom and gloom may headline, but that's not the only thing happening in this society. Knowing there are some who live day to day helping others in selflessness fills me with hope and a sense of comfort.

The warmth of my drink consumes me as it slides down my throat, the mint leaving a film of frost in its steamy wake. Beeping from my watch pierces the air, shattering my daydream and dragging me back to reality. Wiping tea from my chin with the back of my hand, I stand. *If I don't leave soon, I'll be late. And I hate being late.*

I set my plate and cup in the sink, regardless of having not touched the meal. Only after rushing to button up my lab coat do I realize I'm in my sleeping gown. Profanity escapes my lips as I remove it and waste no time back to the lav. Flinging a cabinet door open, I yank the first thing from the shelves and slip into it with ease. I scramble back into my lab coat while rushing to the front door. I pull it open, exposing myself to the morning air.

The door clicks as it locks behind me. With a deep breath, I step onto the gravel and make my way to the Knowledge Research Union Lab (or KRUL) the same way I've done a thousand times before. Most around me are going about their usual day, others stop and whisper as they stare at me, 'The Designer.' The local shop owners and my neighbors are the ones getting on with their normal routines without even a glance in my direction. This offers me a shard of relief.

All the eyes my direction set my gut unsteady. *Why do I feel like a liar when I try to keep myself hidden?*

'They're all watching you. Everyone is judging.'

My stomach turns as Anxiety whispers her dark words. I pull my arms across my chest. *Breathe. Just breathe. Nobody cares.* I avert my gaze to the ground, focusing on my feet.

'Don't kid yourself. If you really believed that, you could look them in the face.'

After a while, I look up at my destination sitting at the end of the gravel path, past the grass field—one of my sanctuaries. Only a few diffusers are on today. Tucking them inside the center of the trees was an ingenious way to hide the gawdy structures, providing a golden dust to capture light and contrast against the magenta tufts. Trees circle the entire field and line the pathways. I pass many of them on the streets in town and still have yet to discover a set schedule of operation. I'm actually lucky to pass through the field every day. It's the one green area left in our city.

The entrance to the KRUL is at the top of a set of stairs, under a stone canopy jutting out from the face of the mountain that houses it. My shoulders relax as I return to a comfort zone standing in front of the doors. Waiting for them to open is like anticipating the sun cresting the horizon.

A blast of cool air dislodges loose strands of hair as the doors open and the building lobby depressurizes. Light cascades through the high exterior windows of the lobby, casting shadows on the engravings in the ancient stone walls. The smooth dark granite floor bounces the remaining light into corners of the room. I close my eyes and sigh, succumbing to a temporary relief checkpoint of calm before convincing myself to press forward.

Nineveh's shrill pierces through the silence. "Aya! You're running late. Are you okay?"

"Mm . . . Yes, I'm fine, Nin. Thanks for asking." Even my quiet voice reverberates off the walls as I proceed toward her oval desk in the room's center. "Just a late start is all."

"Oh my! That's not like you. Everybody's so excited to get started, they're already here. And the news station has called people over to start on interviews."

"Even Tiamet's here?" The skepticism in my tone effectively hides the panic of just how late I am.

Nineveh giggles, turning in her chair to grab a file. "Aya, do you honestly think anything could get Tiamet here early?"

"No . . . I suppose there probably isn't." I chuckle. Even though Nineveh can be bothersome at times, more often than not she helps my emotions equalize.

"You suppose there isn't what?" Tiamet's voice emanates from the entry doors, echoing through every corner of the room.

"Tiamet! You're here, well, rather early!" Nineveh raises her eyebrows and looks at me with surprise. "We were just talking about y—"

"Yesterday." A lie. *I'm not ready for him to know he's a conversation topic.* "At the Zeyo. Sorry I was short with you." I withhold my glare for Nineveh, who looks back at me with a devious little smirk. So devious, in fact, I'm certain she's doing it on purpose, regardless of it being unlike her.

Spinning in her chair again, she grabs another file and stands. She walks out from behind the desk and hands one to each of us. She motions for us to follow her toward two large glass sliding doors at the back of the room. On a normal day, I'm alone when Nineveh provides a brief of the memo in the folder. In fact, I'm never around when others arrive, so I can't even be sure if her receptionist duties require she does this for all employees or if it's just a favor to me. Plus, I'm pretty sure she likes doing it. She gets to practice public speaking, as if she needs any help with that. Seeing as I'm usually alone for this, it will be interesting to share today . . . and with Tiamet, of all people.

"They've isolated two thousand three hundred and twelve different species that could be possible candidates for a genetic match," she starts. "Aya, that should help you and Latif narrow some stuff down during your research for compatibility based on the collected data in your folders. Once we've zeroed in on a region for landing they're expecting you to spin it down even further before the trip to Earth."

Nineveh stops in front of the doors and turns on the ball of her foot to face us. "They're from a variety of habitats but all are top contenders for a successful mix. Tiamet, your team will locate the best habitats necessary for the new species's survival." She looks at us, smiling as though asking if we have questions.

Tiamet follows my lead, holding his wrist out to the scanner, prompting the doors to open. Nineveh takes a deep breath and claps her hands together as the doors hiss. "Good luck to you both!" She turns again, her shoes clicking across the lobby floor.

"Thanks, Nin!" With one hand in a pocket, he proceeds forward. *Well, isn't his morning voice chipper?*

I stand there, looking at him, then glance over my shoulder at Nineveh, her hair bouncing as she walks. My shoes make a popping noise, thanks to the sticky floor, as I enter a clean room encased in glass. The doors close behind us, and I stare at the doors ahead. The silence while waiting for the decontamination spritzer to activate is ear-splitting.

"So . . . you seem to be in the morning mood." I catch his reflection tossing a casual look toward me.

I fold my hands together, clinging to the folder, before looking back at him. His eyes lock onto mine, and I evaluate responses in my head before speaking. "I'm not sure what you're referring to."

A smile slowly draws on his lips as his gaze moves from my eyes to my shoes, then back up. His violet-rimmed, azure-centered eyes go soft, shining like gems under the harsh light. "Just that your coat is crooked." The spritzers deactivate, and the pressure changes in the sealed room.

"Oh." I look down, heat washing over my face with embarrassment as my heart begins thumping against my chest. "It was a late night." I flip the folder under my arm and realign the buttons of my lab coat.

"I know. I remember you leaving." Tossing the cover of his file open, he steps forward to exit ahead of me. How is everything about him so calm and on point? What it must be like to live a life of confidence.

Blinking a few times, I search my memory of the surroundings last night. I don't remember seeing him before I left. After regaining focus, I make my way onto the surveillance deck. White walls on parallel sides go up three stories next to the sealed stone faces of the mountain until they converge with a skylight.

Turning to the right, I waste no time targeting a small door embedded into an alcove of rock. The slap of Tiamet's file on a white glass tabletop follows me through the room as I pass translucent, vertical monitors hovering mere inches above the tables. Upon reaching the door, I input a code on the small keypad, then scan my wrist, prompting the door to open.

After stepping inside, I turn to brave one last glimpse of Tiamet for the day. He's taken his usual position among the monitors illuminated with different images of landscaping. He leans forward with his hands propped against the table and taps at different spots in the photos to highlight contrasts in terrain. Our eyes connect once more when he looks at me before I'm lowered into the sub-basement.

Tiamet - 4

I interlace my fingers, my elbows resting on the arms of my chair. I smile at the reporter and wait for her to speak.

"So, Mr. Osiris, how did you feel when you first received news of being selected as director for this leg of the project?"

"Please, call me Tiamet. And that's an interesting question, Mira. Can I call you Mira?"

She giggles. "I'm surprised you remember my name!"

"Oh, I'm a big fan, easy to remember." I shift my weight and flash a confident smile for the camera. "But, to answer your question, I initially wasn't interested in being director."

"That opens a brand new category of questions!" She sits forward, crossing her ankles.

"Mira, I'm an open book. Ask me anything you wish."

"If not the director, which you're obviously so suited for, what part *did* you want to play?"

"Well, few know this, but my main interest is social behaviors and how they change in relation to geographical region. I created the system we use to collect and sort the data based on those parameters."

She taps her finger against her chin. "Mhmm. That's fascinating!"

"It is fascinating."

"So what changed? Why did you put your name in the hat for the director's chair?"

"Social behaviors," I tell her. "After watching a few people around the building, I was inspired to apply for the position. My goal is to help them grow and be productive in the way I know they can be." I let out a deep breath, leaning back in my chair to relieve weight from my feet.

"It sounds like maybe there are a few people you have in mind that aren't reaching their full potential."

"That's not how I mean it. It's more of . . ." I stop, tilting my head to the side, searching for the correct words. "It's like when you know you can do something, you're confident in your abilities to do it. Right?"

Mira nods.

"Right. So my intention is to help others find that confidence. Their work is not suffering from it, but you can see it's wearing on her soul." My heart sinks. *I just singled her out by the mistake of a single word.* I hold my gaze with Mira as she adjusts herself in her chair again.

"So it's someone specific?"

"I didn't mean to single anyone out. I believe everyone has room for improvement and growth." Inhaling slowly and steadily helps to calm my heart rate. *Maybe she'll accept that answer and move on.*

"It must be someone you care about if you've changed your entire focus of the mission just to help them." Mira's glossy lips smile, but her eyes hold something else. A sadness? No, a yearning. I've seen it many times from young women who shower me with admiration.

"She's a rather private person, so I'd like to respect that. But yes, I care for her."

"That's so sweet." She brings her hand to her chest. "Why is it you care for her so? What is it about her that intrigues you?"

I break eye contact and look to the corner of the room. Longing fills my chest, replacing my cheery smile with a soft one. "You know, I think it's because she reminds me a lot of my mother."

"Your Mother? That's a bit odd to have those caring

feelings for someone like your mother, isn't it? Or are these feelings more like ones you'd have toward a sibling?"

My eyes meet hers again. "No. My Mother is . . . was this amazing person. But she and Ay—also liked her privacy." *Shit, I'm not doing well at keeping her identity unknown.* "To the outside world she was smaller than the bud of a flower. But to those she opened up to, there was an entire world inside of those petals. I've seen glimpses. This person has an entire world hidden away too." My voice threatens to crack as my eyes glass over.

"Oh my! Are you concerned with your ability to remain professional in such close proximity? Deserted on a paradise planet?"

My heart leaps over the previous emotions about my mother. *Vacation? With Ayathesti?* My heart races, and my palms grow sweaty. I take another deep breath. "Being on a paradise planet with someone that deep . . . I hope she can let out that inner nature. But I have no doubt in our ability to remain professional."

"Your confidence in that is quite assuring. So you intend on remaining the most eligible man in Simbhora when you return?" Her cheeks flush with the slightest tint of pink, looking at me with flirtatious eyes.

"I'm not in the habit of making promises I don't know I can keep." My chest tightens, rumbling with a forced chuckle. "But I'm sure you'll want to have me on again when we get back." My lips involuntarily curl into a smirk out of habit.

"I certainly intend to, yes."

"Until then, I hope you find yourself well, Miss Mira." I reach forward and offer a polite hand, putting an end to the interview. She scoots to the edge of her chair and reaches her hand out, slipping her soft palm into my own.

Ayathesti - 5

The elevator door opens to Sub-basement Level Three. It's darker here than in the surveillance room. Three others are here preparing for different portions of their day. Two are preparing to leave—an older gentleman and his lab assistant, both who, working on a different project, prefer the night shift. As they exit, I greet them with a nod before sitting in the rolling metal chair near the elevator door. After adding my file to a disorganized stack of papers on the table, I flip it open and begin reading.

"Most of the selections are amphibious creatures . . ." Latif approaches from behind. I glance over to see him balancing a pen on the tip of his green finger. Being young and fresh out of TASA by only a few years, most of his comments are things that validate him thinking he knows everything. I hear the pen fall into his hand as he stops behind me. He peers over my shoulder, and I can practically feel his body heat.

I blink with annoyance before stopping to look at him. "But they said they identified those most compatible," I say in admitted confusion.

"That they did. But I've already been through that entire file and about sixty percent are amphibious. So I think they just don't want us to 'miss' anything." He folds his arms and leans back against the adjacent table.

I roll my eyes and turn the chair to face him head-on. "Yeah, you know how they are. Trying to pretend they're important by having the final say. How did you get access to the list early enough to have combed through it already?"

Latif chuckles, nodding. "Yes, yes. I know how they are. My father is one of those guys and I have to live with it."

"Answers that question." *What's his fascination with always reminding me he's here because his father is on The Council?* I close the folder and stand. "Well then, let's start the chemical breakdown. If we're already knowledgeable on what we're looking for, there isn't much sense in wasting time."

I push past him, making my way to a locked freezer and pull on a pair of thick gloves housed in a box beside it. Plumes of cold steam escape into the air while I remove a rack of filled sample tubes and a flask of opaque white liquid. After placing the samples into the thaw rack, I walk to the table in the room's center. With a quick tick of my ear toward my shoulder, protective glasses emerge from the ring pierced through the cartilage of my ear.

Latif shakes his head. "When are you gonna tell me where you got those glasses? They're killer."

Slipping nitrile gloves over my hands, I turn and direct my attention to the samples. An angled glass plate clinks when I set it on the table. "Don't know where they came from. I received them as a gift. I told you that." *Another lie today, woo. I'm on fire. But he doesn't really need to know about the nights I spent in my room at TASA tinkering and avoiding being social. Let's face it though—not much has changed since then.*

The plastic squeals against itself as I unwrap a new tip and attach it to a pipette. With precision and grace, my thumb works the pipette as I focus on the tube, extracting a small amount of the sample and releasing it into a petri dish. The solution shimmers after the other chemicals are added for molecular breakdown.

I prepare a microscopic slide without a glance at Latif. "Are you going to stand there jealous of my glasses all day, or are you going to help me out around here?"

"Right, sorry." A sense of satisfaction sets in when I hear him rummaging for equipment.

I gather the petri dish with the remaining deconstructed sample to store in a small freezer. Habit forces me to accurately turn the blue knob to a measurement of twenty clicks. When I get back to the counter, I put the slide under the microscope to examine the cellular structure.

Latif's unsettled posture and change in movements as he returns supplies to their places pulls my focus away from the work before me. After sanitizing his hands, he removes his glasses and places them in a wire rack at the side of the sink and pats his stomach.

"Well, my belly says it's time for food. I'll be upstairs." He makes his way to the elevator and stops just before stepping inside. "You should consider a break. You work too hard!"

"At least somebody works around here." I roll my eyes as the elevator ascends and place my equipment on the glass tray. My heart races in panic as that leads to a beaker of washing fluid jumping from the edge of the countertop and shattering at my feet.

I breathe deeply for a few moments to steady myself before moving a sample to the final empty spot on the shelves in the freezer. While proceeding to clean up the mess, hunger stabs my side.

Leaning against the back of the elevator, I close my eyes to give them rest from the morning strain they've endured and place my hands in the front pockets of my lab coat. I look down, focusing on the buttons, unable to stop a smile, reminiscing Tiamet's words from earlier. "Crooked." I chuckle to myself while the elevator door opens. I walk through the now-empty surveillance room and exit through the clean-room doors.

The eatery is up a set of spiral stairs, which are carved into the mountainside. My hand glides over the cold metal rail as I use it to keep my momentum while climbing the stairway. Hesitating at the top, I stare ahead through the glass wall at those sitting among their standard cliques. My knees buckle when I force myself forward through the crowd to a silver counter. I swipe my wrist over a cubed black recession in the table. A beep sounds, prompting menu options to appear. After making my selection, I wait for a multi-colored glass tray with my meal to extrude from the counter.

I take a deep breath as I turn and see Nineveh waving her arms violently for my attention. I watch my feet as I walk. *Is it a nervous habit, or do I actually feel like I need to make sure there's nothing I'll trip on?* I glance at the occupants of the table ahead to make sure I'm still headed in that direction. *Is that Latif sitting across from her? Great.*

I sigh with slight annoyance before remembering the first time he admitted liking her. "That friend of yours sure is cute! It's a personal goal of mine to get to know her better," he had said.

Knowing Nineveh also has a crush on him puts me in a good spot. *I could tell either of them the secret and watch the mushy stuff start, or I could watch him make an ass of himself.* My thoughts prompt a smile. *Besides, isn't it better when it's drawn out? I can handle him sitting with us, I guess. Unless he says something to make me lose my lunch.*

Ayathesti - 6

"Well, well. Look who decided to leave the cave."

My heart skips, likely because it's now in my throat. I force a swallow, moving my glance to Tiamet sitting where I had placed Latif in my mind. I let out my held breath and roll my eyes in silence, settling myself into a chair before shoveling food into my mouth.

"What, you're not even going to acknowledge me?" he says, sounding upset.

"Oh, I acknowledged you. You should pay closer attention."

Nineveh covers her mouth, stifling a giggle.

Tiamet's eyebrows lift. "Me? Pay closer attention?"

I stuff more food into my mouth and raise my eyebrows to match his, shrugging in response.

His teeth flash in a quick smile before his expression straightens. "Well, the day's work is slow going. Turns out about seventy-five percent of the 'species' they selected for sample extraction are amphibious."

"Yeah, I know." My words come out sloppy as I speak through my food. "Latif told me already."

"Do you guys even listen to me?" Nineveh folds her arms, a particular sulk in her voice "Golly, I swear I don't even know what good I am around here."

"What do you mean, Nin?" I look at her, washing down the chewed contents of my mouth.

"Well, if either of you had paid a little attention toward me this morning, instead of trying so hard to ignore each other, you would have heard me say that."

A laugh bursts from my chest. "Oh hell, Nin, we were walking to the door. And I'm pretty sure you're just convincing yourself you included that, because I have no recollection."

"I swear I said something about it . . ." Nineveh squints, as though it will help with memory recall.

Tiamet is staring at me with one eyebrow lifted, which complements his smile.

I cover my mouth. "Oh, sorry." A giggle slips out. "Too loud?"

His smile quivers, as though struggling to wipe the expression away, while he shakes his head. "Not at all. I was thinking back to it, and I don't remember her saying anything either." He nods toward Nineveh, whose lips pout.

"Come on. Now you two are ganging up on me, aren't you?"

"Oh, stop. You're being a baby," I mutter. "Anyway, Latif seemed pretty smug about knowing the selection was amphibious before I even had time to look over the file this morning. Has your team been able to narrow that down by exclusion of incompatible environment?" I stare at Tiamet, still feeding myself as if on autopilot.

He rubs his chin a few times. "Well . . . I mean . . ." With a sigh, he leans in, resting his folded hands on the tabletop. "It's hard to pinpoint. Compatibility charts correlate species specifically with environment. So, at this point, I need a new search method just to stop feeling lost on what I'm even looking for."

"Didn't you design the system?" Nineveh asks.

"I did, but the algorithm was only set up to analyze the data and plot them with a select few variable options. That's just how the hardware would allow us to work it."

I nod in understanding. "Right now, we're working on breaking down compounds to find the most efficient protein bonds. This will find what works best for testing once we get samples. Then we'll build up from there once we narrow it down."

"Why don't you go through the list and remove all the amphibious selections? Then use those remaining results as your primary target?" Nineveh sounds confused. "Why be stuck on the thought of having amphibious options if they won't work?"

Tiamet turns to her in the chair. "Well, we can't exclude any options before considering them."

"That seems like a large waste of everybody's time!" she says.

He nods. "Yes, but we'd hate to overlook something."

"Unless we find a high percentage option first. I didn't bother looking through the list," I add. "I have to agree with Nineveh on this. Working with non-amphibious data will likely land us on a match before we waste lots of time."

Nineveh's smile carries victory. "I want to see what you've got so far!"

I laugh out loud once more and am thrown into a coughing fit, choking on my own saliva. "Nineveh, we only started today. There's nothing to see." My cheeks grow hot at the sound of Tiamet's chuckle.

Nineveh folds her arms. "I don't care. I'm still attending TASA, you know, and I am interested in your section of work, so I'd like to see!"

"Okay, okay. Come down with me after lunch, and you can watch for a few minutes."

"Well, if she gets to see, I want to see too!" Tiamet says.

"Nope." My response is accompanied by a quick shake of the head.

He throws his hands up in protest. "I see how you are. You'll let her down, but not me? That's rude, Aya."

"Hey, you know the rules of sub-levels. Maybe you should have studied harder instead of goofing off with girls. Then you'd have access down there."

"What's that supposed to mean?"

"Nothing personal. But if you want to see where I work, you'll have to get a pass approved. Or work down there, but that's not likely. Since Nineveh is still a student, she can observe to help her decision." My voice grows shaky as my throat tightens.

Tiamet grasps his fruit from the tabletop, his voice going deep and firm. "First off, I didn't ask to see where you work, I asked to see your work. And second, I wasn't wasting my time with girls, and if you'd ever left your room, you'd know what I was doing." He stands, pointing at Nineveh. "You. Make sure she gets a drink after playtime downstairs. You know how Miss Perfect likes to take herself too seriously by working so hard." He walks away, leaving Nineveh in a giggle.

I'm frozen, watching him leave, with eyes wide from shock before turning to Nineveh. "What . . . what just happened?"

"Well . . . it's difficult to say. But I believe you were just told you're wrong." Nineveh presses her lips together, trying to hide a smile. "Oh goodness, hide me!" Her shrill voice rises in pitch, as if it were even possible, as she throws a napkin up to the side of her face.

"What th—" A slap radiates from my upper back into my neck and ears.

"Well, how's it, ladies?" Latif stands next to the table, his hand on my back.

"Gah." My fork clanks to my tray. "Can't I eat my food in peace?" I shrug his hand from my shoulder.

"No can do, boss." He takes the seat Tiamet just vacated.

Are they working together? It seems too coincidental for Tiamet to leave so abruptly and then Latif shows up like this. Maybe I'm getting too comfortable and didn't notice them signaling one another across the room.

"Hey, Latif. W-what's your work like down there?" Nineveh clasps her hands together in her lap, raising her shoulders ever so slightly.

"Well, why would you wanna talk about work when we could talk about you, and me, *after* work, at the Zeyo." He puffs out his chest, leaning toward her with a pathetic attempt at a smolder plastered on his face.

"Um . . .? Well, I—"

"Besides"—he adjusts his posture—"I'm sure you have already heard it all from Aya here." He reaches his hand toward my back once more.

I list away. "Are you going to let her finish responding before you drown her with more of your words?" I shake my hand at him, an invitation for him to leave.

He throws his hands up. "Fine, fine. I'm going. Cool your head, fire maker." He looks back at Nineveh. "Think about it," he says with a wink.

"Go make yourself useful and get started on the next step for those samples, eh?"

He puts his hand to his forehead and throws it outward lazily. "*Yiss*, ma'am!" he says and walks away.

I shake my head, resisting the urge to roll my eyes. "Sometimes that guy just . . ." I hiss through clenched teeth before looking toward Nineveh.

Her face is pink as she exhales the breath she's been holding in. "Oh, Aya, I almost can't even keep myself composed around him! He's such a . . . such a . . . you know?"

I nearly choke on my food. "Ha, almost? Are you *that* into him?" She nods. "Well, I *am* a bad judge of character these days."

Nineveh pouts and says under her breath. "Yeah, considering you've got a thing for Tiamet, that jerk."

I stare at my empty tray. *I'll just pretend I didn't hear that.*

"Attendance to the front desk," a voice echoes from overhead speakers in the room.

"Well, I guess that's me!" Nineveh stands with her tray and walks to the doors.

"Hold up." I turn toward her. "Don't you want to come down to the lab?"

"Yes, I do, but it will have to be later. I have other duties to attend to! I work here too, you know." Nineveh's shoes clack against the ground as she nearly skips from the lunchroom.

I sigh as I slip away into thought. *Am I a downer? It can't be coincidental that everyone seems to leave suddenly, and those who stick around ignore most of what I say. Almost like I shouldn't be here.* A clang of a tray on the metal collection bin by the entrance jolts me from my pity party. I look at the empty room and stand to deposit my tray on the way out.

I veer from the stairwell toward a piece of paper I spot on the ground and kneel, picking it up. It's soft and worn, with dirty edges from traces of ink enhancing the micro-tears on the corners. I stand and turn to deliver it to the personnel office but am knocked from my feet by another body. Quickly, I slip the paper into my pocket.

"Oh gosh, I'm so sorry."

"No"—he fumbles over himself—"I'm sorry. Are you okay?" He grasps my elbow to help me balance out.

"Yeah . . ." I straighten my coat, focusing first on his shoes and following the length of his body up to his face. Tiamet. A flood of embarrassment drowns me. "I thought you left like half an hour ago?" My throat tightens, struggling to let the words out.

"Yes . . . I did. And that's supposed to mean?"

My eyebrows furrow with confusion. "That you went back to your lab? What else would it mean?"

A chuckle. "Typical Aya, thinking about work. I'm headed there now, and you are . . .?"

"I am what?"

"Going where?" He puts his hands in his pockets.

"Ah! Right. Yes. Back to the lab—my lab." We stand there, staring at each other in silence. *Stupid, stupid!*

He nods with a smirk. "Your lab . . . You sure about that?"

"Yes. Where else would I be going?"

"Looked like you were heading the other direction a second ago." He glances at my hand in my lab coat pocket.

I grasp the paper and expose it. "Right. So, uh, I'll just go that way, then." I look over his shoulder, toward the personnel office, before starting past him.

"Oh no you don't." He playfully grasps my wrist and inches the paper from my hand. "What's this?"

I lick my lip and tuck it underneath my teeth, rolling my eyes while turning toward him. "I don't know. I was just going to turn it in, okay?"

"Ahh, well, aren't we a helpful one?" He holds it up to his face and smirks, flipping it between his fingers.

"Stop. That's private!"

"You'd know because you read it, right?" He cocks a brow, his gaze piercing through me. My lips part and shiver as though to speak, but nothing spills through. "No, of course you didn't."

I yank my wrist from his grasp and take the paper from his hand, clenching it, the hurt on my face impossible to hide. "The *point* is, it could be."

He licks his lips, wiping the smile from his face as he folds his arms. "It's a recipe. And it's mine."

"Yeah right!"

"What, you don't believe me?"

"Should I?"

"Why do you think I'm so untrustworthy? What could possibly bring me up here instead of being downstairs, Aya? Mull that over."

A lock of ebony hair falls onto his forehead and distracts me from the pressure building in my chest. "Oh . . ." My fist loosens, and I hand it to him. He pinches the paper between his finger and thumb.

The moment steals my breath, along with my confidence. *I have to get out of here!* I turn and force myself to head toward the stairwell. Without the use of sight, I use the cold handrail once more to guide me. I'm in a speed walk by the time I reach the bottom. I rush across the room and scan my ID at the clean-room doorway.

"Stupid!" I mutter as I catch my breath.

"Aya!" Click-clack, click-clack. Nineveh approaches from behind. "Your interview was rescheduled for ten minutes from now."

I sigh as the doors open. *So much for riding that wave of relief.* "Thanks, Nineveh. Where are the interviews at?"

Nineveh points to her wrist and makes a few swiping motions in the air with her hand before smiling and walking away. I look at my wrist ID now pulsating with a green luminescence after Nineveh's file transfer. I apply pressure to the center of my wrist with my thumb and reach around with an extended finger, tapping on the back of my hand twice. My palm illuminates with an address, suite number, interviewer name, and time.

Great . . . it's Mira. I groan.

Tiamet - 7

I pull the paper from my pocket and gaze at the contents while waiting for the doors to open. My chest swells while gazing at my mother's photo next to her handwriting. How can something make you feel so heavy yet light enough to float away at the same time? Her smile offers me comfort from the ache of her absence. The sparkle of love for life in her eyes is a gentle reminder of who I strive to be . . . and why.

After the doors to the surveillance deck open, I tuck the re-folded paper carefully into my pocket with a content smile. I peer up at the sun-flooded skylight as I make my way to my workstation. My monitor illuminates with various tiled programs when I sit down. One document shows data of habitat locations. Another lists images and descriptions of potential species candidates. And another coordinates all that data and cross-references it all together, creating different graphs and charts.

"Mr. Osiris?"

I look up from my monitor after what seems like hours of staring, sifting, filing, sorting, typing, categorizing.

"There's is an impromptu meeting with The Council regarding the mission." I look around for a person before realizing the voice is coming from the transmitter on the side of my monitor.

"Oh, yes. Great. Thank you! I'll be on my way shortly."

The streets are busy as I make my way across town to The Council Center. I forgo my typical route to avoid casual conversations with the locals and arrive more timely. I'll be late to dinner tonight. *It was my night to cook too. I hope Pop and my brother understand why I won't be on time for our weekly get together.*

The big glass doors open, and the air displaces, brushing my hair across my forehead. I walk to the tall mahogany desk at the back of the room, examining the intricate wooden carvings on the walls and the olive-green chairs beneath them as I pass by.

A young girl looks up at me and smiles. "Oh! Mr. Osiris, you're here." She stands and walks around the desk, her lavender silk gown reaching her ankles. "This way, please." She motions for me to follow. *That's fancy wear for a normal day at the office.* I examine the dress climbing up her neck, the stiff collar cutting into her hairline and the capped sleeves hugging her shoulders. *It can't be comfortable.* As we start down the hallway, I look toward the entry doors at the sound of them opening to see Latif enter and head to his father's office. *It's the middle of the day. Ayathesti's going to freak.*

There's a large walnut table in the meeting room, surrounded by chairs already occupied by The Elders. As I enter, they look up in mid-hand gesture as though I interrupted their conversation.

"I apologize for the delay." I take the empty seat.

"Thank you for joining us, Mr. Osiris. We were just discussing the necessities for your little journey." Elder Ammon rests his interlaced hands on the table in front of him, his sleeves draping over his arms. "The ship is already commissioned, but we must evaluate the list of necessary personnel and equipment."

"We're looking to cut your hundred ten–man crew by

at least half." I whip my head around to Elder Hager.

My eyes widen. "Half?"

"Yes, perhaps even more by the look of things." Hager's tone is firm but carries a certain level of remorse.

I let out a breath and tilt my head to one side. "Why so many?"

"Our resources are in a worse state than previously reported." Ammon speaks calm and calculated. *So official.*

I sit forward in my chair, adjusting my position, and look back to him. "What kind of resources are we talking here? If it's a matter of funding, I can—"

"It's not the funding, Mr. Osiris." I hold my gaze with his, waiting for more information. "Crops are showing early signs of failure."

"No." I shake my head, thinking to past reports I've seen. "They should still have a good six hundred years before they even start to fail."

"Nutrients in the soil and water are depleting quicker than anticipated with the reduction in sustained atmosphere. They're being bombarded with radiation from the sun where they're exposed. The levels are already on the verge of toxicity for our vegetation."

I interlace my fingers and tuck them under my chin, elbows resting on the table. My breathing is heavy but refuses to shutter. "What will cutting my crew down accomplish for this issue?"

"We are reinstating a plant replenishment project to filter toxins from the air. We'll also introduce artificial nutrients to the plants, assisting with sustained longevity. We'll need some of your best botanists and hydrologists to remain behind for that."

"Only botanists and hydrologists?" I push my tongue to the roof of my mouth, gritting my teeth to keep my concern hidden.

"Yes."

There's a click when the suction breaks, and I prepare to speak. "How long until the toxicity reaches critical?"

"It's estimated at one hundred nintey–five years as levels currently stand."

I take a sharp breath in. "It's at least eighty-seven years of travel to reach the targeted planet with near lightspeed velocity."

All Elders nod in unison. "Yes," Ammon responds.

"That's not enough time."

Elder Shani's soft pitch enters the conversation. "We're working through the set-up of a geoengineering project to create a barrier and apply it as a temporary layer to the exterior of the atmosphere using cloud-seeding technology. It's still under development."

I shake my head and pinch my lips together. "With the time differences involved for our travel, you'll need that to give us at least twenty-five more years of food sustainability. Is it any more stable outside Simbhora limits?"

"It's all still under observation. It's delicate. We don't want to completely cloud off the sun. We do need the plants to grow, after all." She reaches up, brushing a strand of hair away from her slender nose, the sleeve of her tunic sliding up her arm.

"Have you thought to consider artificial lighting on a mass scale while clouding out the sun? We have t—"

"Mr. Osiris." Ammon draws my gaze once more. "We're taking many options into consideration, which is why we need you to select the best of your scientists, outside of those necessary for your journey, to stay behind. They'll work on keeping our people alive until we can get gold back here for our generators."

"We have also assembled a team of engineers to work on a transport gate," Elder Hager adds.

"Transport gate?"

"With the timeline cutting it so close, we need a faster method of getting resources back. We can't afford to wait for a second round trip to attain stability. They are designing a transport gate to skip over the time needed for traveling to get it back to us."

"But that's still cutting it too close. They'll have to at least get back out there and set up the gate before sending anything back." I press my fingers together with such force that they grow numb.

"That's another topic of discussion. You'll need to alter the target landing site," Ammon says.

"Will this push back the launch date?" I ask. They all shake their heads. "I must ask, why are we changing it at this point?"

"While we're cutting your science team, we're sending five to ten new members for an excavation team. They will collect gold resources to bring back. We can stretch it far enough to survive until the port gate is functional."

I nod, taking a deep breath as the pieces connect. "Yes, sir, I understand. I'll have the list of those to cut delivered no later than tomorrow morning."

Ammon bows his head in thanks. "Now, if you'll excuse us, we need to continue discussing other issues at hand."

I stand, excusing myself.

When I exit the building my hands are still shaking. *Cut half the crew? It'll be a late night after dinner, for sure. Shit . . . dinner.* I glance at the sun to see how late I am at meeting Kamal and Pop for dinner. *I have enough time to stop by The Jobi Hut for an apology pastry. Good thing it's on the way.*

Ayathesti - 8

"Dr. Ayathesti Cleoths, you've gained quite the reputation."

I sit in probably the most terrifying moment of my life. And there it is: my face magnified on every screen in the newsroom. Silence cradles me while I stare at the reporter, sweat gathering in the seams of my palms.

"How are you handling all the attention?" she asks. My heart pounds in my ears while my chest struggles to stay in rhythm. "It's normal to be nervous. Why don't you tell us about your contribution to this mission?" The reporter, Mira, crosses her ankles, pushing her posture forward.

My focus shifts to the monitors around the room before settling back on her. "What do you want to know?"

"What does a typical day look like for you?"

"Well . . ." My voice cracks, and I swallow forcefully. "I guess I start out with a morning memo handed out by the lobby receptionist, Nineveh. After that, I go to the sub-levels, where our lab is, and play with chemicals all day."

"Why is your lab located in the sub-levels?"

Relieved she's asking easy questions, my stomach settles a little. "Working with live tissues and chemicals requires a controlled environment. Since the sub-levels are deep in the bedrock, they're better insulated and integrated with regulators to achieve the temperatures needed."

"When you say you play with chemicals, what does that entail?" The reporter folds her hands in her lap and sits back in her chair, as though the voice in her ear is satisfied with my level of communication.

"We break down compounds and regrow them in a culture, testing out different solutions until we get one that works with our genetics to replicate with the correct cellular structure and avoiding any abnormalities."

"Ayathesti, you said 'we.' Are you not the only geneticist working in this lab?"

There's an itch on my cheek that refuses to leave. "No, I'm not. That would be asinine."

Mira's eyes grow wide with either offense or surprise. I can't be sure which yet. "What prompts your word choice? Did you not petition The Council to move The Extension Project to the back of the list for survival options?"

"I did." I shift my weight in the chair, glancing at the monitors again.

"And, Dr. Cleoths, did you also include in that petition that 'it would be too dangerous with so many hands getting involved'? That it would 'open higher risks of error'?"

"Well yes, I did, b—"

"So then why is it asinine to assume you're the only geneticist working in the lab?"

Offended . . . she definitely got offended. "I'm the only senior geneticist working this project. However, I have my aid, Latif. Two sets of hands get more done. There are things to do that don't increase the chances of error." My breath is quaking as sweat crawls down my hairline.

"Is this the same Latif who's father sits on The Council?" Her eyebrows perk up.

I nod. "Yes, but he's per—"

"Just one more question for you. The gentleman selected as director for the first flight mission, Mr. Tiamet Osiris . . ."

I stare at her in silence. Gritting my teeth in annoyance at her ease of cutting me off.

"How do you two get on?" The corners of her lips

snake into a predatory smirk, as if she's ready to strike with fangs at a moments notice.

With my hands folded in my lap, I clear my throat again. "I don't know what you mean."

"Well, public record indicates you both attended the academy at the same time."

"Yes, we did."

"So, how do you two get on?" The excitement in her voice is enough to urge the desire of driving a nail through my elbow.

"I don't know what information you're after."

"You two spent a lot of time in class together. Are you friendly? Or will your seniority status cause a rivalry for leadership power?"

"He can have the leadership power. I don't want it. I want to do my job and come home."

"So you mean to say, on a paradise planet with easily the most eligible bachelor in Simbhora, all you want is to 'just do your job'?" Her face flushes as she fans herself with her hand.

"It *is* possible for two professionals to keep their work relationship . . . professional." I bite the inside of my cheek to keep my fingers from fidgeting.

"So outside of professional work, there's more to your relationship?"

"Really? Are we done talking about my mission involvement? Can I go now, or do you get some sick thrill out of twisting my words to fit your narrative?"

"Wouldn't you like to know what he had to say on the matter?" She sits back in satisfied composure.

"Frankly, no. I don't care. We're done. Excuse me." I push my hands against the arms of the chair to a stand and leave the set. My fingers twitch with fury. After rounding the corner, a wave of panic consumes me. My heart slams against my chest, my breath trying to escape. The recording bell echoes through the hallway moments before the clacking of shoes approaches.

"Well done, dear." Mira's voice comes in like a snake from behind.

"I'm not answering any more questions." I fold my arms across my chest to hide the rate of breathing.

"No more questions. The cameras are off."

"Good. How do I get out of here?"

A hand pops onto her hip. "You'll be escorted out in a moment. We need to get your gear removed." With a snap of her fingers, three people seem to appear out of nowhere and remove the electronics from my clothing.

"Hisef will show you out. Be sure to come back again. That was a fantastic interview!" She turns and walks away speaking with the other two assistants. *How does her voice carry such threatening vibes?*

"Not if I can help it." The words escape in a whisper, my skin crawling.

"C'mon." Hisef starts down the long hallway.

What did Tiamet say about how we'll get on? Was she baiting me for a reaction? Do I care what he said or her motives for doing it? I watch my feet as I walk, habit.

Hisef pushes a door open at the end of the hallway. "Have a nice day." He mumbles waiting for me to leave.

The sky burns orange as the sun sets on the city of Simbhora. A chill spreading through the air erects the hair on the back of my neck. Looking out upon the city, hopelessness drops weights on my shoulders, sending a new list of thoughts running through my mind at a million miles per second.

Will we succeed in our mission? Will our people survive? If we do, how long will it last? What if I disappoint everyone? Will this backfire?

These are only a few things that come to mind as I walk past the doors to the KRUL. Taking a deep breath, I turn and face the doors.

With my hand in my coat pocket, I grasp a ring of keys. I feel the smooth metal of each one before stopping on a thin stem with a T-shaped end. I missed my end-of-day ritual, but closing my eyes allows me to perform it in my mind.

Here is where I'd normally place the key into the crease where the glass doors come together, prompting blue lights to cascade down like the night sky during a meteor shower as they glide over the surface of the glass from the center of the doors to the frame.

Thanks to my imagination, I can get my night back on mental track. I look at my reflection in the window as the light in my mind fades.

Black hair falls like moss tendrils on a tree, getting caught in the jewelry on my ears. Genetic lineage markings intensify the saturation of blue in my eyes and cause the yellow center to appear green under the glow. The fiery sky offsets my lavender skin to an orange hue. In this lighting, I'm unrecognizable. If I hadn't seen myself this way many times before, I'd be convinced I was someone else.

I look down at the identifier tattoo upon my wrist, thinking about my heritage. It's a reminder of the pride I should feel granted through my ancestry. The open teardrop hooks at the upper left corner and emits pulses of dull-blue light. I remember the last day I spent with my father, when he took me to scribble my signature in the center. Typically, signatures are renewed as we age, but I couldn't let go of that last day I saw him alive.

Tiamet - 9

My stomach grumbles in protest of working, dragging my attention from the monitors that are sifting through data and narrowing the options of a new landing site. I look at the clock on the wall, the numbers illuminated blue with two orange dots appearing on the left side and three on the right. I rub my face with my hands and my stomach growls again. *Can I really be that late to lunch? No wonder my side is screaming at me.*

With a double tap on the keyboard projected onto my desk, the screen locks and I make my way to the cafeteria. After retrieving my tray of food, I sit at an empty table, still organizing the landscape data in my head.

I delivered my list of crew cuts to The Council this morning to be reviewed before notices went out. By the look of those around me, it would appear the announcement has yet to be made. *If Elder Ammon hadn't specifically said not to mention it until the list of cut personnel was fully approved and finalized, I would have mentioned something to people this morning.*

A tray clinks in the collection bin moments before a body hovers next to me. I lean to the side slightly, looking up with a smile. "Afternoon, Nineveh."

"May I sit?" she asks. I motion my hand toward the empty chairs around me. Breath escapes her when she sits, and she pinches her hands between her knees as she settles in. "So."

"So." I smile and raise my eyebrows, taking a bite of my orange pasta drizzled in a tang sauce.

She fidgets with her hands, looking out the big windows behind me into the hallway.

"Something on your mind?" Reaching for my glass, I swish the water into my mouth before swallowing, eyes content, awaiting a response.

She looks at me and sits forward. "Tiamet, I—I'm not sure I'm the best person to lead medical on the expedition."

I cock my head to the side, eyebrows perking up. "Medical lead, really?"

"Yes, of course, silly. You recommended me, didn't you?"

"No. I simply gave them a list of our best botanists and hydrologists."

"Oh . . . Well if botanists and hydrologists need to stay here, why did the medical lead get pulled?"

"I based the decision on more than current job position. I looked at the credentials of each person, and our medical lead has a strong background in botany. That's why they selected him initially. He had a dual purpose with medical experience and being able to help in plant collection."

"But . . . I only just applied to work at the medical office here. Am I even qualified to lead on a different planet?"

I set my fork down and tent my hands over my tray, my elbows resting on the table. "Nineveh, you're as qualified as anyone else they could have selected. I know you're still at TASA, but I also know you're almost finished. As top in your class year, no less."

Her eyes sparkle, and her pink lips part in a smile. "Oh, you're just saying that because we're friends."

"Are we?" I raise my eyebrow and smirk.

Her jaw drops and her eyebrows furrow. "You don't think we're friends?"

I chuckle and wave my hands in the air. "Nineveh,

I'm kidding. Of course we're friends. But that's not why I'm saying this." I spin pasta around my fork, maintaining eye contact. "Besides, they didn't include me on deciding replacements."

"They didn't? But you're the director of the mission. They should include you on the final say of who's on your team." She adjusts her position in the chair, sitting back and eyeing Ayathesti as she walks in.

I glance at Ayathesti as she makes her way to the meal counter before looking back to Nineveh, and I shake my head. "The Council told me this morning, after I dropped the list off, that I'm to keep quiet about the whole thing until they agree and finalize the selections. So say nothing to anyone, okay?"

She touches a finger to her lips.

"Even Ayathesti." I tilt my head downward, eyes still focused on Nineveh.

"My word is silent, Mr. Director." She giggles, shrugging her shoulders.

I smile and chew when she sits forward again and shrills across the room, waving her arms around. Glancing to where she's looking, I see Ayathesti walking toward us.

"That guy you like, Nineveh? He's insufferable today." She sets her tray on the table next to Nineveh.

"What's he up to now?" I sip from the water in my glass.

"Oh, you know Latif, same old jokester stuff."

"Did something specific happen, or are you just not in the mood to tolerate existing today?"

Nineveh glares at me. "He's such a goofball, makes me laugh." Her cheeks flush.

"He has his moments, sure," Ayathesti says, examining the leafy greens on her tray. "But he's not funny all the time. You're just twitterpated and don't know better to look past that trait."

"Why should I look past it? He's cute, funny, and he's nice to me, too." Nineveh turns in her chair to face Ayathesti.

"So we're ignoring me now, I see," I say to myself, popping a crunchy purple veggie into my mouth.

Ayathesti only glances at me before turning back to Nineveh. "All I'm saying is, maybe explore your options. Don't limit yourself. Have a little adventure, you know?"

"Oh, I'll be having a wild adventure!" Nineveh turns to look at me when I tap my fork against my tray, raising my eyebrows at her. "You don't think Latif is a wild adventure, Tiamet?" She puts her finger to her lips again.

"Yeah, aren't you two, like, best friends . . . or whatever?" Ayathesti finally speaks to me again but brings her focus back to her food.

"We're good friends, yes." I watch her.

"Good thing you've got connections. That way, you can hold all the power during our trip, huh?"

Nineveh looks at Ayathesti, confused. "I'm sure Latif had nothing to do with The Council's choice of Director."

"It's alright, Nineveh." I smile at her. "Are you going to the Zeyo after work later?"

She bites her bottom lip and looks toward the ceiling. "Hmm . . . I'm not sure. Are you bringing Latif with you?" Her shoulders scrunch up again, hiding behind her curly hair.

"I don't think he'll be hard to convince." I chuckle, sitting forward.

"Then I'll be there! So long as I get my duties completed early enough to leave on time. In which case, would you both excuse me?" She stands and faces Ayathesti. "Are you coming tonight? I'd love to see you outside of the cafeteria!"

Ayathesti stabs her fork into her food and sighs,

letting her cheek sink into her palm. "If Latif doesn't get on my nerves too much, I may tolerate one drink."

"Oh, goody!" Nineveh giggles and turns to leave.

"Now, hold on! That's not a 'yes,' that's a 'we'll see,' " Ayathesti says louder as Nineveh continues to walk away, waving a hand over her shoulder.

"I'll take it." Nineveh's voice trails off as she rounds the corner out of the room.

I watch Ayathesti pick through the berries and lettuce on her tray. "Rough day?"

"No." She pinches the berry between her lips and chews slowly.

"Okay . . ." More silence lingers in the air between us. "You just seem exceptionally irritated with Latif today."

"I didn't get much sleep last night."

"I'm sorry to hear that. Anything you want to get off your mind?" Since she won't look at me, I line the prongs of my fork up on the edge of my tray as a distraction.

"Not particularly, no."

"Not even about my goal to grasp all the power on our trip?" I lick my lips and raise my eyebrows when she glares at me. "Your words, not mine."

"Go ahead and deny it. I know that's what you're after."

"Aya, what are you on about?" A buzzing starts in the bottom of my chest, prompting me to fold my arms over it.

"It doesn't matter. You can have the power, I don't want it."

"I—ok . . ."

"I know you talked about me in your interview yesterday."

I nod, pinching my lips together. "Did you watch it?"

"No."

"So you don't know what I said, just that it was about

you?"

She stabs a berry with her fork, rather violently. "She asked about our *relationship*." The word seems to roll off her tongue with disdain, sending a stab into my gut.

"Ah, well, I didn't talk about any relationship. Just how much I care about people on my team and wanting to see them reach their full potential." I tilt my head to the side, watching her spin her fork in circles over her food. "It's what reporters do, you know?"

"What is?"

"They bait you into saying what they want," I say. She lifts a fork full of glazed greens to her mouth. "Aya, look—"

"It's not worth your breath, Tiamet." She stands, grasping her tray.

"You're finished already?"

"So?"

I shrug. "Nothing. I just—"

"I'm not a child. I don't need you to take care of me."

I nod my cup toward the door without a word. *If I open my mouth, kindness may not come out.* She rolls her eyes and leaves her tray on the bin with a clank before exiting.

Leaning back in my chair, I fold my arms across my chest again when the buzzing returns. *What can I do to make her less defensive? Is it just trial and error over time? Maybe after this entire trip is over. That's assuming I can figure out where gold deposits may reside for a new landing site.*

Sitting forward, I tap my fork against the metal tabletop. Clink, clink, clink. My chest contracts. "If I can recalibrate the image probe to send out a magnetic pulse and can use the camera lens to narrow in on specific areas . . ." I push myself from the table and grab my tray. I leave it at the bin and quickly make my way downstairs.

I swipe my wrist under the scanner at the clean room-doors, where Ayathesti stands waiting for them to open. I'm peeling through layers of coding for the probe in my mind to get a head start on making changes. When the door opens, we both step inside and wait through the endless seconds of decontamination.

Ayathesti - 10

My chest stays tight as we stand in that chamber together, waiting for the doors to open. I can see his smile in my peripherals. *Why isn't he breaking the silence? He always breaks the silence.*

Sweet freedom allows me to escape to the observation floor. I rush across the room, enter the sub-level elevator, and turn to catch his curious glance toward me before I'm lowered. The descending elevator breaks our eye contact and I step back, leaning my head against the wall with a sigh. After the elevator door opens, I hesitate to enter the low-lit room and stop at the paper-laden desk, trying to analyze the entire encounter.

"Woah, what's this?" Latif projects his voice. "Why does the slave driver herself look as though someone has put her back in line where she belongs?"

"Oh, can it, daddy's boy." *I'm far from the mood to be passive toward his attitude for the rest of the day.* Able to take the obvious hint, Latif directs his attention back to the petri dishes. Without another word, he pulls a thin layer of pink film from the bottom of it and drapes it down on a piece of mesh paper with a light-blue film already placed.

"No, no, no! What are you doing?" I rush toward him, my heart pounding.

"Hands off, boss, I've got this."

"That's the wrong process for this, you—" My jaw tightens, holding back my comment. Air hisses through my teeth as I breathe. "Latif, we're not working with plants here. You know that, right? This is a complex biological makeup." I tick my ear to my shoulder and reach for the tweezers in his hand. "Give it."

Latif takes a step back after passing the tweezers over. *At least he'll listen when I work up the nerve to act like I'm in charge.* "Sorry, Aya, you're right. I'm automated to plants . . ." There's a sound of sorrow in his voice, like he's admitting himself to some kind of truth.

"You were working on the replenishment project, I know." I steady my breath and focus. "It might be salvageable." I pick at the edge of the pink film with the rubber-tipped tweezers. "Get me the, um"—I squint and furrow my brow—"white solution, beaker, cleaner fluid, and a syringe."

I lift the paper with care to the workstation at the room's center. Latif sets the tools on the table. I create a diluted solution by pouring a small amount of each fluid into the beaker. With the syringe, I siphon the concoction from the beaker and drizzle it onto a silk cloth held by the tweezers. I let it glide over the top of the films bonded with the mesh, watching with anticipation for them to release. After placing the syringe down on a glass tray, I use both hands to attempt peeling it off.

With gentle pressure, I lift the pink film from the paper as it tears at the edge. I close my eyes and take a deep breath before opening them again to proceed. The pink sample releases its hold on the paper. Hope taps on my shoulder. The moment flees when I watch the sample dissolve right before my eyes. I let out a grunt of frustration before refocusing my attention to the blue film. With the same results, I set everything down, bathing in defeat. The sample is unsalvageable.

"Sorry, boss. I wasn't even thinking." Latif picks up pieces of disposable equipment and tosses them into the trash.

I wave my hand to dismiss his apology. "No, it's fine. We'll just do a new one. I should've been down here sooner. Don't worry about it." I look over to see concern slathered across his face. "What?" I look at the workstation, then the floor.

"Your hand," he mutters, pointing.

I lift my arm into the light and sigh—not a sigh of sadness or upset, but annoyance. "Today can just be over now if it wants. I sure wouldn't mind that right now." My inner monologue spills out as I push myself away from the table. *How could I have been so concerned with salvaging the sample that I forgot to put gloves on?*

I thrust my hand under the sink nozzle to stop the chemicals from eating away more tissue. I clench and flinch in pain, forcing myself not to pull away. After grabbing a small plastic sheet to wrap it in, I walk to the elevator door, twisting my arms around in an awkward position to scan my wrist.

"Go ahead and clean up and head out. I need to file an incident report. And if you've ever been in that office, you know I'll be a while. Just . . . don't try anything smart till I get here tomorrow, if you will." I do my best not to sound condescending, though I'm sure that's how it came out anyway.

"Great. Just great." My voice quivers as the elevator nears the surface. Blood rushes to my head as I imagine the stares and whispers. This is only the fourth incident report I've had to file through all my years working in the lab. The doors open, and I walk through the monitor room, hiding my wrist in my lab coat.

Whose brilliant idea was it to place the incident management office farthest from where any actual work gets done? I think as I drag myself up the stairs of the lobby.

An elderly woman at the medical reception desk

stashes a pencil into grey hair twisted on the back of her head. "Yes, dear, do you have an appointment?" She looks at me over the rim of her glasses, folding her fingers together under her chin.

"I need incident papers for personal injury." I'm relieved that she's nicer than the other girl they had here years ago. It helps keep my voice calm.

She grabs a pen, tapping it on a glass tablet stack at the front of the desk. I take the pen and clipboard to a chair near the front door.

Nearly two hours pass while I fill out the paperwork. *To think I've been here so long and still need to see the medical director.* By this time, the building is nearly evacuated, leaving me wondering what's taking so long. I adjust my position in the chair, straightening my back, and look at the desk clerk.

"Oh, dear, are you still waiting?" She clicks her nails on the desk. I nod without a word. "Right, well you can go on in, then."

"Thanks." I try not to sound too annoyed as I make my way to the examination room. *Did she honestly forget I was waiting?*

Ayathesti - 11

Stinging in my hand drags me from integration with the void. My eyes open gradually, preparing for light to set my brain ablaze. Peeling myself from the comforter, I initiate my typical routine. The motions happen on autopilot: bladder, sink, hair, clothes. I wince at the heat that comes in waves as it radiates through my palm to my wrist, reminding me of yesterday's mishap.

Wanting to continue my usual undisrupted walk to work, I store my hands in my pockets while observing my surroundings. I take a mental note of the people in today's ever-changing flow of business. Indifference rushes over me when I enter the KRUL lobby doors later than my standard arrival time. I make my way to Nineveh's desk and lean one arm on top, resting my chin on my palm while my injured arm stays hidden to my side.

"Good morning, Aya! We were just talking about . . ." Nineveh trails off after turning from her conversation with Latif. "Well, never mind. It looks like you probably don't want to know."

It seems I'm in more of a melancholy mood than I realized, and interrupting their conversation no longer intrigues me. Why ruin their fun start to a great day? I clear my throat. "No, continue. I just wanted to ask if you'd do me a favor. Will you call in a delivery order for me? A three-of-five oojo in a tall glass would do the trick. And if it's not any trouble, would you mind tossing in an anodyne once it comes over?"

"Um, okay, sure." Nineveh's eyebrows contort, her

freshly glossed lips no longer smiling.

"I'll be upstairs for a bit, so no rush." I glance at Latif, then back to Nineveh, before stepping away from the counter. Nineveh is a close friend, always eager to help where she can. Even still, guilt engulfs me in a cold embrace for pulling her away from their conversation for my benefit.

After the typical wait in the health ward and a fresh wrap applied, I make my way down the stairs and meet Nineveh at the front desk with a sigh. "Hey, Nin," I say, my voice just louder than a whisper.

"Aya, I couldn't get anodyne." Nineveh stretches her arms toward me, presenting a thick paper cup and a transparent candy lid.

Heat radiates into my hand when I take it from her. "No, it's fine." I force a smile to my eyes. "I don't need it anymore. I shouldn't have asked in the first place."

"Well . . . why did you?"

I bring the cup to my lips, inhaling deep and slow, taking in the mint fragrance, allowing it to sink into my bones. I tilt it with care till the hot liquid claws at my lips. The aroma fills my mouth more than the flavor does as I hold it there for a moment before swallowing. I lick my lips and set it on the countertop.

"Oh, I was lazy getting back from lunch yesterday," I tell her. "And Latif decided to—well, wait, he didn't tell you?"

"Who, Latif?" Her eyebrows quirk. "Why would Latif know why you're acting weird this morning?"

I nod. "Yes, Latif." The way his name slips from my mouth with sarcasm shows the nature of our relationship. "Isn't that what you were discussing this morning? Aya's newest perfectionist, controlling moment?" I lean forward with my elbows on the countertop, both hands now clinging to the cup.

"No, we were talking about what happened at the Zeyo last night."

"Oh, sorry . . . Well anyway, Latif tried to keep the ball rolling on rebinding specimens but used the wrong process is all. Naturally, I freaked out and got burned. So . . . nothing major." Another mouthful of aroma stops my words, forcing me to think about them before they come out sour. "Just a bit of morning pain to start my day."

"Oh, so the whole upstairs thing? That's what that was about. It was my next question." Nineveh puffs her chest out with pride.

"Yes, that's what it was about." I'm not one for knowing what's going on in others' lives, but I'm not sure Nineveh could live without her daily gossip. In secret, I like her knowing what's going on in my world. She's safe. "Well, I better get back to it. I'll see you in a while for lunch."

Tiamet - 12

Nineveh sits at the lobby desk doing more than her normal amount of paperwork, folding, collecting, organizing and sorting, putting documents into separate folders for each department in the building. I tap on the countertop, sending her into a jolt before she turns to look up. A breath of relief is followed by a giggle.

"Oh, good morning, Tiamet! You scared me. I thought you were my replacement." She reaches for a folder and takes a breath to prepare the occasional morning briefing.

"You can save yourself the speech, oh chipper one." I grasp the folder from her coolly and pocket my free hand, leaving my lab coat hanging from my wrist. "Replacement? You accepted medical lead then?"

"Yes, I did. But it will take a few weeks before the new girl is trained and they complete my move to the medical ward." Nineveh looks down and continues sorting the pile of papers before her.

The light reflecting through the windows bounces off the mirror-like surface of the countertop, catching on her glossy lips. It brightens her jade eyes, urging the red in her hair to shine through the brown hue. "That's alright, time is just one thing that will always stand between now and the future, as long as we're moving linearly. You shouldn't be worried. I'm not too worried about how great you look right now." My brain sends the words to my mouth automatically. *I've lost my train of thought. Did I really just say that?*

Nineveh giggles, looking back at me. "What are you going on about? How good I look?"

I straighten my posture in an attempt to erase my

embarrassment. "Sorry, new lighting, I suppose. It's a great look on you. No wonder Latif finally made his move." Her lips part in surprise before I turn and walk away casually.

The sound of the doors decompressing to the upper deck lab has become one of hushed nuisance. I step through them, muscle memory dragging my feet past obstacles that reside between the doors and my data station. The act of pulling my chair underneath me forces breath from my chest while I prepare for my tasks of the day.

I lean on the glassy white desktop while staring at the elevator door in the far corner of the room. The thick translucent monitor in front of me emits a soft glow around the edges as it powers on. A blue screen flashes awaiting access codes. With a habitual sweep of my wrist, it fades to deep green before lighting up with images and programs holding data about Earth.

My thumb repeatedly flicks the edge of the folder Nineveh provided earlier, causing the corner to curl upward. I hold it in my hand, lifting it to fall open before me. My eyes skim over general daily memo information about safety procedures and our current timeline for the initial flight. I twist my chair side to side while shuffling the papers around to ensure I've seen all the new information before closing the folder.

I push my chest forward, stretching as I come out of a slouch. Clearing my throat, I turn my attention to the screen, ready for the impending battle between my mind and lists of data—images of creatures, topographical maps, temperature maps, graphs correlating all these things into viable landing site options, and the new code to locate gold deposits hidden at the base of everything. *At least the workload is light today.*

A deep voice in a nearby conversation steals my concentration. "Pilet, I still don't understand why you're so shocked at her reactions in public. *Everybody* knows how uptight she is."

"Did you see how out of it she was, though? I figured for sure the amount of liquor she consumed would calm her down," a whiny voice responds.

"I've seen her there a lot, but I'm not really obsessed with her, so I don't count her cups," the other voice says back with a teasing snicker.

"Ah, Jarem, we all know redheads are more your type anyway. Don't tell me you don't count Nineveh's drinks! Particularly when she's seen hanging out with that dark-haired guy. His name always escapes me. You know the one I mean—thinks he's hot shit because his dad is on The Council."

I glance over my shoulder to where Pilet and Jarem stand by a workbench. Pilet is a short, string bean of a guy with a shaggy light-colored mop plopped atop his head. Jarem towers over him in comparison, with his short raven-black hair, granola skin, and honey-brown eyes. His broad shoulders are like slabs of pure muscle.

"Latif?" Jarem's deep voice carries confidence.

"Yeah! That's the one!" Pilet squeaks from his tiny throat. "Bet you'd like to show him how a real man courts a lady!"

Both men erupt in a chuckle before I do a full turn in my chair and catch my feet on the floor to stand. It's obvious that Pilet is hyper-sensitive to movements in his surroundings; his focus whips toward me. Jarem's gaze slowly follows, a smile still on his lips by the time I reach them.

"Interesting workload you've got over here," I say, trying not to sound condescending.

Pilet rubs his hands together nervously, averting his eyes. Jarem turns his full body to me, fearless. "Just taking a bit of a break before we get back into it."

"Ah . . . yes. I see. I have nothing against that. I tend to take breaks myself. But if I recall, this task is better done in the break room, rather than on the work deck."

"You're one to talk about rules." Pilet's shoulders shiver as he finds the courage to speak.

"Excuse me?" I do my best not to snap at him.

Jarem places his hand on Pilet's shoulder. "Tiamet, it's just a passing conversation in the moments between work. We certainly understand the rules and how important our work is."

"I would hope so Jarem. As head of security, it's vital you have all situations planned for." I put my hands in my pockets. "These types of conversations can be a distraction while on the work deck. That's the purpose of having a break room."

Jarem nods. "Yes, we understand that. Our deepest apologies if the conversation was unsettling to you and others in any way."

"I appreciate your cooperation, Jarem." I look toward Pilet and offer a polite nod before dismissing myself back to my station.

The room is busy around me. I keep my chin high, tray in one hand, puffing my chest out in confidence—the kind of confidence a leader would have. I know all too well where the busy tables are, as people group around them with their closest friends. *I used to blend in with them, mingling where I please. But they look at me differently now, calculating their responses. I miss casual conversations.* I think back to Jarem's responses earlier. The words exchanged no longer had the flow and relaxed presence they usually had. *I know he's security and respects authority, but we're friends . . . or at least I thought we were.*

The corner of my eye catches her swaying ponytail and lavender skin as she places her tray near a bin at the cafeteria entrance. I break eye contact with a passerby to watch her walk along the big windows separating the room from the hallway. Her gaze is toward the floor, her hands engulfed in her pockets. *Why do you always look so sad?* I think as I take in the way she moves, as if in slow motion, with precision and grace. *What's weighing on your mind?*

Like a statue, unable to break my concrete focus, I remain where I am until she's no longer in view. Conversations we've shared over the past few weeks flood my mind. Her smile consumes me while I drown in her ocean-like eyes ribboned with the gold our people crave for survival.

The swelling roar of conversations penetrates the silent barrier in my brain. In an instant, I'm drawn away from her soft, high cheekbones and am surrounded by people consumed within their own experiences. I flick my tongue to wet my lips and continue looking around, making brief eye contact with people as they acknowledge me.

I settle in next to Nineveh and Latif, who are deep in a conversation that shows signs of going nowhere based on both their inabilities to recognize flirting.

"Good afternoon, Tiamet!" Nineveh seems to never lose her cheer.

A half smile crosses my lips and I nod toward her. "Afternoon, Nineveh. Latif." I shovel a large portion of food into my mouth.

"You missed Aya by only a moment. She's hardly said a word to either of us all day." Nineveh admires a napkin on the table, twisting the corners to emphasize the design of the bird she's folded it into.

"I'm not sure what world you're from, where Ayathesti ever says much, Nin." Latif smirks. "Working with her, you get used to how quiet life can be without external stimuli."

"Well, she talks to me." Nineveh crinkles her nose.

An uncontrolled yawn forces my jaw open. Blinking my heavy eyes, I shake my head and turn my gaze to the windows by the table. "I want to know what goes on in that lovely mind," I murmur to myself before turning to Latif and Nineveh. "The amount of one's silence has a tendency to reflect the inner complexity of their thought process. She chose her profession for a reason, after all. Having known her back at the academy I can assure you she's brilliant and would have done well in any career. Those glasses she created, for example. I believe she makes her own fragrances as well as stained glass windows. And if you could hear the angelic way she hums in innocence when she's content with a task . . . you'd likely want to dive inside the depths of her mind right along with me, just to explore the wildlife that lives beneath the surface."

Latif contorts his eyebrows. Nineveh, with her hands to her chest, looks as though she's hurting inside, sharing my longing to know more about Ayathesti's inner world.

I look at them. "What?"

"Are you on your mating cycle?" Latif snorts.

Nineveh gasps and slaps his shoulder.

"Ow!" He chuckles, rubbing his shoulder, content with his own humor.

"That was *very* inappropriate, Latif! He's allowed to have feelings!" Nineveh crosses her ankles and turns her back to him, pouting.

"I only mean he's talking as though he got drugged with an entire vat of hormones! 'Delve into the ocean of her mind.' " He inhales to laugh—only to choke on saliva instead.

Nineveh bites her lips together to hold back her amusement.

I can't help smiling at his karmic misfortune. "No, Nineveh. He's right. This feels sudden to me too."

She smiles. "What do you mean?"

"She's always just been another person. Do I like her? Sure, but until a few hours ago, it was merely playful banter." Placing my utensils on the tray, I straighten and stretch my lower back, resting my elbows on the table.

"What happened a few hours ago?" Nineveh asks, perking up with excitement at the prospect of new information. Latif leans forward with one hand on his knee to get closer, as though he struggled to hear me.

"A conversation between two colleagues. They were discussing someone who's interested in someone else. Long story short, I guess it made me realize that playful banter grants no certainties." I quirk an eyebrow at Latif with implication.

Nineveh puts a hand to her blushing cheek. Latif narrows his eyes, pursing his lips. "What are you getting at?"

I run my hand through the locks brushing against my forehead. "Something needs to change." I put my hands on the table and stand. Grabbing my tray, I look at them one last time and step away from the table. "The pieces on this game board need to be moved, and she doesn't seem keen on being the first to move."

I walk away from the table and dispose of my tray before exiting the cafeteria. My heart is pounding in my chest with newfound excitement. My feet lead me down the staircase with determination as I coordinate a plan in my head for how to break the thick sheet of ice between me and *her*.

Ayathesti - 13

The clock hanging above the elevator door changes from light blue to amber, indicating the time has come for the workday to end. I lean against the cold metal countertop, staring at the glow. I fold my arms in slight disbelief that I managed to go through the day avoiding conversations with everyone. Lost in the light, my focus breaks with the sound of Latif sifting through papers on the desk. My eyelids flutter, and I direct my gaze to him.

"Latif, I can handle this if you want to head out." My tone is soft and tired.

He continues as if my words were silent, then I clear my throat. "No way, boss. I've decided I want to be more like you." He places the recently organized folders on top of the desk.

I pop a hand onto my hip, shifting my weight to one side. "What, curvy?" I attempt to stifle a smile, watching for his response.

With a smile and a shake of his head, he reaches for a paper on the edge of the workstation. "No." He turns back to the desk and places it on top of the pile. "Dedicated."

"Ahhh, haha. I see." I pick up a few pieces of equipment and make my way to the sink. I place them under the nozzle from which water flows in a slow, steady stream. The residue of fluids used in them snake their way to the drain.

Latif's elbow nudges mine, pushing me to the side. He reaches into the sink, grabbing a beaker. "Those were my mess. I've got this." He nods his head toward the door. "You should get that bandage changed."

My eyebrows furrow further as suspicion swells inside me. I hesitate but turn, making my way toward the exit. "Right, uh . . . Well, see you tomorrow, then." I stare at him, watching for a sign of trickery or humor. Glancing around the room, I take my time leaving.

After receiving a fresh bandage, I leave the medical ward and make my way back down to the lobby. I look up at the high ceilings as a hiss sounds from the doors to the surveillance deck. *Who could possibly be leaving this late?* My toes catch on the floor when I see Latif stepping into the lobby. My heart races as I regain balance.

"You're still here?" My voice echoes across the otherwise abandoned room.

"Well, no, not anymore. I'm leaving." Latif makes his way toward me.

"Well, yeah, but . . . Oh, nevermind." My mouth and my brain refuse to cooperate with one another in attempting to find a reason for his late departure. I look at the entry doors and start toward them with Latif on my heels.

With street lights lit, our feet against the dirt is the only sound between our inconsistent small talk.

"So is it true you feel that way? That this will all be for nothing?" His lips contort as he aims to kick the same small pebble along the path through the park while we walk.

I watch the tip of my shoes as they occasionally peek out from under the flow of my dress, my hands clasped at the small of my back. "Don't worry about it. What I think shouldn't concern you."

"But it does."

"Why is that? It makes no difference to the mission if I think it'll fail or not."

"Because you're the lead geneticist. What you think should concern everybody." He swings his foot back, ready to kick the pebble harder than before.

My insides clench at the thought of everyone assessing my innermost thoughts, and I squeeze my hands together.

"I mean, you have complete control over our success," he says. His toe hits against the stone, sending it into the base of a tree along the edge of the path. But the purple tufts remain as still as the night around us.

I snort with laughter. "Hardly!"

"Well, Pop sure seems to have a different idea on the subject. He insists your brilliance is the key to everything."

"Your pop being on The Council doesn't make him the smartest man in the room, Latif. It's all more complicated than my job skills. If only it were that easy."

"How would that be easy?" He picks up his pace to kick a new stone ahead of us.

Tendrils of silence grip me while my mind sifts through words to formulate an adequate response. "If that was the only stipulation to our species surviving, I'd just come up with an alternative solution all together." I gnaw on my lower lip. "In fact, if it were up to me, I would say we stop allowing the higher class in our society to be lazy. I don't know what it takes to run the planet, nor do I care to know, but if every citizen pitched in a bit on this new planet, we could gather enough materials to sustain us till we find an alternate solution."

"Wouldn't that just allow you to be lazy instead of The Council?" he chuckles.

"No. Even if it did, that's not the point." I clench my

jaw with frustration at his misinterpretation of my calculated response.

We turn the corner from the park to the street that houses the Zeyo. Latif turns for the entry doors while I maintain a straight path for home.

"No way." He steps backward and grabs me by the elbow, pulling me to a stop.

"What?" I stare at him.

"Boss, you work way too hard! Come have a drink with me."

I pull my arm from his grasp slowly. "First Nineveh, and now you've got some weird thing going on for me? I don't think I'm your type, Latif. If all of what happened back at the lab was to impress me, I can save you some trouble a—"

"Woah! Nooo. Nooooope. Nuh-uh. No way." He throws his hands up defensively. "Nineveh is . . . Wait, how do you know about my affections for her?"

I raise my brow. "Honestly? Latif, I work with you…" I look at him, waiting for him to get it. "It's obvious!" I raise my voice and chuckle at his blank expression.

He averts his eyes to the doors. "Anyway . . . You work way too hard. Like you said, I work with you. Just come have a drink. We can keep chatting, and we'll chill for a bit."

Why is it I spend days arguing with myself about something, but the moment someone else asks me to do something I'm easy to give in?

"Alright, alright! Fine. But you're buying!" A small smile graces my lips after I push past him and head toward the doors, content with my decision to accept the invitation.

I slide a chair out from under a small circular table and look around before sitting down with a sigh.

Latif places a hand on the table, leaning closer to me. "What's your flavor?"

I twinge my lips to one side "Hmm . . . Anything musky. Surprise me."

"You women and making decisions." He shakes his head. "I've got this," he says and heads to the bar.

I examine the faces in the room, those alone and in groups. My eyes catch a glimmer of curly red hair turning the corner from the lavatory. The clicking of shoes match her gait, growing louder on the marble floor as she makes her way into the room. Latif catches Nineveh's gaze as she does a double take at him standing at the bar holding two drinks. Her eyes then meet mine. Eyebrows furrowed, she makes her way to our table.

"What are you doing here?" A breeze blows past my face as she stops right next to me.

"Um . . . Latif convinced me to stop in to wind down." I look at him at the bar, then back at her.

She sits, forcing out a breath. Arms folded, she looks over at Latif. "You *know* how I feel about him. I didn't even see him leave today! You always stay late. How could you ever do this to me! I have tried to—"

"Nineveh, would you lower your voice?" I lean closer to her, and I can't help getting defensive. "What are you talking about?"

"You . . . and Latif. Here. Together. He's buying you drinks!" Nineveh's voice cracks, her eyes glistening with the threat of tears.

"Oh . . ." My defensiveness morphs into empathy as I place one hand on her forearm. "Nineveh." I lean my head toward her, ensuring eye contact. "There are so many reasons why that would never happen. I don't like younger men, for one. I work with him, and let me avoid talking about that mess, even if I *wanted* to like him. And, well, you're my best friend, and I would never do that to you." I glance at him as he makes his way back to us from across the room. "My hand needed a fresh wrap. He volunteered to finish cleaning up. We happened to leave at the same time, and he asked me to join him. Not to mention you're both crazy into one another."

Nineveh maintains the pout on her face and averts her eyes from my glance to the floor just as Latif steps up to the table. She glances up from his shiny black shoes to the three drinks in his hands. She pinches her eyes closed to, I assume, rid them of moisture. A tiny upturn of the corner of her lips appears, and she returns her gaze to me as Latif places the glasses on the table and finds a chair.

I look at the glasses, then back at her. "He seems to know you're stalking him. Do you suppose he wants to have two of those himself?"

An underlying smile breaks across her face. "You're right. I'm sorry! But best friend, huh?" she leans in. "And I'm not a stalker!" The words escape in a whisper when Latif sets a chair down and sits beside her with a satisfied smile.

I was the first to not waste time taking my drink. I bring the glass to my lips, inhaling slowly. A cloud of dust is the first to hit my senses. It's followed by flower petals being blown through a cool spring breeze. A sigh of approval resonates in my throat. I part my lips to allow the smallest amount of liquid to pass through. The smell of musk sits heavy on my tongue, filling the cavern of my mouth, dancing with the subtle sweetness of rose extract. I part my lips further, gulping down the liquid. Warmth radiates in me as it settles in my stomach. With the next breath, a rush of cool breeze from the peppermint fills my lungs.

With raised brows, I look at the glass, then glance at Latif and mouth the word "Wow." I let out a deep breath, enhancing the chill filling my throat before placing my glass back on the table. Latif has an accomplished smile on his face before reaching for his glass and consuming its contents.

"What did the doctor have to say about your hand, Aya?" Nineveh's cheeks go pink as she accepts the glass Latif holds out to her.

I look down at my hand, turning the palm upward. "He said it will heal just fine and to come in twice a day until it does. You know, Latif, I'm rather shocked that you didn't tell anybody." I return my gaze to him.

"Really?" Nineveh giggles.

"Yes, really." I look at her. "I figured he would be keen to brag about his boss's requirement to file an incident report."

"But then I'd have to admit I did something wrong." Latif raises a brow, "smart ass" written all over his expression.

"Ahh, right. We couldn't have perfect daddy's boy get caught doing anything wrong!" I over exaggerate to ensure my statement is drowning in sarcasm.

"Well that's quite an evil look, if I've ever seen one." Tiamet's voice bombs in from the side as he approaches the table. I throw my hand underneath the table to hide my bandages. Tiamet reaches for a chair from another table and positions it between myself and Nineveh before settling in.

"She always looks at me that way." Latif laughs.

"I do not!" I snap before rolling my eyes and slouching back into my chair.

"Yeah, no, she doesn't," Nineveh says, defending me.

"I swear, it's like women don't contain the same sarcasm chromosomes as men." Latif shakes his head.

Tiamet's erupts in a laugh as he leans on the table. His eyes battle with mine in a stare down. "Rough day?"

I look at him and follow his gaze to my near-empty glass. "A normal day. Why do you ask?"

"You need a refill . . . and I've never seen that before.

Especially when I'm just arriving." His hand motions toward my glass.

I tuck the inside of my cheek between my teeth and nibble. My thumb rubs the surface of the glass while I try to ignore the smile on his face. "Well, that just shows how well you know me, doesn't it?" I look toward Latif and Nineveh, who are already engaged in their own conversation. *Relying on them to save me from myself in this conversation is pointless.*

"Hey . . . I'm gonna head out." I empty the remaining contents of the glass and savor it before slamming my glass on the table and swallowing. When I rise from my chair, it catches in a groove on the floor. I grab the table's edge with one hand and the back of the chair with the other to steady myself.

"I didn't mean you should leave!" He is in a mid-rise, reaching to assist with the chair, his hand grazing the fingertips of my injured hand.

"No, I'm getting tired. I'll just see everyone tomorrow." I depart from the table, trying to swallow my embarrassment.

"I guess she's not too fond of me." Tiamet's words grow quieter with each step.

"No, she wouldn't even acknowledge my existence in her lab for months." Latif's comment makes me slow my pace to eavesdrop. *Why do I do this to myself? It never makes me feel better.*

"I don't know how to make the lady have more than a three-word conversation with me." That's Tiamet again.

"Oh, you boys need to just stop. She's shy and reserved! She also gets embarrassed easily, so she . . ." *Nineveh coming to my rescue, as always.* I hadn't made my pace slow enough to hear the rest before I pushed myself through the Zeyo entry doors, meeting the night.

I watch my feet as I walk in the quiet. Even with the drink spreading warmth over my skin, there's a chill in the air. I set a mental reminder to ask Latif what he'd brought over so I can request it again. I turn the corner and stare down the line of houses on my street. Breathing gets easier as I reduce the distance to my home.

"Aya."

I had made it to my front step when the voice called out. I pivot to see who's near. I choke on my breath after realizing who it is, my throat strangling my voice.

Tiamet's pace slows as he draws closer.

"What?" I turn back to face my door, silently clearing my throat.

"Why are you running? You're always running away from me." His chest heaves deeply, but steady. *How long had he been chasing me?*

I'm slow to turn and face him once more. "Who says I'm running away?"

"Your actions. Wait . . . were you crying?" He moves toward me, his shoulders easing forward.

I roll my eyes and shift my weight to one side, sighing. "What do you want, Tiamet?"

He stops. *Good, he can take a hint,* I think as he starts speaking again. "I wanted to make sure you're okay."

"I am." I turn back to my door, fumbling with the code box.

"You're sure? You left in a rush."

"Look, Tiamet . . ." My hands fall to my side, and I stare at the ground. *How do I even start to explain why I can't allow myself to get close to him?*

"I'm not blind, Aya." He exhales, his shoes scuffing across the ground as he takes another step closer.

"I never said you were." I turn and face him, my

breath shaky while I force a swallow to smooth my cracking voice again.

"In all seriousness, Ayathesti. If you ever want to talk, I'd be more tha—"

"I'm sure you would." I lean my back against the door, pulling my arms in to shield my chest. "Is that all?"

My heart shatters as a look of defeat washes the concern from his face. Returning my attention to the code box is the only way to avoid facing his pain—pain I caused. *Why did I say that?* I wonder, pressing buttons in habitual sequence just to keep myself distracted. Beeping sounds disrupt the silence as I scan my wrist and the door opens.

"Aya . . ." he whispers, pleading with me. *I've never seen him this way, so broken and sad. I did this.*

Mustering up the rest of my courage, I lock eyes with him.

"I . . ." His hands fall to his side as he exhales. "See you tomorrow." He tucks one corner of his lips into his cheek, a feigned smile.

I nod, closing my eyes to hide the tears welling up. "Yes, I'll be there. Good night." I close the door behind me and lean my back against it, hand clenching at my chest, trying to ease the ache.

Tiamet - 14

My legs weigh me down as they hang over the base of my bed when I wake, my arm dead at my side as it tilts over the ledge parallel to me. Blinking and staring at the wall, I force myself to swallow. It's thick, dry, and scratchy. I clench my jaw and squint at the pain. Ayathesti and I spoke more to each other that night than we have in the past few months. *This is my new awakened life? Should I even keep trying?*

Pinpricks climb up my fingers and into my shoulder after I move. Grunting, I roll over before hoisting my body up.

Maybe I overdid it last night. I stand and swallow again; it goes down easier this time. While running fingers through my hair, I think back to how little interaction I've had with her since then. *What did I do to make her retreat from me more and more by the day?* While examining our interactions, the voice of my mother plays through my mind. *Only you can consent to another making you feel worthless.* I can't help but smile as the ache in my heart starts to feel less constrictive.

Checking the clock, I realize how little time I have if I want to change my pity habits and grab a pastry on my way to work. After splashing water onto my face and rubbing it into my hair, I toss my lab coat over my shoulder and start toward The Jobi Hut.

I arrive just as the owner tacks open the shutters over the order window. "Good morning, Sayali!"

"Oh, good morning, Tiamet!" She beams.

"Do you want help with that?"

"Still as kind as ever." She chuckles and dusts her hands off. "But you're a few minutes too late, dear."

"Well, I'll try to be more timely in the future." I smile and lean on the counter.

Sayali walks through the little hut door and stands on the other side of the now-open window. "What can I get for you, hon?"

"Oh, you know my favorite. Just set me up with that?"

The wrinkles at the corners of her eyes enhance, and her nose crinkles as she smiles. "You bet, sweetie. How's your father doing?"

"Well, you know Pop." A blinding light pierces my peripherals. I look over to find the cause, landing on Ayathesti closing her door and starting down the street toward me. "He's the reason we're all okay."

Sayali places a berry pastry and a cup on the counter. I hand her payment and she holds her hand up. "Pay me later when you come back in tonight."

"Sayali, I can't possibly."

"Hush. Go get the girl. We'll talk later, hon." The sly smile on her face ignites a fire in me.

Pop must have spoken with her recently. I grab the items and smile at her. "Thanks. I'll see you tonight, then!" I turn and jog across the street and slow my pace just ahead of Ayathesti. I sip my oojo and walk, listening for her footsteps to approach.

She passes me within moments, her quick steps not even faltering with an ounce of recognition. I sigh. *You are in control of your worth.* I think and move at a slight jog to catch up before maintaining a small distance between us.

I'm about to close the gap when we arrive at the bottom of the KRUL stairs, but a low mumble of voices spills over the top of them. I start back into a jog up the stairs, shouting on my way up. "Hey! What's going on?"

She spins around, startled, and clutches her arms to

her chest. I climb the stairs, flashing a toothy smile as I pass and say, "Morning." When I reach the top of the stairs, I stop at the back of the group.

"Who knows?" A voice shouts back.

"It's the new girl. She keeps forgetting to unlock the door!" another voice adds.

I catch Ayathesti roll her eyes before pushing her way through the group. Within a few moments, the group starts filing inside. Making my way toward the front, I spot her standing to the side, allowing the others to enter first. With one hand in my pocket and the other still holding my morning oojo, I mosey over and linger next to her.

"So, you're the 'new girl'?" I say, smirking.

"Oh, please." Ayathesti rolls her eyes again before following the last of them inside. "You know for damn sure I have access to lock and unlock the doors."

"Come on, Aya, I was making conversation. Honestly, you've been so . . ." I hesitate. *Watch yourself, Tiamet. Don't want to start a nuclear war.*

She stops and faces me. "So . . . what?"

Her stare surprises me, but our eyes remain locked. "Well . . . distracted."

"Distracted . . ." Ayathesti mumbles, almost as if she's not even aware she's talking to a person. "Distracted?" she repeats louder.

"Yes, distracted. Your work is important, I get it. But really, I'm concerned it's getting out of hand." I finish my oojo and walk past her, making a straight line to the clerk desk where Nineveh used to reside.

"Hana, would you throw this into recycling for me?" I place the cup on the counter and pocket my other hand.

"Um, no, Tiamet. That's not my job. Besides, you're close enough to do that yourself! Unless you think you need my help to just get over there . . ." Her giggle is shy as her short brown hair falls in front of her narrow, flirty eyes.

"Oh, I'm capable. But Hana, I've been thinking . . . the *long* journey to the other side of the room would be more enjoyable if graced with good company." I lean on the counter and gaze at Ayathesti, who stands at the clean-room doors.

Another shy giggle echoes through the room. "Oh, Tiamet! You're such a flirt." She shrugs her shoulders up, tipping her chin to one side as her cheeks blush rose.

I smirk once more and grab my cup from the counter. "Well, I'm just doing my civic duty of spreading smiles throughout the office. Catch you later?" I toss my cup into the recycle bin before standing next to Ayathesti.

"Oh, Nineveh," she says in a mere whisper.

"What's that?" I pocket my hands again.

"Nothing." Her response is monotone, lifeless.

Looking over, I spot the corners of mutilated papers protruding from her folder. "Feeling anxious lately? Those documents look like they've been experiencing some therapy."

"I don't really think that's an appropriate conversation for an office setting. Do you, Tiamet?" She hugs the file folder closer to her chest.

"Sorry, I'll break the silence another way, then." I tap my foot and whistle a lighthearted tune.

She sighs, and I look over, expecting a scowl and a scolding. But she only looks relieved as the doors open and we're allowed to enter the surveillance deck.

"Great talk! See you later." Sarcasm threatens to drown me while optimism holds my head above water as I pretend we just had a titillating conversation.

Ayathesti - 15

The door opens, and Nineveh appears, stopping me from entering the elevator. "Aya!" After months of not hearing her peppy morning voice, it's as sweet as birds singing on the first day of spring. "It's been so long! I've missed you. How have you been?"

With a halfhearted smile, I look at her with tired eyes, my voice mellow. "I'm doing well, Nineveh. It's nice to see you. A friendly face is always welcome."

The smile on her face melts into concern. "You don't look like you're doing well. Is everything okay?" She reaches forward, resting her hand upon my shoulder.

I nod, an unconvincing sigh escaping my lips. "Yes, it's just this new girl, Tingle or whatever her name is. I haven't been able to take a liking to her at all."

"I noticed you've been skipping lunches and keeping yourself isolated in the lab throughout the day. That's not healthy. I haven't seen you at the Zeyo recently either. Oh! You should come out with me tonight! I'll even blow Latif off so it can be just us!" she giggles, her posture perking up again.

The corners of my lips fight gravity. "You know, Nineveh, that sounds nice. How are you liking your new position?"

"Oh, it's fantastic! I'm glad I decided to go to the medical ward. I get to see pretty nasty stuff, but making people feel better is what I'm all about!" She straightens her already perfect posture, exhibiting pride.

"You are superb at it too, Nin." My happiness for her

having found her calling runs through my core. A pain stabs through my chest upon recognizing that I have relied on her daily interactions to keep me sane, though. It seems like ever since she graduated from the academy and took her new position, I can't seem to find my way out of this hole.

"I'd better get upstairs. Paperwork doesn't like to fill itself out!" Nineveh giggles, turns and walks away. "Oh!" She stops and looks over her shoulder. "You're coming to the ship walk-through today, right?"

I nod.

"Oh goodie! I can't wait to see you there, then. We should get lunch after!" She continues out of the room while I watch her. I smile a genuine smile, happiness radiating through me for the first time in what seems like months.

After navigating the hallways of the Engineering Advancement Building, I walk into the room housing the craft commissioned to take us to Earth. The voices of the tour group echo against the tall ceilings like a rumbling waterfall on rocks. I look around to find some source of comfort in the foreign space. The craft appears to be comprised of a flat black surface. *That's disorienting . . .*

The magnitude of this dark object dangles a piece of calm for me to grasp onto. The ship towers over my anxiety, shooing it into the shadows of my mind. *Once again, my insignificance offers solace.*

"Ayclee?" I whip my head around to the deep, unfamiliar voice approaching. "Ayathesti Cleoths?" His eyes glitter like honey in the sunlight, his blond hair rounding out his forehead. His lips, poised in a smile, are plump and pink against his beige skin.

"Yes?"

"Oh, come on. You don't recognize me?" Our eyes lock

as he moves closer. He looks familiar, like I know him somehow, but I can't figure out from where.

"Sorry, I don't."

He laughs, shaking his head. "Typical. You haven't changed a bit! Other than growing up, of course. And man, did you grow up!"

"Excuse me?" I retreat into myself, folding my arms over my chest.

"Aya, it's me. Rothe," he says as I stare at him, searching my memory bank. He sighs. "We used to play together at the riverbank between our farms? Our Dad's worked at the generator plant together."

I'm flooded with memories of my childhood days at that stream with a nerdy, blond-haired boy and am overcome with a smile. "Shut up! Rothe? Wow, your teeth really grew in!"

"Gee, thanks." he laughs.

"Sorry, that was rude. I—do you work here?" I shake my head. *Get back on track, Aya.*

"No apologies necessary, though you're still stuck in that habit, I see."

"What habit?"

"Apologizing for things that aren't necessary."

"Oh . . . I'm just being polite."

"Does it not lose the value of sincerity if overused?"

My heart slams against my chest. "I suppose you're right."

He stands with his hands on his hips, shifting his weight. "Ayclee! What are you doin' here?"

I cringe at the sound of his childhood nickname for me. "I'm looking for the pastry shop."

He smirks. "Is that so? I think you took a wrong turn."

I chuckle. "Obviously I'm here to check out the ship, Ro-ro."

"Yikes. Nobody's called me that since I last saw you."

"So are you touring the ship too or . . .?"

"You bet your britches I am!"

"Do you know where we're all meeting?"

He points to a group of people gathering at one side of the room. "That large flock over there."

"Oh, good. Why wouldn't it be the giant group of people." I raise my eyebrows and sigh.

"Still don't like them all that much, eh? Thought maybe you'd grow out of that, what with all the attention from the mission and such."

I shrug. "Yeah, some things you can't grow into, I guess."

He looks me up and down. "Well, you're definitely not a child anymore."

My cheeks grow warm. "I . . . Well, no. But neither are you!"

"There you are, boss!" I look over my shoulder to find Latif and Nineveh walking toward us.

"I've been here for a few minutes," I reply.

Latif snorts. "How did you lose us?"

Nineveh smacks his arm playfully. "Stop it! She's capable of asking for directions if she gets lost."

"Actually, I wasn't," I tell her.

Nineveh falters. "You . . . Are just talking to some random person for no reason, then?"

"He was talking to me too, Nin."

"And it's not like you talk back," Latif remarks. "So you literally just let this guy talk to himself while thinking you're a real person who will respond?" He gets another deserved smack from Nineveh.

Rothe puts his hand forward. "I'm Rothe. Ayclee and I grew up together."

"Ayclee?" Latif's eyebrows perk up, and he opens his

mouth to laugh.

I clench my teeth and lock eyes with him. *Don't even think about it.*

Latif changes his route of teasing to a safer one. "Ayathesti was never a child!"

"Do you mean she never grew up?" Rothe smirks at me again.

My heart beats faster again. "More like *you* never grew up until I left! You were still no taller than a workbench when I moved to Simbhora."

Rothe puts his hands on my shoulders and steps closer, his chest brushing against my back. He leans in and squishes his cheek against mine. "Ohhh, you weren't so tall yourself there, Ayclee."

His sweet, musky scent seeps into me, calming my heart rate somehow. I roll my eyes. "Oh my, don't even get me started!"

"Dr. Pentro, can we get started with the tour?" Tiamet makes his way over.

I peer over my shoulder at Rothe. "Doctor?"

Rothe straightens but leaves his hands on my shoulders. "Certainly, Director Osiris. It seems we may have allowed enough time for any stragglers to find their way in." He squeezes my shoulders.

Tiamet's gaze stays firm on Rothe, and he nods. "Yes, it would seem that everyone is here." His eyes wander to mine.

I bite the inner corner of my cheek and stare at Tiamet's stone face. "Sorry, Tiamet. I was just getting directions from Rothe."

"Dr. Cleoths, I advise we address everyone formally in this professional setting."

My eyebrows dip. "Yes, sir, Director Osiris, sir . . ." A pang hits my heart. *What's up with that?*

"Dr. Pentro, if you please, after you." Tiamet turns, extending one hand outward, inviting Rothe to lead.

Rothe nods and walks toward the back of the group. "Aren't we an enthusiastic bunch?" His voice fills the room, and he has a smile that's contagious throughout the group as they part to let him through. "Maybe I was wrong? So much silence."

A voice buried in the group yips.

"That's more like it," he says. "Let's have some fun here! I know we're at work, but there's no reason we can't enjoy it. There are just a few safety guidelines I need everyone to follow while we're walking around in here."

"You were getting rather cozy with Dr. Pentro," Tiamet whispers, leaning over to me, drowning out Rothe's safety instructions.

"We're friends," I respond, keeping my gaze focused forward. The heat of Tiamet's stare bores into me before I turn and look at him. "What?"

"Ayathesti . . . you don't *have* friends."

"What happened to Dr. Cleoths?" I fold my arms. "And that's a rude thing to say. I have friends."

"Name three outside of Nineveh, Latif, and myself."

"Rothe."

Tiamet shakes his head. "Nope. You don't converse with him regularly, so he doesn't count. Who else?"

I look at the floor, trying to think of anyone I even talk to outside of the three of them. "Sayali, the woman who owns the oojo shop near my house. We talk all the time." Tiamet scoffs, shaking his head. "What?

"You really expect me to believe you're friends with Sayali?"

"Why can't I be friends with Sayali?"

"What's her son's name?" He smirks.

"She doesn't have one."

"Oh, doesn't she?"

"No, I don't think so . . ." My chest grows heavy. *Does she?*

"She does. His name is Aljio. He's not even in entry school and likes to kick balls around."

"How do you know that?" I look back at Rothe to distance myself from the shame.

"Because I actually *am* friends with Sayali."

My cheeks burn with embarrassment. "Okay, fine. I *don't* have friends. But you could be less of an ass about it."

He folds his arms, likely in satisfaction. "I don't care if you have close friends, Aya. In fact, it's probably better that you gain more friends. But while we're on work hours, I can't have you flirting with contracted staff."

I click my tongue, scoffing. "I was not flirting. Rothe and I grew up on neighboring farms. We played together when I was little." His silent stare is unbearable. "Say something."

"I'm just taking that comment in."

"It's the truth. I didn't have to explain that to you, but I did anyway. It's none of your business what company I keep, *Director*." I move forward and follow the group, with Rothe's voice booming explanations about our transportation to Earth.

By the end of the tour, it's clear they recruited the best minds on this commission. Based on our lifestyle and how we walk everywhere to reserve atmospheric resources, one would never guess we possessed this level of technology. Rothe tells us the ellipsoid-like ship is covered in carbon nanotubes that absorb light, external temperature, and radiation, converting it into energy for propulsion.

When entering the shell, we can see the core structure

of the exterior wall. Rothe explains how there are giant magnetic rings that will create an electromagnetic field. It pools the energy into the same area where the nanotubes convert radiation into energy, and the way they interact with each other results in enhanced propulsion.

Most of the interior is still an open space, exposing the magnets and the shell. Though there's framework to separate compartments and the flooring is placed already, there's still work to be done.

"We expect completion with plenty of time leading up to the launch." Rothe stands in the middle of the echoey space with his hands on his hips, smiling at all of us with pride and joy in this creation. "Does anyone have questions?

Hands shoot up around me. "Okay, now, before I answer any of those questions, let me mention that while making great progress, we're nowhere near completion. If you have requests for specific requirements for your team, let your manager know, and they can see if it's on the list or if it should be." Most hands in the air drop. Rothe points to a young girl close to the front. "Yes, your question, ma'am?"

"Did you design this all yourself?" she asks.

A chuckle shakes his shoulders. "I'm part of the design and engineering team, yes. But all myself? Absolutely not. Something of this magnificence could never be conjured up by only one mind." Rothe locks eyes with me. "It's important to utilize the strengths of everyone you work with. This helps reduce the chances of gaps or failures in design."

I smile at him, my cheeks blushing, before gazing to the floor.

Tiamet walks forward, pushing through the group of people, stopping near Rothe. "Thank you, Dr. Pentro. This tour has been invaluable. Is it possible we can come back in smaller groups to examine different portions once they have progressed?" Tiamet's arms bulge as they fold across his chest.

Rothe nods. "Absolutely, Director. We'd love to have everyone back in whichever manner you see fit."

Tiamet turns and faces us. "I know this was a lot of fun, but I expect to see everyone back in the office in a reasonable amount of time to finish out the workday. I'll keep in touch with the team here while they progress and discuss our next visits with each manager. You'll have plenty of notice before your group comes back for another tour."

People file out of the metal room and I go along with the flow, all the way to the building exit.

"Aya!" Rothe's voice echoes behind me.

I stop and turn, hugging my arms to my chest.

"You're in a hurry to get out of here. Everything okay?"

I nod without a word.

"Good. It was great to see you, Ayclee! I hope we find time to catch up." His warm smile melts through my fear barriers, and I grin.

"That would be nice, Rothe." I glance at Tiamet approaching from behind him. "But I'm rather busy. It might not be for a while. Maybe during my next tour?"

He puts a hand on my shoulder and pulls me in for a hug, engulfing me in his arms. "Any time I can get will be cherished."

Something pulls on my heart. *What is going on? Why do I suddenly want to cry?* The tightness in my throat prompts me to pull away from his warmth and smell. I smile and nod. "Yes, probably will have to wait until my next tour."

His smile shows concern but no hurt. "Get home safely!" He backs up a few paces before turning around, walking toward the engineering bay, nodding at Tiamet as he passes him on the way.

Tiamet smiles and nods back at him before looking at

me. As he approaches, my heart stops in anticipation for the reprimand. Words to respond to his inevitable comment formulate in my mind, but he passes me without any acknowledgment aside from a glance before he exits the building.

Ayathesti - 16

I glide my thumb back and forth over the engraving in the glass while we sit at a table in the far corner of the Zeyo.

"So what's Hana done to spark your dislike for her?" Nineveh sips from her tall, slender glass of bubbly, her pinkie reaching into the air.

Bringing the rim to my lips, jealousy threatens to spill over my threshold as it swells inside. I lift a finger and point toward the door where Tiamet and Hana just appeared. "That. Precisely that." I hold my breath and force my hand to ease the glass back to the tabletop.

Nineveh gasps. "You mean to tell me you haven't made strides with him yet?" She leans against the table, a hand to the corner of her mouth.

I lower my gaze, shaking my head. "I know. It's horrible. . . and likely too late now. I gave up hope the first week of your absence. Nineveh, I didn't realize how much light you bring to my life!" My eyes sting with the familiar threat of tears when my heart fills with appreciation for her. I find a smile, one in relief that she's here, with her eyes so intent and focused on listening.

"What about that cute engineer you grew up with?"

"Rothe?" A soft grin dances on my lips.

"Oooh, I sense a romance!" Nineveh giggles.

"Oh, stop. There's nothing there. We grew up together, that's it. I didn't even know he lived in Simbhora."

"But you know now! And he's clearly into you." She shrugs a shoulder, smirking.

"Ugh, gross! It would be like . . . I'd say a brother, but I wouldn't know since I have none. Anyway, I wouldn't get involved with someone while I'm still hanging on to someone else." I sigh and look back to Tiamet.

Nineveh peers over her shoulder. "You know . . . for how smart you are, it kills me you can't take a hint!"

"What do you mean?"

"Isn't it obvious he's flirting with her to make you jealous?"

I blush when I look over to see Tiamet staring in our direction, leaving Hana conversing with herself. "Well... no..."

"That's your problem! You don't see what you don—"

"I've been a bit preoccupied! But enough of me. How is it going in your new position?"

"Oh, it's perfect, everything I wanted it to be! I'm just lucky I didn't have to wait long before it opened for me." Nineveh takes another sip of her bubbly.

"I was very proud to hear you transferred. I only wish you would have told me yourself that they asked you to be leading medical officer on Earth!" I perk up in my chair.

"You know how they can be. I had strict instructions not to tell anyone until decisions rolled down from The Council. Have you reached a point where you're excited to go, then?"

"Yeah. Think I'm more excited to take a break while we journey out there. My energy levels are so low as of late." I shift in my chair to avoid eye contact with Tiamet.

"That's too bad. You've always been great about taking care of yourself . . . but you do look rather tired." Nineveh's eyebrows furrow. "In fact, we should get you home so you can rest for tomorrow." She stands.

"But I haven't even finished yet!" I'm swift in bringing the glass to my mouth, draining it before she grabs my arm.

"Oh, just leave it!" She pulls me from the table.

"You're bossy tonight!" I quicken my pace to keep up with her. "Wait a second. What's tomorrow have to do with anything?" Habit has me looking at the houses on the street as we walk by, catching our reflections in the windows as we pass.

"You think it will be a normal day, but they planned surprise physicals and some training sessions to make sure everyone can stay on their feet after the long flight."

My footing falters at the thought. *What am I worried about? I always do well on exams . . . but I usually know I'm prepared for them.* A surprise *anything* is almost guaranteed to throw my anxiety levels into an unmanageable level. "From what I understand, not everyone will sleep the entire time."

"Well, that's what we're hoping for, but we've been getting things prepared so that no harm will occur if the time extends beyond what's intended."

"Are they expecting something to go wrong?" It dissipates, the temporary relief from my old friend darkness.

"No, no! Of course not! It's just that . . . Well, sometimes, things are out of our control. We finally got allowances for better equipment in the pods."

"Well, that seems fair, considering I've been telling them all along that this whole thing will end up out of our control. We could all die because of what we're doing, but nobody wants to listen t—"

"Aya!" Nineveh's voice echoes, offering a ledge of sanity for me to stand on. "Take a breath. Tiamet said himself, everything will be fine. And Latif mentioned you've narrowed down to only forty species! Isn't that exciting?"

We reach my front door, and I lean against it, my body going limp while I slump to the ground. "But why did you have to bring him up? How will I cope with being stuck on a tiny ship with him? And next time, the trip will be even longer."

"Come on. Don't be that way!"

I reach for the handle and pull myself up. After fumbling with the keypad, I stumble forward as the door gives way under my weight.

Nineveh grasps my arm with both hands and steadies me. "Besides, you'll both be sleeping this whole time around, remember?"

"Right . . ." I smile through the little voice inside telling me to give up. I lean against the frame of the doorway. Nineveh stands next to me in silence. "Hey, Nineveh . . . Thanks for tonight. I really needed my friend."

Her painted lips beam. "I'm glad you still consider us friends!" She pats me on the shoulder a few times before turning around, starting away from my door.

"Get some good rest. I'll see you tomorrow for testing!" she shouts at me over her shoulder as she walks away.

I enter the KRUL at the usual time. Word must have gone around that we're testing today, as lines form to go in. The voices of conversation reverberate outrageously loud off the high walls. I pick a line that seems shorter and stand at the end.

My eyes grow heavy, my knees aching with the desire to move quicker. My chest tightens before each expansion. I yawn and glance at the inside of my new wrist watch to check the time, calculating how long I've been waiting. A hand lands on my bicep, delivering a jolt of alertness as it drags me away.

"Hey! I've been waiting like everybody else. Now I'll have to wait even longer!" The promise of an end disappears as I look at the place I stood only moments ago.

"Calm down. You won't have to wait longer. You shouldn't even be in line." The familiar voice stills my heart. *Why do I never expect him to show up?* It's as though he only exists as someone I've made up when we're not together.

I seize gumption and look Tiamet in the face. *And now I'm short of words to respond? Just talk to him!* The firm grasp he has on my arm releases, though his hand remains in place. We stand outside of a door I've somehow never noticed before. The strained mechanics moan like an overstretched rubber-band before it finally opens. The light flickers dimly, growing with intensity as time passes. He pulls me through the door, and we stand there in silence.

"Tiamet, what are you doing?" My back presses against the wall of the tiny utility closet.

Releasing the grip he has on my arm, he stares me down. "You're the top researcher in this entire facility. Why wouldn't you assume you've got priority over everybody else out there?" His tone is hard, frustrated.

I avert my gaze and stare at the ground, again trapped by silence.

"Honestly, Aya . . ." His chest heaves.

My eyes shoot up, looking into his, and I'm overcome with a sudden sense of the pain he's been feeling for the past few months. A pressure builds in my chest, threatening to suffocate me, intensifying with each additional breath. *What am I feeling? His pain . . . His eyes used to sparkle when we conversed, but ever since I got stuck in this hole, it's been gone.*

It was like watching a light dim over time before flickering out. You know it's happening and the darkness is inevitable, but you're powerless to stop it . . . for it's not your light to keep alive.

Anticipation builds as I await his response. "Honestly, what?" There's a hint of desperation in my voice, and I refuse to look away.

The heat radiating from his body teases my skin. His breath sweeps through the hair hanging in my face. He shakes his head, breaking our gaze. "Ah, never mind. You're just growing to be annoying, that's all."

"Excuse me?" My building excitement grows into hurt and confusion. My eyes scan his face, searching for a tell—his words don't match what I'm seeing.

He turns his back to me, standing there in silence before the door opens.

"If that's all you wanted to say, why did you drag me all the way in here?" My voice quivers, my eyes stinging as heat crawls up my neck. I swallow to keep the flood of hidden emotions buried.

He rubs the back of his neck and stands there, letting the door close once more.

"Well," I start to say, "at least let me leave if you're not goi—"

His hands land on the wall beside each side of my face. I flinch, clenching my eyes shut. "I tried," he whispers.

I peer up to see him staring back down at me. My breath flees. "Tri—"

"Don't even open your mouth because I don't think I can take it anymore." His head hangs, hands sliding down the wall to fall at his sides. He leans in, resting his forehead against the wall. Chills crawl over my skin when his heavy breath hits my neck. Butterflies flap against my stomach with anticipation as I take in his dusty aroma. The automated lights turn off, leaving only a dim illumination filtering through the frosted sidelight.

"I'm sorry," I whisper back. *Move your arms! Touch him. Hold him. Give in.* One arm reaches for his side.

"Sorry?" He stands upright. "I've been trying, endlessly, to find the right words in every moment between us to pour my heart out and all you can say is 'sorry'?" He scoffs, shaking his head.

"What do you want me to say?" My arms come to a fold across my chest.

"I don't know. I don't think I can do this right now." He turns away.

"Why are you always like this?" I straighten, inching closer to him. "You pop in and out of my life, acting as though I'm supposed to lie at your feet, dismissing the possibility that I have feelings at all! Then this . . . rudeness?"

"Oh, I'm the one who's rude?" He faces me again.

"Yes! I don't even know—" A lump invades my throat, choking my will to speak. I lean back against the wall for support, trying to swallow.

"I guess . . . just do what you always do." His shoulders drop, his tone becoming softer.

"What's that supposed to mean?"

"Figure that one out on your own. I'm done playing your fucked-up game." Again, he prompts the door open and steps out.

I stand there alone, the lump growing harder. My knees collapse beneath me the moment the door closes, my back sliding against the wall until I'm sitting on the floor, unable to keep the floodgates closed.

Tiamet - 17

I make my way across the lobby and lean against the doorway of the testing room I know Nineveh is working in. I look around at the walls with patience while waiting for her to acknowledge my arrival.

"T! You're finally here for the day. I have a few documents to finish up, and then we can get you started. Come on in." Her focus returns to the tablet in hand.

I smile and enter the room, closing the door behind me. I make my way to a chair, sit, and look at the equipment to distract myself.

"How goes the testing?" My fingers tap on the arm of the chair. She's sitting with crossed ankles on a tall stool.

"Oh, you know, as expected. Except . . ." She sets the tablet down, folding her hands together.

An eyebrow piques. "Do we need to do some reorganizing?"

"Well, no, everybody's fine. I just haven't seen Aya yet this morning. Last night I told her to just come right in when she got here."

I direct my attention toward a painting on the wall. Children playing in the park, and the sky is actually blue. Tall purple trees surrounding the area allow gorgeous plumes of gold dust to fill the atmosphere. There's a clear line of mountains that surround the field where the gold dust morphs into the Mediterranean sky. It is a world of the past, a world nearly forgotten—a world I've been longing to see since Mom died. That ache of desire and hopelessness is ever so present today.

"Yeah, well, you know she never listens to anybody.

Not even those supposed friends of hers." I reel in my contempt for our conversation topic.

"What is going on with you today? She listens. She's just hard to talk to. *And* she's in a rough place right now. You remember that she's against everything we're doing, right?" Nineveh's readiness to defend Ayathesti is evident in her scolding tone.

I look at her, arms folded against her chest and eyebrows furrowed in disapproval.

"I know that, Nin!"

"She told me last night she's not smiled in weeks."

"Okay. She takes life a little seriously. So what? That's no reason to act the way she has been lately."

"She's not like us. She lacks the ability to socialize without being forced into it." She stands from the stool, placing her hands on her hips.

"That's her own damn fault. You can't expect everyone to wear a hazard suit around her because of the chance she'll go nuclear." My chest constricts with the rush of adrenaline.

"It's not that simple! Her mother provided copious neglect after her father died in a generator explosion. She had only herself to talk to for years!"

"I get it, okay? You don't need to go over her entire sob story, Nineveh." Her words saturate my mind, providing insight to the unreachable center of this person I've been chasing.

"I'm offering a different perspective to how hard it is for her right now."

"She's not the only one in a rough place. So why don't you get this over with and we can stop kicking that dead animal in hopes of it moving again." I release a controlled, slow exhale, forcing myself to calm.

Nineveh sighs and picks up a glass tablet before

walking around her table to an elevated bed. Pulling a hovering saucer from under the table, she sits and pats the bed. *I guess that's my queue to move.*

I sit on the bed and stare at her. "Okay, doc. Just be gentle, it's been a long time!" I smirk, trying to lighten the mood.

Nineveh smiles and places my arm inside a tube with a hard white exterior and a velvety black interior over some heavy padding. With a quiet hum, the cushion inflates, conforming to my arm. The outside surface fades from white to black before lighting up with an outline of my arm and all the interior characteristics. The precision is so dialed in, I can see the pulsing of blood as it moves throughout my fingers.

"Cool! I thought this tech was torn up and used for parts!"

Nineveh holds her clipboard over the capsule and presses a button. "Isn't it, though?"

"So, what's the verdict, doc? Am I a goner? I knew it!"

"Shhh! Hold still. You're being obnoxious." She removes the cuff and pushes my head down with a fingertip on my forehead.

"You've only just noticed I have a tendency to be obnoxious?" Pinching my lips together is the only thing to stifle my chuckle.

"Tiamet, it's part of your nature to avoid uncomfortable situations by being obnoxious." My jaw drops in exaggerated surprise. "Oh—come on. Get serious! This is my job, and yours, on the line here."

She maintains her focus on the clipboard. One long beep squeals at the touch of her fingertip on the surface. "Good. Now, stay." She places a finger to my forehead once more.

I furrow my brow and follow orders, wriggling my body into comfort on the padded table. The lights dim, and the bed inflates, molding to my backside. The ceiling above me replicates the imagry effects of the cuff still snuggling my arm. "Woah. I've never looked inside of myself before." I chuckle.

Ayathesti - 18

After a few moments of shock and some silent tears, I collect myself in the tiny utility closet. I stand, leaning my back against the wall, and clear my face from signs of moisture. The muscles in my cheeks twinge when I force a few practice smiles. I open the door, the piercing light forcing my eyes to narrow. After a few moments of blinking to adjust, I step into the lobby. The line I had been in is now only a few people long.

Lost in my own thoughts, I walk toward the testing office, jumping ahead of the line. My heels catch on the floor when I pull myself to stop at Nineveh's closed door. Even though I can have the test performed by any available practitioner, I wait. *Maybe if I am with someone I trust, I won't bomb the test by being a sweaty, nervous mess.*

While pressing my back against the wall opposite the door, I dig my hands into the pockets of my lab coat. The soft edges of a paper brush against my fingertips. I'd forgotten this was here. I clench it in my fist and take a deep breath, attempting to keep myself composed. Diverting my gaze to the floor, a rush of sadness takes over me once more.

Where do I start examining what I've done to push him to act this way?

The question processes through my mind over and over in as many ways as I can think of to rephrase it. *You're getting annoying.* His voice rings in my head. A wave of heat crawls its way from my heart to my face.

I close myself off to the world around me by hugging my arms to my chest. My chin quivers while moisture stings my eyes. Reaching with a trembling hand, I brush the soft paper against my lips, closing my eyes to hold an image of Papa in my mind. The way his smile made his eyes gleam. How his voice was so tender and encouraging, it would melt every worry away. *If only Papa could be here. Everything would be okay and I could smile again.*

A click comes from the door and laughter spills from the room. I force myself to swallow and look up at the door, awaiting the patient to vacate.

"You're good to go!" Nineveh's peppy voice protrudes from the opening doorway.

"Yeah, hey, sorry about earlier. I'll see you tonight, right?"

"Oh, yes, definitely. I wouldn't pass this up for anything. I'm in much need of a break!" Nineveh's voice rings again as Tiamet smiles and exits her office.

All I can do is stand there, staring at him, unable to move, speak, think, or even breathe. I wish I knew what to say to heal what I have broken between us. Tiamet stops and looks at me, all the previous joy fading upon my sight. The smile in his eyes fades, leaving false happiness and forced courtesy in its place. My heart threatens to break. He nods in my direction while stepping out of the doorway. I know now, for a fact, I've lost him forever. He stops and extends his hand behind him, as if granting me permission to enter.

"She's all yours!" He turns, swaggering in a gait I've never seen before.

I enter the room and immediately sit on the edge of the bed. My head slumps with my posture.

"Aya! Where have you been? I figured you'd be here like . . ." Nineveh looks at her coder and gasps. "Well, a long time ago! Have you only just arrived?"

A subtle shake of my head without a word. Still clenching the last letter Papa wrote me, my hands cover my face as the threat to lose composure creeps up again.

She turns from closing the door behind her. "Well, at least you're your usual quiet self this morning. Tiamet was being—"

"I don't care about anything he's involved with," I snap through my hands.

"What changed since last night? You were upset about the lack of interaction between you recently." Nineveh steps forward and sits on the hovering saucer next to the bed. "You're both in bad moods today. What happened?"

Laying back on the table, I close my eyes and let out a long shaky breath. My fingertips dance around the edges of the paper in my hand while they rest in my lap.

"I don't even want to go on this dumb trip. Can we get this test over with, please? I'd rather not talk about it." My voice cracks.

Nineveh nods, starting up her equipment. The lights dim, and we go the entire test without another word spoken.

Tiamet - 19

I tend to always arrive at the Zeyo first. The people watching is good, and it gives me a chance to be social without the pressures of being at work. Typically, I jump from table to table, engaging in conversations. Tonight, though, a different mood looms in the air. No, tonight, I sit isolated in a dim corner.

"Am I not as smart as I thought I was?" I stare at the untouched beverage on the table, thinking out loud.

"You are!" Nineveh giggles as she approaches.

I shine her a confident smile. "Yeah, I know. I was just replaying a memory." Motioning to a chair across the table, I invite her to sit.

She joins me, unloading an armful of papers to the table. "I don't think there could be a moment in your life where you didn't feel smart."

"Well, you're misconstrued, young one." I bring the glass to my lips in a chuckle, the first one of the night.

"You should slow down for the next few days before our trip."

"No, I'll be fine. You know me, after all." I give her a teasing wink.

"Yes, I do know you. Both you and Latif never seem to have any trouble functioning after being out all night." She swats the air at me, crinkling her nose.

"All I can say is I'm glad this initial species collection will be a short trek compared to the colony mobilization, once we get a few prototypes made." My smile fades.

"What? I thought you'd be excited!"

"Yeah. Well, I was . . ." I look at the door as Ayathesti

comes in.

Nineveh turns in her chair "Oh that's weird, she was depressed today. I thought she'd just go home. AYA!" She shouts, waving her hands around.

Ayathesti looks over and makes her way to our corner.

Depressed . . .? I watch silently as she draws nearer.

"Nineveh, I'm just gonna quit and not even go." Ayathesti drags a chair from a nearby table and sits. Her elbows rest on the table, hands covering her face.

"Ahhh! You can't *not* go!" Nineveh turns to her.

"Well, why not?"

"Because you're the bioengineer. You need to confirm specimen compatibility! You're the only one qualified to use the equipment unsupervised!"

"Well then, bring them all back and I'll do it here. There's absolutely no way I can put myself through any more anguish." Lifting her head, she blinks a few times.

I slouch, leaning back in my chair with arms folded across my chest. "Now, don't think you're off the hook because somebody you don't care for will be now joining us." I grin.

"What do you mean?" Ayathesti asks.

"Oh, you didn't hear?" Nineveh places a gentle hand on the table.

"Hear what?" Her confusion is obvious by her expression.

I maintain a smirk. *This is gonna be so juicy.* I sit forward, resting my folded arms on the table. Ha—"

"Hana made her way onto the passenger list for this flight." Nineveh interrupts, leaning toward me.

"Seriously?" Ayathesti holds her breath. "I wouldn't let something like letting fresh meat join us get to me. Just because she doesn't make mornings as bright as you,

Nineveh, doesn't mean she doesn't deserve it."

"Well, thank you, Aya! I'm thrilled to know we built a true friendship during that short time!" Nineveh's eyes brighten, her smile beaming from ear to ear.

"That's the kind of smile I like to keep for myself." Latif appears, holding his hand out for Nineveh. "I'll be taking her away now. You kids have fun."

"You're becoming see-through, Aya." I stare at Ayathesti, as though we're the only ones present. "Ouch." I chuckle and rub my shin where Nineveh just kicked it under the table.

"That was crass," she says, placing her hand in Latif's before standing. "I'll see you tomorrow." Her gaze moves from Ayathesti to me. "Be nice." After collecting her stack of papers in one arm, she latches her other around Latif's, and they leave.

"At least I don't have to degrade every person I come in contact with just to feel better about myself, Tiamet." Ayathesti trembles.

My smile drops as I sit forward in my chair and point at her. "What the hell do you even know about what I do to keep going every day? Honestly, what's wrong with you lately?" My heart races, chest heaving to keep the rage from building.

Ayathesti folds her arms. "What is wrong with *me*?" Slouching down in her chair, she averts her eyes to the floor. "What *is* wrong with me?" The words repeat in a whisper. Her eyes close, and she buries her face in her palms.

"Aya . . . That's not—"

"No, you're right. There has to be something wrong with me." She looks back at me. "Every person on this planet looks forward to the mission's completion. They long for how things were years ago. Everyone other than me. There must be something wrong with me. Maybe I'm just cracking under the pressure." The moisture in her eyes glistens as it catches the light.

She swipes at a tear crawling down her cheek. *Cracking under the pressure? She can't be that stressed about it, can she?* My heart fills with guilt.

"Well, thanks for cheering me up." Her lips quiver with a feigned smile. "I'll leave you alone now. I think Hana was right behind me, so you two enjoy each other." She stands and turns to make her way to the exit.

"Aya . . ." I sigh, reaching out to her as her ponytail sways behind her. A familiar flutter fills my chest.

Is this hope? I think through all the moments I've tried to get close to her. Realization strikes as I sit with palms on my cheeks, fingertips buried into my hair. *She hasn't lost care for me. She's lost care for herself. And I've done nothing to help.*

Ayathesti - 20

I sit at my table near the door, staring down into my cup of oojo. My entire body is stiff, full of dread for the day to begin. The only thing anchoring me to sanity is watching the speckled leaves swirling around in the cup I cling to. I lift it to my lips, taking a deep breath in. The aroma pulls me into a moment of peace, a false sense of security telling me the day won't begin as long as I don't finish this cup. I can just stay here, all day, thinking about when I was little and I woke up with the sun to spend time with Papa before he left for work.

Sweet pastries in a dish would be on the table, placed in the space where generator schematics weren't covering the wooden surface. Fluffy slippers would hug my feet as I crawled onto a chair to hover over the diagrams and Papa would explain each component and its functions to me.

"Oh, let her be a child, Harvat!" Mother would scold while I pointed to the different parts, asking, "What's this one do, Papa?"

We'd pour over them until the sun shone in through the colored glass windows next to the kitchen table. Mother would always try to peel me away from them.

"She needs to spend time with other children. There's time for learning when she's older!" I'd hear her say to him when I would walk up the hallway to change into the coveralls he'd made to match his work jumper. Then I would return to soak up the rest of his attention before he had to leave. I'd sit on his lap and watch his oojo leaves steep in the hot liquid of his cup, and mimic his motions with my warmed milk. Mornings were our most cherished time together, Papa's and mine. Even Mother would join in some days. But after the explosion . . .

With only one more moment of hesitation, I tilt the cup and allow the liquid to flow past my lips, holding it in my mouth before gulping.

"Okay, Aya. Stop it. Self-pity is over. You have a job to do now." I place my hands on the table, pushing myself to stand. Draping my lab coat over my arm, I pick up the glass and walk it to the sink. Now is a moment when I would set it down and leave, allowing the automated system to clean it. But I had shut it down in anticipation for the extended journey.

I slip my arms into the sleeves of my coat and grasp the cold metal handle of the door. A look over my shoulder makes my stomach flurry. *Nerves.* I examine everything I hold dear, the place that's been my comfort zone for many years. My heart free falls. My throat swells, and I exit.

Stepping outside, the door locks behind me. I look around: The sun is just peering over the hillside. The streets are more empty than usual for this time of day. *Everyone must be at home to watch the launch.* The thought of empty streets releases some of my tension. *A walk to work without their eyes on me?* This thought offers a sense of relief I didn't know I craved.

Arriving at the Engineering Advancement Building, one would have thought it was just another standard workday.

Standing in the entrance, countless voices tower over me as I examine all the familiar—and unfamiliar—faces in the room. I grip for their excitement to feed my own.

"Aya!"

I sigh and turn around. *I don't know if I'm ready for this…*

"Here, put this on and come to the lounge outside the loading bay." Nineveh holds a soft bundle against my chest.

I look at her—hair pulled back, lips lacking their usual gleam of color. "You look different."

"The first thing on my mind is getting everyone prepped for launch." She looks around and then back at me, and smiles.

"Your excitement is contagious. Thank you." I hold up my new suit, and she nods before walking away with another in hand.

I look around for an indication of where we're to change. A line pours from the restroom. *Avoid.* Across the room are some offices with the blinds drawn but no light coming around the edges. *Against the rules? Go now, or you won't do it and you'll be waiting in that bathroom line.* With a deep breath, I make my way over to the offices and peek my head in through one of the doorways. I slip inside and shut the door quietly.

I hold the garment to my chest and examine it—a white bodysuit with green markings. I strip from my clothing and fit into the suit. Light floods in from the door opening as my hands glide over the fabric hugging my curves to ensure everything is in place. My heart jumps, and I hold my breath, turning to see who I owe an apology to.

"Oh, I'm sorry," Rothe says, rushing a maneuver to leave.

I'm rendered motionless. *Say something.*

"Aya?" he chuckles, stepping inside and closing the

door.

I bare a wide, toothed "oops" grin, still unable to speak.

"We have a locker room, you know."

I clear my throat. "Sorry. I didn't want to wait in line for the restroom."

He crosses his arms and leans against the door. "I mean, we have actual changing rooms. With showers and everything."

I open my mouth. *Say something, anything.* "I didn't even think to find one of those."

He quirks a brow and smiles. "Still not one to ask when you need something, eh?"

My breath trembles and I look around the room. "I didn't anticipate being in here long. I'm sorry, Rothe."

He shakes his head. "Stop apologizing to me."

"Sorry."

He chuckles again and walks toward me. "Well, let's have a look." He circles his finger around in the air.

I roll my eyes, grin, and put my arms up, spinning once.

Rothe sits on the edge of the desk, nodding. "It's a good fit."

I tug the cuffs of my sleeves into my hands. "It's a little tight."

"Well, yeah. Compared to those coveralls you never stopped wearing as a kid, it's a little tight."

I smile bigger. "You can't possibly remember those things!"

"How could I not? It's all you ever wore!" He laughs.

I shake my head, licking my lips. *You're kidding. That is the thing he remembers about me?*

"Crazy to think we've never run into each other before this project, yeah?" He crosses his arms again.

I shrug. "I mean . . . not really. Simbhora is a big city and—"

"And you rarely leave the house outside of going to work." I inhale sharply at his comment and open my mouth to retort. *Nothing. He never had any flaws like me.* "I didn't mean it that way, Aya. I was clarifying a thought," he says.

I bite my lower lip. "It's true."

"You can't do that. It's not fair." He smirks.

"Do what?" I ask.

He tilts his head.

"Don't you look at me in that tone of voice. Just say it!" My cheek twitches as I try to keep my smile hidden.

His chest heaves with his sigh. "You can't keep being so hard on yourself."

I look at him and shrug. *Oh well, stop me.*

"And I'll look at you in whatever manner I please," he says, raising both eyebrows and examines my suit again.

My cheeks grow warm, and I smile. "I should probably get out there."

"Yeah, me too." Rothe stands, walks around the desk, and opens a drawer. "Can't launch you into space from my office."

"Well, you could try. Heaven knows you would have back in the day." I smirk. "Then again, your ideas never worked out back then."

"Hey, at least I was trying something." He puts an object from the drawer into his pocket.

"Do you remember trying to get that rocket you made into space?" I snort, covering my mouth to hide the burst of laughter.

"You're not allowed to bring that up!"

"And it singed all your hair off!"

He stands there before me. Cool. Confident. Steady. And with a big smile, making his eyes gleam as he steps toward me. "Your laugh is infectious."

"Promise you won't light us all on fire?" I take a few deep breaths to compose myself.

He nods and places a hand on my upper back. "It's time."

I breathe in deeply again and turn to the door. Rothe walks ahead of me and opens it, offering me to leave first.

We walk to the lounge in silence together, rounding a corner to see the crew in different lines for boarding.

"C'mon boss! You're the only one we're waiting on!" There's no hiding the excitement in Latif's voice as he grabs my wrist, dragging me behind him into the room. I look around at everyone in excited conversation with one another.

"All the leaders are in this line. Don't you worry your head about me! I'll be over . . . there." He points to a line a few rows back.

"I'm glad you're concerned for me to know which line you're standing in, Latif." I nod, watching him walk away before turning around to see Rothe has disappeared. I sigh and look to the front of the line. *Only 3 ahead of me. Great, this should be quick.*

Clenching my jaw with my insides buzzing, I look around for Tiamet's face in the crowd. But it's the one face I don't see. *Maybe he's in a different line? I mean, he is the director.* I rehearse what I want to say to him in my head, hoping to apologize before the journey begins. Now is as good a time as any. *He was probably the first one inside.*

I press my palms together, warming them up before rubbing my left one with my right thumb. There's been an ache I can't seem to shake for the past few weeks, perhaps from the accident I had months ago.

I turn around when there's a tap on my shoulder. "Sorry. I guess everyone was waiting on me," I say to Rothe.

"What did I say about apologizing to me?"

"I know, I know. Sorry."

He chuckles. "Don't worry, I'll break you out of it . . . eventually."

"Shouldn't you be off somewhere practicing how to light us all on fire?"

"The fire will be so big, you can see it from space once you get up there."

"Actually, I think I might be asleep by then." I shrug.

"I just came by to say good luck. Not like you'll need it. I'm one of your engineers, after all." He puts his hands on my shoulders.

I roll my eyes. "Yeah. Thanks."

"Ayclee." He stares at me.

When I look up at him, he slides one of his hands down my arm and into my palm. "You deserve to have this. Wait until you're alone to look at it. Don't ask questions. Don't object." He closes my hand into a fist over the object and presses it against my torso, slipping his finger into a hidden pocket at my waistline.

"Ro—" I begin to speak, when he puts his finger against my lips.

"No questions." He raises his eyebrows and nods.

I nod back and slip the long, hard object into my pocket. The smile he gives reminds me of all the times he asked me to trust him when we were kids.

His hand moves from my lips to my shoulder again. He pulls me in against his chest. "Safe travels. Let's catch up when you get back."

I wrap my arms around him, clinging to his sweet smell as my heart pounds. "Yes, let's."

As he pulls away, he squeezes my shoulder and then walks through a set of doors on the far side of the room.

After what seems like a lifetime of waiting, the door to the ship opens, allowing us to enter one at a time at ten-minute intervals. I close my eyes and rub my hand; the pain hasn't let up at all, and now I'm stuck wondering what contraband is hidden in my suit.

Another person enters and a foot stops my progression forward as someone cuts in line ahead of me.

"Excuse me!" I stare at my foot in disbelief.

"Excuse yourself, then. Someone saved this spot earlier this morning." Tiamet's voice is hoarse as he settles in ahead of me.

I avert my eyes back to the ground, taking a step backward.

"Oh . . ." I continue rubbing my palm, adding pressure to it. "Sorry T—Director. I didn't know it was you."

Tiamet shakes his head. "Aya, you need to stop being a pushover. Take charge. You are in a position to do so, after all." He glances at my hands. "Nervous?"

"Of course I'm not nervous, why would you ask me that?" My response is quick. *Too quick.* I look at him to see if he caught my tell.

He smirks and points to my hands.

I look down, face burning with embarrassment. "Oh!! No! No, I started rubbing it a while ago . . ." I put my hands behind my back.

"Are *you* nervous?" I ask, looking around the room to see if other lines are moving faster. *Of course they are.*

"Yeah, I guess you could say I'm nervous."

"You are?" I catch his smirk fading into a calm smile. *That's the last thing I expected to hear from him.*

He shrugs. "Why wouldn't I be?"

"Well, you've been the one saying this whole time it'll go according to plan. I guess I assumed . . ." The warmth from his hand wraps around the side of my arm, sliding down to my wrist. With a gentle pull toward him, my palm is placed strategically between his fingers.

"I'm not nervous about any of that." He chuckles, attention focused on what he's doing with my hand.

The gentle pressure being applied by his fingertips makes me quiver, my skin crawling with static. "But you just said—"

"I know what I said. But that's not what I was referring to."

I grit my teeth, cringing when he rubs over a painful spot. The smile fades from his face, and he brings my hand closer for inspection, his eyebrows set in concentration.

"Last time I was this close to a girls' hand, my face was prickly for three days."

A vision of him being slapped manifests in my mind, forcing a grin. "I didn't need to know that." I resist the urge to retract my hand from his grasp due to the pain, but I settle for gritting my teeth once more.

"But you asked." After lowering my hand from his face, he eases the pressure off.

"Wait, what?"

"You just asked if I was nervous, and what about." After he stops rubbing, he continues holding my hand.

I slowly pull it away and hug it to my chest, applying slight pressure with my other thumb.

"Better?" His eyes refuse to falter.

I look at the ground, nodding. "Tiamet . . ." I put my hands behind my back.

I look at him when he places a hand on my shoulder. "Shh," he says softly as the door lets out a hiss and opens behind him. He looks over his shoulder before turning back to me. "Well, here we go! See you on the other side!" His eyebrows perk up, and he walks through the door.

What just happened? I stand there, a big smile painted

across my face. The heaviness in my heart takes a sudden turn, adopting light and hope. *I have been wanting to apologize but . . . he stopped me. Did he know what I was about to say?* Minutes turn into seconds, when the door opens before me. I look around, being among the last few still needing to board.

Taking a deep breath, preparing for the next part of the journey, I step inside.

A deep purple light illuminates the walls of a tiny room. White fog fills the air, making my exposed skin tingle. It swirls around my uniform before being absorbed by it; the prickling sensation now radiates over the skin under my clothes. Within moments, the fog retracts through tiny holes in the side walls.

The door before me creeps open, allowing light to flood the room. I blink, forcing my eyes to adjust. The circular room is much larger and is lined with sleeping pods. Only a few people stand outside them while others strap themselves in.

Looking at the pod closest to me, I see the name *Dr. Ayathesti Cleoths* printed on the side. Hesitant at first, I walk toward it and peer in. There are gel-filled compartments lining the entire interior, and a clear plastic piece covers the front. My eyes land on Tiamet across the room as he looks up at me. My hesitations melt away. I open the pod and climb in to get settled. I'm securing the straps around my legs and chest when Nineveh enters and stands at a console in the center of the room.

"Everybody ready?" After a unanimous nod, she pushes a sequence of buttons.

The plastic face lowers before me, clicking as it latches into place. My eyes grow heavy as a purple fog falls from nozzles above my head. When it settles around my feet, it solidifies into a gelatin-like substance, then crawls its way up the remainder of my body.

Keeping my eyes open to watch proves difficult—the last thing I see being Nineveh leaving through double doors.

Ayathesti - 21

My head is heavy, bobbing around while I regain consciousness. I blink, the moisture in my eyes tacky, leaving my vision blurry. The sound of my breath reverberates against the clear shield.

I look down, examining the restraints on me. A thick rope teases my hand, and with a tug, the tension around my torso releases. I tug once more to free my arms and legs as the shield retracts. The outside air meets my skin, sending a shiver up the back of my neck. Ringing silence replaces the sound of my breath.

Where is everybody? I look around the room with empty pods, my focus landing on large doors across from me. *Nineveh. She left through that door.*

With my head groggy, I stumble my way across the room to the door. I lean against the cold metal, chest heaving and shoulders hunched. My stomach lurches, and I sigh, placing my hand over it. My backside throbs with pain radiating up into my back as the door gives way behind me and I slam into the ground.

"There you are!!" Latif calls out from above me.

"Ow . . ." My voice is coarse, fighting through the sticky film clinging to my lips. The pungent aroma escaping my mouth saturates my nose, shocking me into holding my breath.

A hand reaches down from above to assist me off the floor. I look at it and up to the face of its owner. *Hana.* Placing both my palms on the cold floor, wiggling them to check for grip, I close my eyes and push my screaming muscles to get me off the metal floor. I rub my hands together as if to dust them off, grimacing at her.

The hurt on Hana's face soon becomes a fuzzy image as I notice the gawking state of the others in the room. All eyes are fixated out the window spanning the entire wall of the room. Overcome by curiosity, I push through the crowd. With each movement, I glimpse pieces of the view. Breaking through, in near desperation, I am rendered silent and breathless.

There she stands, surrounded by darkness, like a beacon of light calling. A smile quivers across my lips as tears swell. She's more beautiful than my imagination could have tried to comprehend.

Earth. The small marble glows, enhanced by the colors of her surface—hues and shades that were invisible to our probes back on Naratu.

I gasp, catching my breath, and my knees weaken. Breathing deeper, I swallow to steady myself and hold back the barricaded emotions within. For the first time since The Council's decision to send me on this journey, happiness spills over me. *This sight alone is worth everything I've endured to get here.*

"Listen up!" Tiamet calls out from the side of the room. "I know we're all very eager to get down there and get to work, but as discussed back home, we have formulated the best course of action. We'll be descending in groups, with the pilots remaining here to sustain the ship. I have issued an individual travel pod to each team. We will only green-light entry once the security detail has confirmed a safe environment on the surface. The patch of cloth on your wrist is your team color. Find your section and await further instruction."

The room seems to shift around me as people migrate to their respective sections. I look down to my wrist. An orange cloth. *Strange . . . I didn't notice this before.* After locating the orange section, I make my way across the room to see no one else upon my arrival. *Am I the only one in my group?* I lean against the wall, looking around, waiting for someone—anyone—to join me. Anxiety creeps in, slowly filling every inch of me as I realize there is nobody left.

"Each team has one member of different specialty groups," Tiamet says from the center of the room. "Look around. This is your family for the next five months."

Looking around, I still stand alone, folding my arms in an attempt to hide my embarrassment.

"Why is there somebody in Orange? Orange is the quarantine bay!" Tiamet's tone takes on one of frustration as he makes his way over.

"Hey, I just went to the section with the color on my suit, like you said." Closing my eyes, I take a steady breath to shut out all the eyes staring at me. *Keep calm. Keep it together. This is not a big deal. They'll fix it. It was a mix-up. Nobody cares.* Repeating phrases of strength is supposed to help. That's what that book told me.

'Everyone is watching,' Anxiety whispers. But she is a liar.

Nobody cares.

'That's not true. Everyone is judging you.' She holds my face in her palms, preventing me from seeing that, in fact, nobody is watching.

"Ahh . . . Dr. Cleoths." Tiamet makes subtle clicking noises with his tongue as he approaches me. He reaches out, taking my hand in his own and looks at it. Our eyes lock and he grips the orange cloth with his other hand, yanking it off to reveal a fuchsia patch underneath. "Right, well . . . You're on Fuchsia."

After locating the team section, I sigh upon noticing Hana in the group circle. I walk over and push through the people in my group to lean against the wall, using it as added support for my still-weakened knees. *The last thing I need is someone trying to help me off the floor again.*

Tiamet makes his way back to the center of the room. "Just so nobody gets confused, know that security has black tags with a small stripe of each color on them. Your team security contact will be assigned once we arrive. They've already gone ahead of us, and we should be hearing back soon."

"Oh, isn't this so exciting!" Hana's eyes sparkle.

"Yes, it is!" Nineveh's response has no delay, and she looks at me. "Aya, cheer up! Get excited. We made it just like Tiamet said we would!"

"Oh, Nin, please let me be for a few moments, would you?" I can't be bothered about hurting feelings, still focused on my inner battle.

"Well, well, somebody woke up on the wrong side of the spacecraft, didn't she?" Tiamet joins the group.

"I'm sorry, Director, not feeling that great. I'd like to know whose 'funny' idea it was to give me a quarantine tag anyway?" I ask in a failed attempt to keep my tone calm, the taste of disdain on my tongue.

"Well, it was Latif's, actually," Tiamet says. I push myself from the wall and look for the perp. *What a disgusting joke.* "Easy . . ." Tiamet's hands land on my shoulders and guide me back to the wall. "You're still tired from the trip."

I break my concentration from the green group where I spot Latif. *It's so easy for him—speaking to people he's not familiar with, fitting in.*

My feet go numb, and my knees give way. My back slides down the wall till I'm resting, once again, on the floor.

"Like I said, Aya, take it easy." He offers his hand.

I look at it, sliding my palm into his, accepting the offer.

He supports my elbow with his other hand. "You look surprised to see me."

"No, I . . ." Pausing for a moment, I look at Hana while regaining balance. "I just thought you were too busy to hang out with us anymore." I put my hand to my head, as if to zap away the fog in my mind.

"Regardless of how busy I am, I am still assigned to a team. I do need to get to the surface." Tiamet leans one shoulder against the wall, folding his arms.

"Surprising," I say.

"Oh? Why surprising?"

"I just thought you were too important to ever get your hands dirty, that's all."

"Aya!" Nineveh covers her mouth with her hand.

"What? Everyone made a huge deal about it! So why do I always get bitched out for telling the truth?"

"You're never honest unless you're in a bad mood or alone with me." Nineveh steps toward me. "And I'm not *bitching* you out, I—"

"No, she's right." Tiamet's tone bleeds sarcasm. "She's always right. And who would know the truths of my personal situation more than someone who's never around to witness any of it?"

"Tiamet, that's not helping!" Nineveh sighs. "Why can't you two just be nice to each other?"

"I can't be nice! Not if being rude is the only way she'll talk to me."

"Well, just go ahead don't talk to me," I snap. "Because I—"

"I won't 'go ahead' and not talk to you. I'd go crazy." He rubs his temples.

I close my eyes with shame. *Why can't I just get the words right!*

Anxiety starts with her lies again. *'If you could, people*

would pay closer attention to your failures.'

"How much longer till we get to go down?" Nineveh stands by my side with a hand on my shoulder, offering an anchor to reality while she redirects the conversation.

"Oh yes! I am so hungry, I could eat a Fliphnod!" Hana wriggles with excitement, giggling.

Imagine this twig of a person sitting next to a creature with talons the size of a notebook and fluffy wings as big as a house. I clench my eyes in an effort to hide my frustration with being placed in the same party as Hana.

"So, Hana, what exactly is it they brought you along to do?" I feign interest but lack the ability to hide my sarcasm.

"I'm a cook!"

"Oh! Perfect!" I say.

"We're so lucky to have you in our group!" Nineveh places her hand on my forehead.

"Why is your hand on my face?"

"You're definitely not yourself. I'm checking your temperature to make sure you're not sick." A beep echoes repetitively from across the room where a small green light flashes.

"Ah, good!" Tiamet claps his hands and rubs them together. Smiling, he announces to everyone that we've been given the approval to descend.

All doors around the room let out a slow hiss before opening in unison. I turn and examine the space before me. The chairs are spread out in equal distances from one another in a circle around the exterior wall. I follow the lead of my colleagues and step inside the smaller room. The sound of my feet against the floor is hollow, as if the metal is thinner. Approaching a seat, I notice shapes on the backs matching the pattern on the backs of our suits. As I sit in the chair, it guides my torso into position and contours to my body, taking a firm hold of me.

"Ooh, nice design." I nod in approval, speaking to myself.

Tiamet sits in the chair next to me. "No tech was spared." I look at him to watch the chair suction to his body. He looks back at me, the corners of his lips pressing into his cheeks in a smug smile. "It's designed to absorb any movements we may experience."

"What kinds of movements?" Hana sits next to him, jolting at the sensation of the chair growing around her posterior.

He looks at her. "Those such as turbulence or, in the worst-case scenario, an unexpected impact."

I slowly blink to hide my eye roll.

"Is there concern we will crash?" Her voice quivers, and her face twists into an unrecognizable emotion.

"Unexpected practically means it's not regarded as likely to happen. Calm down." I'm snappy, but focusing on shutting her up keeps my internal world quiet.

"We had to plan for every scenario." Tiamet keeps his attention on her.

"But if we do crash, these things will keep us from getting hurt, right?" Her worry stays evident in her voice.

"They're designed to absorb a percentage of the impact to minimize harm done to the passengers." Tiamet places a hand on hers. "That being said, there's also no guarantee that being impaled with something won't happen just because you're in the chair."

"Are you serious!" Her eyes grow large, and she attempts to wiggle in her chair.

"It's not likely to happen, Hana," Nineveh says. "It's like using an apron over your clothes when you cook. You rarely spill on your clothing, but if you do, then they won't be ruined because they're protected."

The look of panic fades. "Oh, I understand now. It's a

precaution." She smiles "Thank you, Nineveh, for explaining it so I can understand!"

"That's just part of what I do." Nineveh lifts her hands nonchalant.

Tiamet - 22

The green light in the other room stops flashing. We have the go ahead to close the doors and initiate the descent to the planet. With eyebrows raised, and an excited smile, I lock eyes with Ayathesti. The visual tension on her face dissipates. With a hiss, the doors close and lock.

A purple light flickers on, illuminating the cabin, and a red light above the door flashes. I lean my head back and count in my mind, eager to feel our disconnection.

Five . . . four . . . three . . . two . . . one . . . and . . .

I furrow my brows. "Release?" I stare at the light, waiting for it to turn green.

Fingertips brush my forearm, and I look to Ayathesti. "What's going on?" she mouths.

With a small shrug and a finger to my lips, we meet an understanding, and she nods. I look at the screen panel in the wall behind her chair to see a red warning symbol flashing. I slam my fist into the disc shape on my chest, releasing me from the chair. My feet clink on the floor as I walk to the panel.

"Director, is everything okay?" an unfamiliar party member asks.

"Fine." I read on the screen: LOCKING SEQUENCE FAILURE.

The internal pressure of the cabin is not secure. Navigating through the menus on the screen feels like second nature, and I easily find everything needed to reset the sequence. Three quick buzzes come from the small speaker next to the screen as another warning symbol reappears on the screen. INCORRECT AUTHORIZATION CODE USED.

"Oh, come on. Work with me, DARLA." I mutter, going through the menus again. The pitter-patter of feet on the floor is quick, and then Ayathesti is next to me.

"Trouble, Director?" She kneels, leaning forward. *Does she actually think she can be helpful in this situation?*

"Return to your chair. It'll just be a moment while I reset the sequence to begin. Once we get a proper seal on the cabin, we'll be good to go." I glance at her, hiding my disappointment in the system failure.

A sympathetic smile. "What's it doing?"

"It thinks I input an incorrect restart sequence. Which is false. I've done this so many times in the simulator."

"Talk me through it while you navigate?" Her eyes are bright even under the dim lighting, providing me with a confidence I haven't felt since the academy.

"Okay, but then promise you'll get back to your chair." I do my best to sound authoritative.

She nods, her hair brushing across her forehead.

I look back to the screen. "Okay. To restart the failed sequence, first we need to locate where it failed. We do that by pressing on the error warning. The next screen will prompt me to select starting at a specific point of the sequence or to restart the full sequence. We want to select 'full sequence' and—" A jolt of the vessel lurches me forward.

Ayathesti looks up, then back at me, confused. "Um… that was easy?"

I shake my head and grasp her elbow, ushering her back to her seat. "Stay."

I hurry back to the screen to finish the sequence, pushing through menu after menu to ensure the seals are in place before we detach from the ship. Hana screams at another jolt, breaking my concentration, and I hesitate.

"T, hurry." Aya's calm voice pulls me back. I check

over my shoulder to ensure she's still in her chair before I finish the last pages of the sequence. Another jolt sends me to the ground. Hoisting myself back up, I hit the final button and press my thumb against the scanner panel to open the approval prompt for an override.

The air blowing from the ceiling vent is deafening as the capsule lurches again, throwing my body to the floor. *We've detached . . .*

The purple light is now flashing red, and a roaring siren echoes against the empty metal walls of our temporary safety zone. I slide a few feet across the floor. Our capsule is listing away from the main ship, the artificial gravity pulling me away from the security of my chair. I look around for something to grab ahold of. *Aya . . .* Our eyes find one another's. There's no fear emitting from her. Rather, her eyes are full of concern. Her expression is soft yet confident and strong.

The floor is so flat, there is nothing to grab hold of, and it's hard to see with the flickering red lights. I squint, trying to adjust. The sweat on my palms is the only thing keeping me from sliding to the other side of the capsule.

Something brushes the top of my hand. Instincts take over, and I clutch it, pulling myself closer. Reaching higher on the object, it grows thicker, increasing the difficulty of holding on. When I look up to see what it is, I'm met with an ocean of blue and gold. Ayathesti is grasping onto the arm of her chair, unsecured, and extending her foot out. I'm holding onto her leg while she attempts to lift it higher for me to get up.

Both of our efforts have brought me close enough to grab onto the chair itself. Climbing onto the slick white backing of the chair, I slam my hand onto the control panel screen, confirming an override.

The sounds stop, and we're thrown into complete

darkness. The only thing we hear is our breathing. A low electric whirr follows as the lights charge up before flickering back on, filling the room with a purple hue. The tilt of our capsule equalizes.

The screen reads: OVERRIDE SUCCESSFUL. AIRLOCK SEALED. LANDING TRAJECTORY INITIATED.

A silent sigh of relief washes over me as I smile, walking back to my chair. A glance confirms that Ayathesti's secured in her seat. I sense her eyes on me as I slide in. I sense all of their eyes on me, but when I look at her, a flood of warmth takes the place of any doubt I had felt. She holds a smile for me—a smile I didn't know could exist until now. *I am the luckiest guy alive to have her smiling at me that way.*

Ayathesti - 23

I grip the arms of my chair as the capsule fights air turbulence during our descent. The thrusters ignite to slow us down, the force causing a turn in my stomach. *This is all normal, right?* With no windows in the cabin, it is impossible to tell if we're close to landing.

With a small jolt, all movement stops. *Touchdown.* I lock eyes with Tiamet, smiling with anticipation to see the outside world. I snap the release on my chest and step onto the floor. My increased weight slows my movement. *Maybe I just feel slow because of the resistance?*

My head and gut are still adjusting to everything. The cabin light turns white, the brightness causing me to squint. I flash back to the moment we detached from the main ship. The blaring echo of the alarm repeats inside my head. The room spins with a wave of terror twisting around me, dragging me backward. I reach for the chair for balance as my vision goes white before fading into darkness.

There's a hand on my shoulder, and a muffled voice speaks. Another hand assists me as I sit. It moves to my upper back, pushing my head forward, urging me to bend over.

The muffled voice is slow but starts coming in clearer. "Deep breaths. That's it. Breathe." Nineveh is on one side, talking me through it. My vision slowly comes back, and I straighten up.

"Easy, Aya. Take it easy." Tiamet's voice is full of calming reassurance.

I look at him with a defeated smile, realizing he's the

one rubbing my upper back.

"Are you okay?" His soft voice draws me into his eyes.

With my breathing still heavy, I nod and take a deep breath. "Yes, I am fine. I think the rush of everything hit me all at once."

"It's important not to push yourself." Nineveh presses her hand to my forehead with concern. "You should wait here as long as you need before coming out."

"Speaking of which"—I prop my hand on my knee to pick myself off the floor—"if we've landed . . . how long do we have to wait before we get to see what's out there? The anticipation is almost worse than being trapped in this tiny can." *Hopefully my enthusiasm will show them my head is coming back together.*

Tiamet stands with me, a hand under my elbow. "It won't be long now. Have a little patience."

He walks to the control panel. Following a few beeps, the lights dim and a hiss resonates from the doors again. Arms folded, he walks around the chair and stands next to me, waiting for them to open. "We're just lucky that the air is breathable."

My eyebrow quirks upward to accompany my smirk. "You're sure?"

He beams his flirtatious smile at me. "Really? You pick the moment we get here to doubt me?"

"Ah! That's not what I meant!" I look away to hide my embarrassment.

"Oh, you two." Nineveh taps her foot, hands on her hips. "Can we just get the door open already?"

"It's working on it. Cool your jets." Tiamet's laugh erupts, only ceasing when a short beam of light breaks through the crack of the doors.

Silence falls as we all turn to face the doors. Light

floods the compartment, the brightness forcing me to squint. *I can't miss this moment.* I force myself to ignore the discomfort of the light entwining with my lingering lightheadedness. Putting my hand up to block some light, I walk to the edge of the cabin and stop right before the doors to peer outside.

A rust-colored powder covers the ground, speckled with clumps of the same color. Small green plants grow in large sporadic patches. The trees look strange with branches starting mid way up, stretching outward, fanning toward the sky. Beyond the close trees, all the way to the horizon, are wide plains accented with more trees and other plants. The colors bleed together more the farther away from view they get. The sky in the distance starts as pale blue, becoming more fierce overhead, and is accented with a fluff of white and gray clouds casting shadows down upon the land.

Eruptions of dust escape the weight of my foot as I take my first step into this new world.

Tiamet - 24

The air is clean and smooth, unlike anything we've felt for years. And there she is, soaking in the gleaming sunshine, absorbing the warmth and energy from such a majesty. She cocks her head to the sky, embracing the radiance of her new surroundings. She closes her eyes and smiles.

I can't drag my eyes away. Her skin glows as though her inner shine is coming through for all to see. The breeze blowing through her hair casts a dancing shadow on the ground. My heart pounding against my chest harder than usual makes it difficult to catch my breath. *Hopefully, nobody can hear it.*

I lean against the wall of the module, watching her enjoy herself completely for the first time. In this moment, my concern for her wellbeing fades slightly and I know . . . *Everything will be okay.*

"Are you coming or what?" Ayathesti shouts back at us as she makes her way farther out, her arms up.

"What is that stupid smile on your face!" Nineveh shrills with laughter.

I straighten my posture and take a deep breath. "What?"

"I have never seen a look like that on your face! I know the air is fresh, but really, out of everyone, I'd expect you to be the most composed."

I give Nineveh a slight push on the shoulder as we make our way out of the capsule side by side. A small puff of dust wraps around my boot when I step into the dirt. I look around to see the other teams have already emerged from their capsules and are unloading supplies. Scanning the crowd, I spot Jarem. Making my way through my group, I put my hand on the small of Ayathesti's back as I excuse myself around her with nothing more than a glance in her direction.

I make my way to Jarem and fold my arms. "Jarem. It seems everyone's landed. There were no incidents reported?"

With his hands on his hips, his shoulders bulge out. "That is correct, Director. There were no reported issues on entry. You guys took the longest to land. To alleviate the anticipation of waiting on instruction, I advised each group to pick a location to unload and set up equipment."

I nod. "Yes, we had an issue with detaching from the ship. I appreciate you keeping things on track."

"Is everyone okay?" He leans to the side, looking at my team, worry on his face.

"Just some heightened nerves, but we're all good."

I spot a large rock over Jarem's shoulder. *Higher ground.* "Excuse me." I make my way around him and head for the rock. Upon reaching the top, I dip my tongue toward the bottom of my mouth, pucker my bottom lip, and blow. An ear-splitting "yip-yip" whistle drowns out the voices and sounds of the soon-to-be camp. Everyone stops and turns to me.

I rub my palms together, smiling. "Well . . . we made it!" I put my fists in the air in victory. A few hoots and hollers sound out from the group. "Yeah! That's what I like to hear. Excitement. Motivation. Every single one of you worked your ass off to get here. You deserve to be here. We each have a role in this mission, and it's important we stay focused on that! However . . ."

I lift my hands and look around. "Look at the spectacular geography of this place. We are at work, but I want all of us to enjoy our time here! Be friendly with your coworkers. Hang out after work. Try to establish a routine to help you enjoy our time here. I'm always available for any issues that arise. But we also have an amazing staff, and we're all each other has.

"Each security team member has a broad range of skills, from temporary medical attention to de-escalating situations. As with your group, I have assigned each residence a security member for ease of access at any hour. We don't require you to stay directly in the confines of the camp, but I recommend you stay close enough to see the security tent. Your proactive work until my arrival is appreciated. So please continue and have a great first night!"

There are a few more hollers and some applause from the group as I jump down from the rock, dust kicking up in my wake.

Ayathesti - 25

I can't help getting lost in the new hue emitting from Tiamet as he stands on the boulder. My breaths shorten, almost to a point of pain. A breeze blows through his short black hair like a whisper. I can practically feel every strand wrapping around my fingers as they whirl around harmoniously.

"Go figure, eh, Aya?" Nineveh elbows me, smiling.

I take a few breaths to regain composure. "What?"

Hana looks at me. "Um, are you okay?"

It's like she's in a perpetual state of unawareness. I glare at her, clenching my teeth in frustration. "Why are you in my business?"

Hana's smile fades, and Nineveh furrows her brow. "Ayathesti, you're being rude. She's concerned because the color has faded from your face." She folds her arms.

I know that look. She's waiting for an apology. Rather than argue, I give in to avoid the headache. "Oh, sorry. I was lost in thought."

Tiamet walks up to us, placing a hand on my shoulder. "Well, let's get started, shall we?"

I nod and wait for the others to start moving before I follow them. *What are we getting started?* Nineveh and Hana walk toward the capsule, chitchatting with one another. I hold a slower pace behind them, alongside Tiamet.

"Hey, Tia—Director?" I watch my feet as we walk but catch his nod in my peripherals. "Well, I was just wondering, how is this going to work? Well, I mean, I know how it will work. But how are we doing the logistics of staying down here? Are we rotating in shifts or . . .?"

A smirk snakes its way onto his face, his eyes piercing through my comfort shields.

I swallow hard, my voice growing shaky. "I'm . . . just concerned with the accuracy of work if everybody's not getting enough rest."

The snake parts, baring his teeth in a chuckle. I stop and stare at him as he slowly stops, turning back to look at me.

"I guess after what happened right before we left, I probably shouldn't expect you to listen to anything I say." He shoves his hands into his pockets before walking to our shuttle and unloading supplies.

What the hell does that mean? I bite my lip and stare at nothing while attempting to evaluate the words and his body language. *I listen.* I look over to see him delegating instructions to the girls when a surge of anger slams into me. Clenching my teeth, I make my way to the group and grab one of the big silver boxes stacked outside the capsule.

"We're this far from home and you still find time to be a prick, Tiamet. I swear, I'll never get used to it." With a supply box in hand, I stomp away. *Deep breaths.*

"What did you say to her?" I hear Hana asking as the distance grows between us.

"Don't trouble yourself, hun. That's just . . ." Nineveh's response fades as I set the box down and sit on it, staring toward the setting sun as it crests the horizon.

The sound of footsteps grows louder as they approach. Nineveh comes around the side with two smaller silver boxes in her hands. She sets them down and heads back toward the capsule.

Moments later, more steps approach. A waft of air

from a large box being placed on the ground behind me pushes his scent forward. A nudge on my shoulder has me sitting upright. I whip my head around and glare at him, but he's focused on opening the box he'd just hauled over.

"The simulator's in that one, so stop moseying about and help us out here, huh?" Tiamet fidgets a few moments before the box clicks and pops open in front of him.

I kneel and apply firm pressure to the metal latches on the face of the box. The lid pops with a click as it detaches. Placing my palm on the face of the lid, I push it open, looking down at the contents.

"I thought you said this was a simulator?" I lift some canvas and examine the contents more. "All I see is a bunch of metal and canvas."

After careful examination of the individual pieces, I have a clear schematic in my mind of how the pieces should fit together. *Ah, yes, it's here.* Looking at the assembly booklet confirms my assumption of how it's put together. I pull out a loose piece of fabric, set it on the ground, and strategically connect the pieces on it.

I catch Nineveh in the corner of my eye as she begins inventory of her medical supplies. Tiamet has begun preparation on building the shelter. Shame crawls through my insides. *Tiamet wasn't being rude, he was joking, finding a moment to tease me for not paying attention to what he'd said up on that rock. Then I explode at him? What is wrong with me?* I sigh and clench my jaw.

After attaching the final piece, I look around for somewhere I can go to process things alone. *I need to apologize . . . again.* Endless scenarios play through in my mind. *I can't force it. Not tonight. I'll wait until we find ourselves alone long enough for me to get it out. Meanwhile, I need to redirect my shame into another emotion. Anger. Yes, that's good, though I can never stay mad at him. No, this time, I'm angry at myself.*

After placing the simulator back inside the box, I shake dust from the fabric and place it on top before closing the lid. I look toward Tiamet, who, to my surprise, made quick work of the shelter and is fixing the final corner post to the ground. The large frame is cloaked in canvas, with clear plastic pieces on the roof to let light in. You'd think they would have put some windows in the sides as well. It wouldn't be that hard, considering they were able to engineer a full door and frame into the canvas, heavy enough to latch shut against strong winds.

I watch him a few moments before observing the other tents coming together. I look over to where I'd seen Latif earlier, wondering if he and Nineveh had found each other yet.

The sky is reaching a deep blue with a haze of orange lingering in the distance where the sun had just set. My heel digs into the ground when I turn and make my way back to the capsule, longing for a few more moments of isolation before venturing inside the tent.

The metal is cold under my hand as I place it on the frame. I look at it, examining the structure in its simplicity. A smile touches the corners of my lips as I imagine Rothe's design contribution. My feet emanate a light tapping sound on the floor as I walk inside. I stop in the center to look around for anything that would be helpful. Once the door is locked, only Tiamet can get in. *All our personal belongings were below. There's nothing in here for me.* Still, a calm embraces me when I check. *It just feels right to make sure.*

A long awaited sigh releases some tension I've held in my shoulders for the past hour. I make my way over to a chair and drag my fingertips along the contours as I walk around the back.

"Why didn't I just listen? Out here, things felt promising, like we were starting over . . ." The words slip out in a whisper.

Leaning my back against the backside of the chair, I look down at the fuchsia fabric on my wrist before thinking of the orange one that was there earlier. A rush of isolation fills my stomach, reminding me I have nowhere to belong.

A knocking echoes through the compartment.

"Mm?" The soft pitter-patter of shoes grows closer before warmth radiates beside me and a strong, confident hand grips mine. It's a familiar grip that stutters my heart.

"I know," Tiamet's whispers.

I close my eyes, taking in a deep breath, slow and shaky, attempting to keep my composure before looking at him.

"Aya, I—" His eyes intent on me, he squeezes my hand, as though hearing the pain hidden in my breath.

"No. Let me." *This is my chance. Sooner than anticipated, but I can't let myself hold onto this guilt.* "I wasn't listening to you earlier, and I overreacted to your teasing. I'm sorry."

"I know." His voice remains as gentle as before. "Aya…"

The hurt in his eyes pushes me to break contact, and I look to the ground, attempting to hide the moisture lingering on my cheeks. His other hand cups my chin, and he directs my gaze back up to his, wiping the tears away with his thumb.

"I wanted to tell you . . ." His breathing grows shallow, but his eyes refuse to waver.

"We can't."

His thumb strokes my cheek a few times. "Let me say this. Please?"

I look down again, attempting to dodge answering, silencing my mind to ensure I hear every word he says.

"You are . . . I can't find the words, Aya. I never could. You take my breath away. My heart beats out of time so loudly, I can hear it in my head when we're close. It throws my focus, and I find it hard to speak my mind. I never seem to say the right thing . . . Mostly because I want to say everything all at once but get lost on where to start."

My eyes blur from the tears building again.

"Aya I—just . . . You have to know how important you are." He stares at me.

I close my eyes, sending tears down my cheek and onto his hand.

"What's wrong?" he asks.

With a hard swallow, I shake my head, placing my hands on his and push them away. But I refuse to let go while I force myself to speak through the tight pain in my throat. "Can't. We can't."

"What's the hesitation?"

"Work. It's unethical. It's . . . a terrible idea." I find courage and look at him. "I'm sorry . . ."

"Aya . . . Don't pull that crap on me. I'm the one in charge here, not The Council." The confidence in his voice makes me want to be reckless and break my morals.

"Oh, so because you're in charge, fraternization is suddenly appropriate?" I turn away, and he catches my wrist, melting the frustration in my chest. He pulls both my hands between his, holding them with tenderness, as if they were a fragile treasure.

"Ayathesti, the only reason we don't get along is because of this tension between us." He lifts my hands, brushing his lips against them.

"You think it's different for me? The torture of seeing you, knowing I'll never get the words right? The torture of imagining *us*?" I step back, hugging my arms against my chest. "It's just not something we should do. It's not good for me to think about how soft your lips could be, or how much I want to feel you touch me."

I reach for his hand but pull back right before touching it. With eyes closed and eyebrows furrowed, I sigh and bite my lower lip. "I want us to be together, Tiamet. It's just—" Tiamet's arms wrap around me, pulling me close. Our lips connect.

Electricity explodes. The world melts. All that remains is us. Past fantasies become reality as my fingers curl into his hair, my chest floating in weightlessness.

Tiamet pulls back and says in a trembling whisper, "I want us too."

My heart leaps. I pull his face back to mine, the space between us diminishing when he draws my hips in. Doubt vanishes as my chest pushes into his. The electric connection grows, enveloping my entire being as his taste seeps into me. The relief of giving in to this moment is one I've avoided dreaming of for the longest time. In a rush of elation, I latch onto it, silencing the inner demons telling me to wake up—because it can't be real.

Tiamet - 26

At long last, I experience her velvety lips pressing against my own. I succumb to the wave of satisfaction when I remember I can't stop time. I open my eyes and look at her with a side smile.

"I want us too," I whisper, my breath shaking. She draws my face back to hers. Pulling her hips in drives my desire deeper, her scent pushing me to intoxication. Just when my chest nears the point of bursting, she sighs into my lips and delivers one last kiss before pulling back.

I take a deep breath and put my forehead to hers, the lingering want pressing my fingertips into her hip. Ayathesti looks at me.

I smile. "You have no idea how long I've waited to do that."

"Was it worth it?"

I stare at her lips. "It's taking all I have not to kiss you again right now."

"They'll be wondering where you are."

"I came out here to find you. They know where I am."

She bites her lip. "Well, we should get back then."

"Not yet. Please, I—" I take a deep breath and wrap my arms around her. "Can't I just hold you for a second?"

Her face presses into my shirt. "You smell nice." She pulls back, squinting. "When did you find time to change?"

"I changed before I came in."

Straightening her posture, she clears her throat. "Why didn't you say something?"

"That was my initial mission." I lean against the chair

with folded arms. "Then I saw you and . . . Well, I felt like we should talk."

She stands there, looking at me as though in disbelief of what just happened.

"Actually, I looked for you for a few minutes before checking in here."

She looks away, folding her arms. "I'm sorry"

"Stop being sorry." I reach for her hand.

She pulls back at my touch. "I didn't think I was gone that long."

"It's not like it takes me long to change, Aya."

She turns her back to me. *To hide her vulnerability, perhaps?* "Well, thank you, Tiamet, for letting me know the tent is up. I'll go change now." She starts toward the door.

With a quick step, I reach for her hand and hold it. She turns to face me.

"It was my pleasure." The smile on my face refuses to leave. I bring her hand to my lips and let them brush the surface before I loosen my grasp. Her fingers tingle against my palm as they slip away, and I watch her ponytail sway as she exits. Sitting down in a chair, I take a moment to process what had just happened.

The mere thought of her creates a brand new craving. The scent of her lip balm lingers in my nose, as does the warmth of her body on my chest. *I need her lips on mine again.*

Ayathesti - 27

The smell of food pierces my nose when I open the tent door, erasing any traces of Tiamet that may have lingered.

"Aya, have you seen Tiamet?" Hana stands behind the table on the left side of the room.

"Huh?" I look at her as I return from my daze. "Oh . . . Yes, he's locking the capsules." There are empty plates on the table. Nineveh sits with two unfamiliar faces.

"Great! Dinner is ready," Hana says.

I nod and look to the hallway in the center back wall of the tent. *Sleeping quarters.* I glance at the lounge chairs on the right side of the room as I walk toward the hallway.

Reading the name tags on each door as I pass them, I brush my fingers over my lips. At the end of the hallway, I see my name and push my way inside. The walls are canvas. *At least there's still a little privacy.* A cot sits to the right of the door, with my chest at the base of it, leaving about a foot of space between them. *And enough space for a path.*

I make my way to the chest, kneel on the ground, and open it. My belongings. With a deep breath, a wave of relief washes over me. My items are safe. I reach in and untie a stiff string that holds my clothes together. *Lucky my comfort clothes are on top.*

The restrictive binds of the suit ease away within the first few inches of the zipper being unfastened. After getting dressed, I reach for my hairbrush and run it through my hair, smoothing it out before pulling it into a loose tie at the side of my neck. I lay my suit on the cot and flatten out where seams would be to make for easier folding. Brushing my hand along the waistline, Rothe's words come to mind as my fingers glide over the lump in the pocket.

"Wait until you're alone," I whisper and slip my fingers inside before pulling the object out.

With a deep breath, I bring the long crystal closer for inspection. "A holo?" I sigh. "A lot of good this does me, Rothe. I didn't bring a projector." I look around and hold it up to the light. "But maybe I can at least see what might be on it."

Bringing the crystal up to my eye, letting the light shine through, I twist it slowly. With one eye closed, I squint to get the image into focus. My chest floods, and I struggle to catch my breath.

"P-papa?" Chest heaving, my eyes swell, and I pull the crystal to my chest in a fist. "Oh, Rothe—where—how?" I sit and allow the tears to flow. "Thank you."

I walk down the hallway, voices of conversation growing louder as I reach the open room. Nineveh, Hana, and Tiamet sit in quiet conversation, their words inaudible even as I approach and welcome myself to an empty seat.

I look up from my plate, catching the eyes of each person around me: Nineveh to the left, dazzling like her usual done up self again; Hana, sitting across from me, staring down at her food creation with admiration; and Tiamet to my right, glancing back at me, holding my gaze with his gentle eyes and a soft smile.

Time seems to flow around me as I sit there, motionless. Hana is the first one up from the table, taking empty plates with her to the sink. She washes them before heading down the hallway. Nineveh leaves next, retiring down the hallway as well. Tiamet avoids going to bed by making himself comfortable in the lounge area. Me? I'm still at the table as though in a trance.

Dragging myself back to my surroundings, I stand up and push my chair in before walking out the tent door for a fresh breath.

The crisp night air tightens my skin, making the hairs at the base of my neck stand on end. I look up at the foreign moon with its calming, bright glow. It's so different, but somehow the vast size provides a familiar comfort. Taking a deep breath of the chill air offers my lungs a sense of being cleaned, refreshed. A glance around the area we'd landed in reels me in from the sky. The tents all show no signs of consciousness, only being consumed in darkness. I draw a pattern in the dirt with my foot before walking inside. *For you, Papa.*

I catch a glance of Tiamet from the corner of my eye and turn toward him. His feet are spread apart as he slouches in a relaxed position in his chair. He holds a file in his hands, hiding his face. A flashback of our shared moment consumes me, and I can't kill the smile it gives me. The buzzing in my gut intensifies just thinking about his lips on mine again.

"Tomorrow is the big day, huh? It all starts tomorrow." I let out a quiet sigh and stare at him, rubbing the sides of my arms.

The folder lowers toward his chest, and furrowed brows of confusion sit atop his blank eyes.

"Never mind." I start down the hallway. *Stupid. Why say anything at all?*

"Hey, wait a sec." The lights shut off behind me, and his hand grasps my wrist, stopping me from entering my room.

I turn to him. "Yes?"

"Good night." His smile threatens to consume me as his thumb glides over the top of my hand.

With a shy smile, I nod. “Goodnight.”

My hand slips from his before he walks back up the hallway and enters his room. *I could get used to that.*

Ayathesti - 28

I wake to a faint tapping outside my door. The light pierces me like a thousand needles as I blink my eyes open to the new day. I shoot up, remembering where we are. I rush to my chest, grab whatever lies on top, and put it on. After slipping into my boots, I unseal the door and open it while pulling the strap of my pack over my head.

"Morning!" Nineveh's peppy voice greets me along with the scent of a sweet-creme oojo filling the air.

"Oh!" I stumble over myself to prevent knocking it out of her hands. My hand rests on my heaving chest. I reach out and grasp the cup. "Thanks, Nineveh."

"You're welcome! I trust you slept well?" Nineveh attempts to step aside in the small hallway so I have room to walk ahead.

I bring the cup to my lips and savor the liquid before swallowing. "Can't complain—mm, that's good." I make my way to the end of the hall, taking another mouthful.

"Oh, I'm glad you like it. Hana is a great cook!"

My footing falters with hesitation before I swallow again. I look around at seating options before making my way to the table. The chair drags on the floor as I pull it out and set my pack down next to it. A shock of cold crawls up my back through my shirt when it rests against the metal chair. The files spewed over the surface of the table make it difficult to locate a place to set my cup.

"Do we have an agenda today, boss?" Latif's voice comes in from the lounge behind me.

Turning halfway in my chair, I glance at one of the

open files before looking at him to respond. "Give me a look, Latif. Do you think I've had time to make an agenda? Besides, I haven't received direction yet. I have no idea where we'll even be working."

I twist back to the table, catching the script on the top sheet. *Transmission 42-38: to implement any means necessary against unknown indigenous beings that may—* The cover is flipped closed, cutting it off mid-sentence.

"What is that . . .?" My eyebrows furrow as I follow Tiamet's hand to his face. *Where did he come from?*

He slides the file to the edge of the table before picking it up. The motions are slow, almost cocky, but hold undeniable secrecy.

"Don't worry about it." He tucks the folder under his arm and walks to the counter to refill his cup.

I glare at him, heat building in my chest and spreading to the rest of my body. "Seriously?" I hold my breath to keep calm. "It was right here for anyone to see, but we're not supposed to worry or be curious about it?" I grip my pack and forcefully stand, knocking my chair to the ground before stomping out the door.

Burning not only in fury but with the heat of the sun as it rains down on me, I look around the tents to locate my work station. One catches my eye, with its canvas door tied to the exterior pole and cages stacked to the ceiling.

I stop in the canopy shade, examining the containers full of animals and critters of various sizes. It appears that collecting specimens for sample extraction has already begun.

Words echo in my head as I look at the piles of cages. *'Unknown indigenous beings.' What does that mean?* I stand with folded arms in the tent's entrance, staring out. *'Beings that may…' May what?* With a repetitive blink, I shift my focus back to the contents of the room. With there being so many options, I look around for any indication of categorization. I flip through various files and notes clipped to one cage. There's a label with a number tagged around one of the bars. Under the top sheet is a chart with a percentage of compatibility.

I smile and lift the cage from the top of the pile and set it down on a small table on the opposite side of the tent. I crouch down, placing my face near the cage opening to get a better look at the creature inside.

It's on the smaller end compared to the other animals, looking to be about the length of my forearm. It has pure-black eyes, a slit in its snout, and big buck teeth sticking straight down from its mouth. The body is covered in sandy brown fur, with the tip of its tail and long ears dark, looking as though they had been dipped in ink. It sits on two curved hind legs (obviously used for jumping) and front legs curled up next to its body. I stare at it, intrigued, before being overcome with sadness for the creature and placing it back on the stack of cages. I walk out from under the canopy and stop. Staring at the ground, remembering that I don't know where my work tent is, I crush a dirt clump with the toe of my shoe. *Satisfying,* I muse before spotting a rock with a good view of the horizon.

I cross my ankles and stare at my shadow on the ground. Animals in the nearby bush chirp a beautiful tune. The sound is foreign and loud but not invasive. It's soft yet lively. Unfamiliar but so calming, it engulfs me in a blanket of reassurance. Sitting up straight, I close my eyes and pinch my hands between my legs, taking a deep breath. A wave of silence washes over me.

A shadow cools the heat on my back.

I observe Tiamet by his shadow as he inserts his hands into his pockets. "Hey."

"Hey . . ." I uncross my ankles and kick a small stone away from my feet.

"You okay? Calmed down a bit?"

My eyebrows furrow, throwing a glare at him. "Excuse me, calm down? Why would I need to calm down?"

"Those files are confidential. I had been going over them before you sat down. Direct instructions from The Council." He turns his head, looking at the bush with small blue winged animals fluttering playfully inside.

"It was your tone. You could have told me that without being so condescending." I rub my hands together between my legs.

"I didn't intend to be condescending or make you feel left out. I know how much you like to be in control of everything. And I feel like we're finally in good standing. I don't want to hinder that by upsetting you."

Now I'm a control freak. "I understand." I bite my tongue to prevent myself from being petty and saying more.

"I knew you would." His hand rests on my shoulder.

I pull back slightly, retreating it from his touch. "Do you know where my workstation is? I should go set up." I stand and stare at him.

"Bio is in the tent under the wide-top tree," he responds with hesitation. "Are you okay?"

I nod, quirking my head to the side—an attempt to look more bubbly. I kick another small stone.

"Yes. Excuse me." As I make my way past him, our arms brush and the tension lingers until the moment the residence tent door closes behind me.

With a deep, frustrated sigh, I plop into a chair in the lounge, sinking into it.

"Control freak," I mutter, rolling my eyes. "What an ass." I hold up my left palm and examine the small scar still there from the accident in the lab back home. I grip it and pull it to my chest when the door swings open. I hesitantly glance up, dreading the possibility of seeing him emerge from it.

"Oh, there you are! We've been looking everywhere." Nineveh says as Latif follows her in, closing the door behind them.

"Why?" I look back at my hand, applying gentle pressure while I rub it.

"Well, if the boss doesn't wanna work"—Latif takes a seat in a chair next to me—"then I'll take that as my cue to go ahead and relax!"

"Oh you!" Nineveh giggles. "I'm sure Aya wants to work!" She looks at me with an eager look on her face, as though waiting for an equally enthusiastic response.

I shrug a shoulder. "I was just here to cool off before heading over to the bio tent."

"See, Latif, I told you!" *Is Nineveh . . . gloating?* Her hands are on her hips, and a smirk is on her lips. "Oh, did you see those cute fuzzy creatures they've found? I've seen pictures, but I didn't think they'd be cuter up close!"

I slowly nod, avoiding eye contact with either of them. "Yeah, I saw. Poor things are about to go through hell for who knows how long it takes to get this right."

"Oh, c'mon, boss! It's for the greater good of our species." Latif interlaces his fingers across his chest.

"I'm not sure this will even work." I scoff back at him with a glare.

"Well, why wouldn't it? We've all worked so hard!" Nineveh says.

"Since when does hard work equal success?" I shake my head. "I'm just not so sure anymore."

"You just need to stop worrying! Calm down and enjoy our time here!" Nineveh offers me a reassuring smile.

"Yeah, boss. You should work on being less of a control freak," Latif says. Nineveh gives him a small kick to the shin. "Ow!" he chuckles, leaning over to rub the spot.

"Be nice!" Her hands are on her hips again as she

scolds him.

"Nineveh, it's alright. I'm beginning to embrace that term." I push myself up from the chair. "Well, you know where I'll be."

I walk to the door and open it, nearly knocking Tiamet to the ground. "Oh, excuse me," I mutter while squeezing past him.

"What did you put in that girls drink this morning?" I hear Tiamet say before the door latches shut behind me.

Ayathesti - 29

A rush of cool air flows past me when I push the door to the bio tent aside. I didn't think being placed under a tree would add such a variance in temperature. *That's good. Helps regulation for samples.* The layout is pretty basic—a table in the center of the room, coolers and other supplies stacked around the walls of the tent. I walk to the table and place the animal cage on top. I grab a lab coat hanging on the side of a tall cabinet and fasten it closed. A bin next to the coats holds an assortment of goggles, and below are gloves. With a tap of my ear to my shoulder, my earring materializes my goggles as I pull on gloves.

When I lift the lid of a big metal chest on the ground, a plume of vapor escapes and sinks to my feet. A rush of comfort washes over me as my toes vanish in the cloud. *It's almost like being in the lab freezers back home.*

After locating the amber-colored fluid in the disorganized chest, I place the bottle in my coat pocket and snap the chest lid shut to keep the cold in. I secure the latch before rummaging through the chest next to it to grab a syringe and test tube. After placing the items on the table, I unwrap the syringe and tip the bottle of fluid before inserting the needle through the seal. The plunger is smooth when I extract the fluid and dispense it into a water tray in the animals cage.

The creature sniffs the air, noticing the change. I lower myself to its level and watch with fascination as it makes it way to the water, dips its curled paws in, and licks the moisture from them. It repeats this a few times as I clean up my supplies. After placing the bottle back in the metal chest, I return to watch as the critter makes its way to the other side of the cage and curls its back feet up to its abdomen, seeming to turn into a little ball of fur.

A whistle drowns out the rhythmic breathing of the animal when the door opens, blasting the room with light. *Latif, perfect timing!* I reach into the cage and maneuver the creature onto my palm. Its soft and limp in my hand, warm and unresisting.

"Oh good. Get gloves and goggles. You can hold this while I extract," I say to him. Panic washes over his face as he stops right inside the door. "Well, don't just stand there. Gloves are to your left."

The impatience must have carried in my voice. He quickly makes his way over, pulling gloves over his sleeves up to his forearms. He extends his hands toward me. *It's not like you'll be any safer if you stand as far away from it as possible.* I place the animal in his hands and watch his shoulders relax when the body fills his palms.

"What are we calling this thing, anyway?" he asks.

I reach inside one of my pockets and unwrap a new syringe. "We're not calling it anything other than it's accession number." I grasp the now-thawed test tube and open the freezer bin to grab a colder second one. *Can't be sure if it needs to be cold or not. Better get both.*

After fastening the colder test tube to the syringe, I look at Latif and motion my head toward the table. "You can set it down."

He looks at the table and places the creature on top. "Why did you tell me to hold it if you knew I'd be setting it down?"

I turn and examine it to determine where to extract from. "I didn't realize you'd look like such an idiot while you were holding it."

I push the tip of the needle through the fur and surface of the skin. I then extract the sample. My brows crinkle, and I bite the corner of my lip, tilting my head with intrigue. The blood is a deep red.

"What?" Latif looks at the tube.

"Nothing—I . . . just wasn't expecting this color."

He chuckles. "We're not—"

"I know we're not at home. That much I understand." I pull the tube away from the extraction nozzle. A milky film covers the opening to seal it from contaminants. I place it down and repeat the process.

After retracting the needle from the animal, I examine the tubes before placing one on a tray on the counter and the other back inside the chilled chest.

"Um, boss?" Latif's voice is coarse and shaky. "I know I'm not as smart as you, but I don't think this thing should still be bleeding . . ." He stands, staring down at it.

I rush over to see a steady stream of blood draining from the animal.

"Oh no." I press my finger over the wound, attempting to suppress the flow. "Get me something, like swabs or gauze to close it up!"

Latif looks around. It's clear he has no idea where to locate any of these items.

"For the love of—here!" I grab his hand and force his finger onto the wound. Rushing over to the chest of dry contents, I grab a packet of gauze squares. I rip the package open and rummage to find something to keep the cloth secure on the animal's fur. With nothing non adhesive-based in plain sight, I tap my finger on the rim of the chest. *Ah! My coat.*

I rip the bottom hem into a long, thin strip and tie the gauze around the animal.

Latif gawks. "How did you know what to do?"

Rolling my eyes, I pick up the animal and gently place it back in the cage. "Oh, please." I rinse its water tray and refill it with fresh water.

"I'm going to keep it in here to make sure it stays alive without having to battle the heat. I guess I need to alter the sedative formula to prevent this for our next extractions." When I pull my gloves off, droplets of blood stain the hem of my ripped coat. I close my eyes and lean on my hands on top of the table, letting out a deep breath.

"You okay, boss?" Latif disposes his gloves and rinses his hands.

"Yeah . . . Just puts me behind schedule is all." I turn around and lean my back against the table, folding my arms, waiting for him to finish.

"So do you want me to fetch you another specimen?" He shakes his hands dry and points toward the door.

"Well, you can leave, but no more extractions until I examine this sample for cell structure behaviors and can identify the coagulation response." I toss my gloves in the bin before washing my hands.

"I'll be going, then." He rubs his stomach and pushes through the tent door.

After pulling my hands free of the spritzer, I pat them against my face. My heart pounds in my ears, and I take another deep breath to slow it down. *I almost lost my cool back there.* I clamp my hands together to stop the shaking.

Tiamet - 30

I peer over my paperwork, watching her enter the doorway.

"Where have you been?" My voice carries through the open room.

The bottom of her ponytail swishes as she shakes her head. "Just research." She walks to the kitchen and opens a cabinet door. After grabbing a glass, she reaches for the oojo pot.

"I wouldn't." I place my files down and stand, watching her movements as she continues on. "That's been there since early this morning." Pocketing my hands, I make my way to the table. I pull out the chair next to her and sit.

"I really don't care how aged it is." She holds the cup under her nose and closes her eyes. "I could use the kick."

"You okay?" I lean back in my chair, folding my arms.

Her focus stays on the fluid approaching her lips. Her eyes grow wide before she swallows and puts her hand on her chest, coughing.

"Told you." I smirk.

"It's fine. I'm fine." She peers over the rim of her glass and mutters. "Unknown indigenous beings?"

I tilt my head, furrowing my brow. "What was that?"

"I should be asking you." She lowers the cup to the table, staring at me. "Unknown indigenous beings. What are we doing with them?"

"You're still on about that?" I lean back in my chair, lifting the front legs from the ground.

She slams her hand on the table. "You may not care what kind of mess we leave behind, but I, on the other hand, do!"

"It's just a precautionary guideline, Aya. Don't look too much into it." I clench my fist to dial back my frustration.

"Are there beings we should be worried about showing up?" The corners of her eyes droop, drowning with desperation.

Examining her, I shake my head with near hesitation. "No. There are no beings for you to worry about." *Hopefully that will satisfy her. That's the truth, but not the whole truth.* My heartbeat grows heavier.

She looks away. "I'm sorry, I—"

The front legs of the chair return to the ground as I sit forward. "Aya, I know that you like to be in the loop, and you're a great asset to have in this endeavor . . . but you need to stop worrying about things that aren't in your job description."

"Wait, what? Before we even got here, you were telling me to step it up, take more responsibility. And now you're telling me to stay out of it?" Her body movements become more animated as she continues, lifting her hands in the air. "What the hell is going on with you, Tiamet? What are you not telling me!"

I raise my brow, taken aback at how assertive she's being. I place my hand on top of hers. "Aya, I just need you to be safe. I need everyone safe. That's my main concern for this mission. Please promise me you'll stay out of this one?"

Her lips part as though to speak. "I won't go looking for trouble, if that's what you mean." With a defeated sigh, she slides her hand out from under mine, then points at me. "But don't expect me to not pay attention to information laying around in front of me! Got it?" She grabs her glass and tips the remaining contents into her mouth, then coughs once more at the strength of the fermented tea.

I lean back in my chair again and smile as I clasp my

hands together at the back of my head. "It sure doesn't take long, does it?"

"What doesn't take long?" She stands and walks her glass to the sink.

"For you to stop being mad at me."

She smiles and returns to her chair, avoiding eye contact when she sits.

"What happened there?" I point to her torn lab coat before seeing red spots on it.

"Huh?" She looks down. "Oh, just . . . experimenting."

"With your coat?" I quirk a brow.

"I guess you could say that." She reaches for a stray thread and tugs on it.

"And what are those red speckles?" I lean to the side of the table to get a closer look at the hem and the red on her coat, reaching out to grasp it.

Ayathesti lifts the coats edge to examine it. "Oh, that? It's blood." She releases the corner.

I straighten up, chest growing tight. "What? Blood? Whose blood?" *How can she be so casual about this?*

Her ponytail sways as she lets out a soft chuckle. "I took a sample from an animal. I guess they bleed differently than us, but nobody knew, so I didn't know to adjust our narcotic to help with clotting." She looks to the empty side of the room, as though reliving the moment. "We had a little bleeding incident . . . But I think it'll be fine."

"Ayathesti, you need to tell me about these things, okay?" I reach for her hand, the tightness in my chest compressing further when she pulls away.

"Seriously, Tiamet?" Her face goes flush. "You act like I've never done this before."

"That's not it." I return my hand to my lap, pressing the fingertips into my leg. *You're the boss, act like the boss.* "I want everything to go smoothly, and in order for that to happen, I need to have reports of everything. Particularly things going wrong, so we can avoid future mishaps."

Ayathesti rolls her eyes. "Well, I expect the little thing to survive, so there's no harm done! I'll be sure to call you over next time something unexpected happens."

"I'm serious, Aya!" My chest tightens as anger bubbles up. "How can you expect others to do their jobs using proper procedure, yet you refuse to do yours!"

"First I'm a control freak, and now I think I'm better than everyone else? How am I supposed to know you want details on every little aspect of my life?"

"It should be obvious by now."

"Obvious? Please." She scoffs, folding her arms.

I dig my fingertips through my hair, and a deep breath reduces the pressure building in my chest. "You just… don't get it, do you?"

"Sorry, but I don't know what I'm supposed to be 'getting.' " The chair squeals as it drags against the floor when she stands. *This conversation is about to become a conflict.*

I look up at her. "Where are you going?"

"I have a narcotic to mess around with. That is, if I have approval, *sir*." Everything about her response seems calm—her posture, her expressions, her tone.

This is unlike her typical emotional outburst. Staring with disbelief, I collect myself, replacing my rage with concern. "Just . . . be careful."

"Right." She rolls her eyes and leaves, not bothering to stop the door from slamming behind her.

Ayathesti - 31

Taking a deep breath, I close my eyes, once more feeling bad about how I'd left things with Tiamet. *Should I swallow my pride and crawl back to apologize, yet again?*

After a few moments of internal debate, I decide against it. Shifting my weight away from the tent pole, I head back to the bio tent to check on the creature. The light flickers on when I push through the door. I look at the cage and walk toward it. The animal appears to be still. Lifeless.

"Great . . ." Placing my elbow on the table, I rest my chin on my palm and stare into the cage. "Poor thing."

After slipping into a new pair of gloves, I lift the latch and pick up the lifeless animal. "Sorry, little guy," I manage to whisper as my heart sinks, placing the animal back down.

Vapor spills over the top of the cold chest and drapes around my feet when I blow on it to see inside easier. Grasping the sample, I tip the vial to ensure it's frozen before placing it on top of the closed, adjacent chest and rummaging around for other supplies I need for testing.

During my search, I catch movement in the corner of my eye. When I look, the vial rolls over the edge of the chest, plummeting to the ground. My heart leaps and panic kicks me. I throw myself down to catch it.

Fire and needles claw at my knees when rocks on the ground dig into them. I catch my breath and smile, sitting back on my heels, cradling the vial in my hands. With closed eyes, I sigh, succumbing to relief. When I look at the vial, a deep colored fluid is pooling in the air pocket inside my glove. A drop pushes through the slit in my glove, dripping onto my pants. I turn the vial over to see it's cracked, a glass shard sticking straight out.

"Damn it!" I can't stop the words and they erupt with an impulse to throw the vial at the ground. Anything in tact before is now shattered in the dirt around me.

Defeated, I peel my knees from the ground and sit back with clenched teeth. The pebbles I landed on had cut through my pants and broken through the skin. Small droplets of dark green blood shine in the light. Propping my elbows on my knees, I press my forehead against my wrist. The tightness in my throat is unavoidable as I surrender to tears.

After a few moments, I collect the strength to clean up. I remove my gloves and wash my hands before applying a gauze square over the cut and placing an adhesive strip over it. My chest stays tight the entire time I clean the rest of the mess. My pride won't allow me to expose the truth and face the embarrassment of an incident on the first day. I flip the light simulator off and leave the lab.

The light inside of the residence tent is blinding when I push the door open. Tiamet, Latif, Hana, and Nineveh are all sitting around the table, eating and conversing. I clench my teeth with each step to hide the pain.

"There you are!" Nineveh beams.

"We saved you a plate," Hana says.

I disregard them, walking straight to my room. Closing the door behind me, I whimper to myself. I lay on the bed, content with the solace of privacy, before a knock at the door rips it away.

I hold everything back. "Yeah?"

"Aya, are you going to eat?" The door muffles Nineveh's voice.

"Yeah, I'll just be out in a minute, Nin."

"Okay . . ."

I sit up and reach for a fresh set of clothes to hide the scrapes on my knees and a pair of fingerless gloves to hide my hands and the bandage.

I plop into a chair, staring at the plate Hana places in front of me.

"Dig in!" Her voice drips with happiness.

I look up at her, unenthused. "Thanks."

"Where were you all night?" Nineveh leans onto the table.

"Working."

"Go figure. Can't even let me know so I can help." Latif snorts.

"I just wanted to check on the animal, but I got . . . distracted." I stare at my plate, avoiding eye contact with everyone.

"Distracted? That's so like you!" Nineveh giggles.

"Any news on it yet?" Latif perks up.

"Well, it's dead if that's what you're asking." I shovel food into my mouth, hoping that they'll stop asking me questions if my mouth is full.

"Oh no!" Nineveh's eyebrows tilt. "What happened?"

I close my eyes, chewing slowly, not responding.

Latif cocks his head. "I meant with the new narcotic."

"Oh . . . Yeah, I didn't get to that yet." I speak through mangled pieces of food before swallowing and spooning another mouthful.

"You were out there 'working' this long and haven't had time?" Tiamet quirks a brow.

I raise my gaze to glare at him before lowering it back to my plate, determined not to answer as many questions as I can.

"When did you start wearing gloves?" Nineveh

reaches for my free hand.

I pull it under the table and into my lap. "I've always had these. They keep my hands warm. Thought they might be useful, so I snuck them in."

"You're allowed to bring your own comforts, Aya," Tiamet says. "Nobody said you had to sn—"

"It's a figure of speech, Tiamet."

"Well, boss, how much longer until you have something done with the new narcotic and need my help?" Latif straddles a chair, draping his arms on the backrest.

I push my heels into the floor and lean my chair back, folding my arms. "Why the sudden interest in working?"

His mouth hangs open, feigning shock and offense. "I can't believe you would even consider that's what my intentions are!"

"Well, then, what is it?" My chair falls back to rest on all fours as I lean forward.

"I think he wants to start a countdown of the free-time he's got left before being enslaved once again." Tiamet chuckles.

Everybody lets out a small laugh. I look at my plate before standing. "Thanks, Hana. Dinner was satisfying." I take a deep breath and tuck the chair beneath the table.

"C'mon, Aya. I was teasing!" Tiamet's eyes plead for me to stay.

I turn away from the group and start walking. "I'll just see you in the morning."

Ayathesti - 32

A faint tapping draws me from the cradle of sleep.

"Aya." The door muffles the voice on the other side as the tapping continues.

I clench my eyes tighter, tucking my blanket under my chin as a chill crawls over me.

"Ayathesti, wake up."

I sigh. *Maybe if I don't answer, they'll go away.*

"Hello?" The voice continually interrupts my solace.

"Whaaat do you want?" The words slide over my tongue in a lazy, frustrated whimper.

"It's almost time for breakfast!"

"Coming." I slide my legs over the side of the bed and slip into my boots. I sit up and hug the blanket tightly to my body before standing. I shuffle to the door and pull it open, peering out, awaiting an excited monster to jump out at me.

Hana's expression proves that my appearance reflects how I feel. "Well, it's not ready yet, so you can get dressed first . . . if you want."

With nothing more than a glare, I push past her and make my way into the lounge, taking a place on one of the softer chairs. Leaning my head back, I pull my feet up into the blanket, hugging my knees to my chest. I close my eyes and shiver.

"Woah," Tiamet says from beside me.

"You okay, boss?" Latif's voice carries from across the room.

I open my eyes, dragging my head up to glare at Latif.

"Right, I'll take that as *no*." He looks to the door as

Nineveh walks in.

The color drains from her face when her eyes land on me, stopping her dead in her tracks. "Oh my! Aya, are you feeling okay? You look terrible!"

"Gee . . . thanks." I slouch, putting my chin on my knees, and adjust the blanket so it's airtight around me.

"Medically speaking, of course. Come on, I'll check your vitals!" Nineveh nearly skips as she turns around to leave, only stopping at the door to wait for me.

I sit there, motionless. *She's really excited about this.* The thought of moving any part of my body prompts every muscle to ache. My head throbs under the pulsating whoosh in my ears.

"Well? Come on!" Nineveh's eyes are begging now.

"I'm fine. Would you all just calm down." I murmur into the blanket under my chin.

"Boss, I've seen you nearly every day for years now. This is not 'fine.' " Latif coaxes.

I roll my head to look at Tiamet. He nods once with a sympathetic shrug.

"Ugh, fine." I let my feet slide from the blanket back into my boots, and I stand. Hugging the blanket close to my torso, I drag my feet to the door, following Nineveh to the other tent.

I spare no time getting comfortable in a new chair, watching as she brushes a thermometer over my forehead.

"Just as I thought. Elevated." She returns it to its home. "Well, that explains the sweating. But why the blanket?"

"Are you serious? It's freezing."

"No, actually, it's not. It's very warm! Did you sleep last night?"

I start to nod but hesitate as I think back. "Well, I woke up once."

"Do you have any pains or aches anywhere?"

Taking a deep breath, I pull my gown up past my knees to expose my new scabs.

"Oh my!" Nineveh's eyes grow wide. "What happened!"

"I fell."

"Well it doesn't look deep. It's already scabbed over. No swelling. That shouldn't be the issue." Nineveh pulls the blanket away and places it on the empty chair.

"Hey, give it back." I grab for it, but she moves it further from reach.

"You can have it back in a few minutes, but I need to check you first!"

I cross my arms in protest.

"What's on your shirt?" Nineveh says, pointing.

I look down at a stain on the torso of my gown, pulling it away from my chest for a better look. I shrug. Nineveh grabs my hand to move it and get a better view of the stain. I wince as pain shoots through my palm and up my arm. She turns my palm up, revealing the swollen wound.

"Aya! What is this?"

"I already told you, I fell."

"Why didn't you report this?" She gently lifts the bandage, shining a light over it.

"I didn't think I had to report clumsiness when walking around." I can't help the sarcasm that spills from my mouth.

"It's already really infected."

"It was oozing everywhere last night too." I hiss as she applies an antiseptic.

"You mean you knew it was this bad and didn't tell me?"

"I went to the lav in the middle of the night, Nineveh. Got rid of some puss and stared at every mistake I've ever made suddenly looking back at me through the mirror."

"Aya, this is a clean cut. It likely didn't happen when you fell."

Eyeing the blanket, I yank it from the far side of the other chair.

"Well, I did fall. *And* that *is* when it happened." I pull the blanket around my shoulders, sighing when the warmth returns. "Don't tell Tiamet." I stare at the floor, my heart threatening to shatter.

Anxiety whispers her dark words to me. *'He'll hate you forever if he finds out you lied to him . . . again.'*

Nineveh raises her eyebrows. "You mean lie?"

"Yes, Nineveh. Lie. He's too concerned about what I'm doing right now, I can't handle it! I can't keep myself composed when he's around, and then I get mad because I can't talk to him the way I want to, and that makes him mad, and that makes me even more mad!" I take a deep stuttering breath. "It's a vicious cycle, and I wish I could stop it, but I don't know how!" My face grows hot, my eyes burning with tears.

"Take another breath, Aya. I won't tell Tiamet, but I have to put this in your file. You should tell him."

"How am I supposed to tell him?" I sniffle and swallow hard.

"Do it the way you do best with all conversations—one on one!" She finishes wrapping the cut and pats the top of my hand gently. "He likes you. It's not like he will get mad."

"Uh, yeah right! That's exactly what he'll do. He'll tell me I should have told him right after it happened blah, blah, I'm the boss . . ."

Nineveh giggles. "Is that really how you hear him talk?"

I nod, the pulsing distracting me from Tiamet. "Why

is it oozing puss? It's disgusting."

"Hm . . . So it is. That's what infections do. But, Aya, he doesn't talk to you that way. That's just the way you want to hear it. You know, compared to how he used to talk to you, he's actually quite charming now."

I scoff. "You have been having too many conversations with Latif if you think the way Tiamet talks to me is charming."

Nineveh hesitates. "Well . . . maybe it's more of the way he talks about you. Now that I think about it, you're never around." She disposes of the puss soaked gauze. "I guess you'll probably have to stop working for a few days so that doesn't get worse."

I sigh. "But that'll put me so far behind!"

"Latif can help. You should probably let him, too! He's been getting a bit comfortable in the last few days." She giggles.

I can't help but smile. "I suppose I could let him do the easy stuff . . ."

We both stand to make our way out of the tent, and she says, "Think breakfast is ready?"

How does she manage to stay cheery in any situation? I don't understand it. "Not like I feel like eating. Anyway, I have to eat with my other hand so Tiamet doesn't see my bandage."

Nineveh shakes her head.

"What? I don't want to tell him before I'm ready. And in front of everybody at the table? No. Unfathomable."

After taking my seat at the table, I hug the blanket around me, hoping to escape the density of guilt shrouding me.

'He knows.'

Tiamet - 33

"Feeling better?" I flash a concerned smile at Ayathesti when she sits in the chair beside me.

"Yes, but, Director, my doctor says I can't work for a few days." She responds with a nod, avoiding eye contact.

"I figured as much. I've never seen you in such a state of exhaustion. Which is concerning, seeing as we just got here!"

She glares, finally looking at me. "What's that supposed to mean?"

"You work too hard, Aya. Relax a little bit. Enjoy the scenery." I shrug. *Maybe if I sound more casual she won't get offended.*

She looks at the plates Hana sets in front of us.

"Dig in and tell me what you think." Hana's voice is soft.

"Hana, this looks great. Won't you join us?"

Hana shakes her head. "Thank you, but I already ate! Sorry, I got so hungry I couldn't wait anymore!"

Lifting my hand, I shake my head. "No apology necessary."

"I'm going to finish getting ready for the day, if you'll both excuse me. When you're finished, feel free to leave the plates in the sink. I'll take care of them when I get back."

I nod and pick up my fork, examining the contents before stabbing a white cube and bringing it to my lips. Savory flavors burst over my tongue as I chew. I smile with approval before digging in.

"I have to tell you something." Ayathesti shifts in her chair.

I place my fork down and lean in, resting my forearms on the edge of the table.

"I . . ." She lets out a deep breath. "Yesterday, I don't know what I was thinking. You're right. I work too hard and—"

"Aya, everyone appreciates your hard work. But you don't have to keep apologizing for the way our conversations end."

"I'm not trying to apologize, Tiamet. I am trying to tell you something. Would you just—please listen?"

"Okay."

"Last night, when I was working . . . I got hurt." Ayathesti lets the blanket loose from her body, slides her hand out from under it and rests it on the table.

"What happened?" I look at her hand. *Don't reach for her. Not yet. It's too soon.*

"I was trying to adjust the narcotic using the sample I got from a critter yesterday—the one that died. But the tube broke. I didn't notice and I fell and . . . I'm sorry I didn't tell you. I was embarrassed."

My chest warms and I smile sympathetically. "Aya, I know you feel you have to be perfect all the time, and that's okay, but you're just making everything harder on yourself."

"I know . . . I don't know what's wrong with me."

"There's nothing wrong with you. Just learn to not sweat the small stuff." I slip my hand under hers, placing the other one on top of it.

"I just need to get this right the first time. What happens if I get something wrong?" Her voice cracks.

"I know your job is serious, but let others help you. You're already a mess, and this is just the beginning of our long journey."

She sighs, a tear trailing down her cheek. With a shiver, she drags her hand back to the inside of the blanket, pulling it in around her. "Why can't we do this all the time?" The corners of her lips turn up.

"Do what?" I watch her tear flow down, practically begging me to wipe it away.

"Talk like this. Most of the time we end up fighting."

I put my hand on the side of her face. My thumb carries the tear away with one swipe, along with everything it represents.

"You know it's true!" She looks at me, cheeks flushed, eyes glistening.

"Yes, I do know it's true. It's just one more small thing you worry about all the time. Aya, please don't avoid me because you're worried we'll fight."

"Would you rather we make a scene and everybody around us be uncomfortable?" She lifts her uninjured hand and places it on the back of mine, holding it against her cheek.

I shake my head, hair brushing across my forehead. "No. I'd prefer you talk to me. Just like this."

"It'll be too obvious . . ."

"Obvious?"

Ayathesti looks away. "You know, that we kind of…"

"Like each other?" I raise an eyebrow, sitting back with crossed arms.

She nods.

I smile. *Don't laugh. Don't do it*. "You're too cute."

"What do you mean?"

"I'm pretty sure everybody already knows you're into me." I smirk.

"Well, somebody's full of himself."

"Confidence isn't ego, Aya."

"Sure could have fooled me. Besides, who says I'm the one who's into you and not the other way around?" She lifts her fork, pointing it at me. I lean forward with one hand on my knee. "I'm serious!" She insists, gripping the blanket tighter around her.

"Because that's not as . . . what's the word I'm looking for here . . ."

"Obvious?" Hana says as she returns.

"Ah, yes! Thank you, Hana. It's all so transparent!" I chew the last bit of food while watching Ayathesti's face twist around as she thinks through the statement.

"You mean that . . . my feelings are obvious?" She finally says, her eyebrows quivering.

I nod with a smile before I look at her. My heart sinks when her eyebrows quiver. *Obvious, Tiamet? Really? Use your brain. Backpedal. Save it!* "Wait, no . . ." I sit forward. "Just that—you don't do well at hiding your emotions."

"I would think I do well enough hiding my emotions, thank you very much." Her voice cracks again.

"No, actually . . . When you act too happy, you're mad. And when you're mad, you're mad at yourself and silent. When you are working, you're content but a smart ass. And when you're happy . . . Well, you actually look almost sad and annoyed."

"Well if you don't like it—"

"Let's not jump to conclusions. Nobody is saying that." I reach for her hand. *Can I salvage this?*

"Just that your moods are transparent," Hana chimes in again, nodding.

"Oh, and that cute pout face you get when you're mad. It's one of my favorites." I smile at her as she pulls her hand inside the blanket, glaring at Hana.

"I don't pout!" She nibbles on the bottom corner of her lip.

Don't laugh. Don't. It erupts from my chest regardless of my efforts, Hana giggling from the other side of the room.

"Shh . . ." Ayathesti looks at the door.

I look over at Hana and answer her comprehensive smile with my own.

"Not a cha—" I start.

"*Shhh!!*" She stands and walks to the door. She pushes her head closer to it. "Do you hear that?"

Concerned, I stand and walk to the door. I hold my breath to listen. I shake my head. "Aya, what are you talking about? I don't hear anything."

"It's a faint rumbling noise." She reaches for the handle.

I'm quick to catch her hand under mine. "Let me check." I open the door and peer outside, looking around. "Well, it's cloudy, that's all." I open the door wider and step out, the wind blowing around me.

Ayathesti follows, looking around as lightning shoots from one end of the sky to the other. She gasps and falters backward. I quickly catch her arm, steadying her balance. "You still don't hear that? It's getting louder too," she says louder, as though to talk over the absent noise.

I look back at her and shake my head. "I think you need to get some sleep." Putting my other hand on her other arm, I direct her back inside.

"Tiamet, stop. I'm serious!" She pulls herself free of my grasp and looks around, squinting her eyes toward the distance. She points toward a darker portion of sky on the horizon. "There. What is that?"

My heart races. *Is that . . . smoke?* "I have no idea. Go back inside." I urge her toward the door again before turning away.

"But where are you going?" She hesitates at the entrance.

"Aya, no arguments. Go inside. I'll be right back." I stare at her and wait for the door to close before I walk to the surveillance tent.

"Director?"

I stare at the one who'd just spoken. "We have a perimeter set up, right, Johi?"

A short girl with most of her face covered by the brim of her hat nods. "Yes, sir. We put up a perimeter as instructed."

"Good. I need to see it."

"Okay, but—"

"Just turn it on." *I don't think I'll ever get used to demanding things.*

She reaches for a green button on the table, and a few monitors flicker on, showing various checkpoints around the perimeter. I stand motionless with my arms folded, eyes bouncing from one screen to another until the plume appears.

"There." I step forward, pointing at the screen. "What's causing that? Can we get a closer look?"

Johi lifts a cloth off the table and taps a few buttons, zooming in on the cloud.

I squint, getting closer to the screen. My tongue seems to swell in my throat, and I choke. "Do we have a file on this creature?"

She shrugs. "Not our department."

"Keep that image up." I storm out of security and into the canopy of caged animals.

After spending too much time looking through the files with no success, I groan. I force the door to my tent open and walk to the crate of files I'd been looking through earlier. I pull out paper after paper in no specific order, tossing unsuccessful searches to the ground.

Ayathesti approaches, stopping just outside my paper

cluster. "What are you loo—"

"Nothing, it's fine." I growl, still flipping through papers that were once stacked neatly in folders.

Ayathesti bends over, picking one up after it lands at her feet. I look up at her, her eyes narrow, brow furrowed, and mouth gaping. Moments later, she thrusts the paper into my face—a picture of a tall, lean, muscular creature with almost no hair standing upright as we do. The paper has five stars stamped across the top: high security.

I sigh and close my eyes, biting my lip in regret before looking up at her. She stands over me, looking down with confusion and disappointment. I look around the floor at the scattered papers and files. Ayathesti puts the toe of her boot on the file closest to her and flicks it at me before turning and walking out the door.

"I guess she still doesn't feel good, huh?" Hana watches me pile the papers back together messily. "Do you want me to sort those for you?"

I stand, tucking the file under my arm. "No, those are classified documents. I'll fix them up later."

I walk back to the surveillance tent, holding the photo next to the image still on the screen.

"It seems the event has ended." Johi's feet are elevated on the desk I'm now hovering over.

"That's beside the point." I straighten, looking down at her. "Can we get this image enhanced and printed for my report?"

With a sigh of annoyance, she lets her feet fall to the floor and presses a few buttons on the monitor, prompting the system to clean up the image. I step forward and tap the screen. "Perfect. Now, I need a printout."

"We didn't bring printers, sir."

I look at her blankly, growing frustrated. *What's with her attitude*? "Then get it to the server." I clench my teeth and take a breath. "You know what, it's fine. Just—keep that up. I'll be back."

I walk to our capsule and unlock it. At the power panel, I fumble through the screens. "I just need to . . . Ah!" The capsule lights flicker a few times before growing in intensity to their full luminescence. *All this back and forth is making me turned around.*

Back in surveillance, I click a button on the monitor. The screen returns to the live feed, and I turn to leave. "Great job. Keep me informed if this happens again."

I stop by the residence tent and grab my report generator before heading back to the capsule. The metal floor clunks under each footstep as I make my way to the panel again. I put my tablet next to the screen for a file transfer. *Shit . . . Ayathesti's seen the photo. This one is clearer, but you can tell it's the same type of creature.* I lock the door, the documents secure in my hand, and turn.

With arms folded and a scowl on her face, Ayathesti stands behind me. *Here is it, the moment I have to explain to her why I'm not required to provide answers.* Uncertainty of how to go about this has me nodding in her direction before passing her, shame eating me up inside as I walk away.

Organizing the folders I'd messed up earlier, I look at her after she lets the door slam and she stomps to the corner.

"What the fuck is going on?"

"Calm down, it—"

"*Don't* tell me to calm down, Tiamet. You're hiding a big part of this mission, and I don't think *you* even know what's going on!"

"Aya, let me jus—"

"No! I don't want to hear excuses or bullshit lies about any of it! They sent me here to do *one* job! That's all I expected to do!" Her hands wave in the air as she paces the floor in front of me. "Apparently, this entire trip is pointless because that *thing*—"

Pushing away the anger swelling in my chest, I toss the file at her feet. "Aya. Believe me when I tell you this creature only had a rumored existence. I have the only file—a *classified* file, if you remember. They included it on a need-to-know basis for safety reasons only. To be frank, we didn't think they would even still exist."

"Still? And since I'm the one who is murdering helpless animals, I suppose I didn't need to know you had knowledge of a perfect match this whole time and I needed no further research!" Her solid-stone expression sends my neck hairs on end.

"It's not that simple."

"It is that simple if you let it be."

"It's too dangerous to attempt getting close to one of these things." I stand and take a step toward her.

"Dangerous? Did you even see the same thing I did? It is a primitive being! And we have all the means necessary to get a sample!"

I step closer, clutching her shoulders. "Listen! We don't know how far they've come since their discovery. I'm telling you! It's. Too. Dangerous." I had done well to keep my tone under control until this point, but now concern and fear slip through.

Ayathesti purses her lips, crossing her arms again. "And what do you mean 'still'?"

Losing my patience, I turn and rub my forehead, growing annoyed at her new child-like tantrum. "I can't get into this, Aya. You're not even supposed to know about these things." A sigh lingers on my breath, and I look over my shoulder at her.

Face red with fury, she rolls her eyes, turning her back

to me. "Fine."

I kneel to pick up the file from the floor, watching her storm from the tent.

"She's still not feeling well?" Nineveh asks as she enters with Latif, opening a canteen to sip on. "She nearly knocked us over, running out of here."

I shrug to hide my distaste for our most recent quarrel. "How am I supposed to know what's going on in that brain of hers. Honestly, Nin, you ought to give that one a sedative so she gets rest for a few days."

"So can everybody else!" Latif snorts.

"I think she may be hallucinating," I say.

"Are you sure?" Nineveh's concern rises. "What makes you think she's hallucinating?"

"She was yelling at me for hiding hairless creatures from her." I linger on my words. *Should I lie to them? And how much should I lie about?* "I asked around, and nobody else seems to know what she's referring to. Other than Latif being said creature, of course." A grin tugs at the corners of my lips.

"Solid burn." Latif chuckles as the front door opens and Ayathesti hurries across the room and down the hallway.

"I know that the antibacterial I gave to her might have effects on cognition . . . but actual hallucinations? I'm not sure. I should talk to her before giving her something else." Nineveh peers down the hallway, as if waiting for Ayathesti to emerge.

"Well, go ahead and try if you want," I tell her, "but once that girl gets an idea in her head, it's impossible to sway her. At least, that's what I've found." I switch my focus from the hallway to sorting papers.

"Yeah, she can be a bit stubborn. Thanks for telling me. If she's still acting strange in the morning, I'll talk to her about it. Otherwise, it may be an effect of the medication and will dissipate once it leaves her system."

Ayathesti does emerge from the hallway, with an olive-green bag slung across her chest.

Nineveh turns to her. "Hi, Aya."

Ayathesti stops and slowly looks in our direction.

"You're still looking a bit pale. How are you feeling?" Nineveh asks.

Ayathesti clutches the bag to her side and nods slowly, a blank look on her face, before she turns back to the door and leaves.

I put my hands up in the air. "Do you see what I mean?"

Ayathesti - 39

The *sun set a while ago.* Even with the dark sky, I can see. A chill sends a shiver up my spine. I take a pause, leaning my back against the trunk of a tree, looking back in the direction I've come from. The air carries the scent of dust, just before water spills from the sky. I rub my arms to bring some warmth back into them while whisking away the moisture. I look around in the darkness for somewhere to take cover from the rain.

Squinting, I sigh with hope when I spot a cliff overhang not far off in the distance. But hesitation catches me for an instant.

'You're never going to make it.' the voice whispers to me while I ponder slipping into my jacket.

I clutch the bag to my chest. *No, I need to keep it dry for when I get there.*

'You're too weak. Just turn back.'

My feet pulse, the ache shooting up my legs, into my hips and back. The amount of energy needed to keep going grows with each step. I watch my feet as I walk, occasionally glancing at my destination. Light fills the sky in a brief flash, and the rain falls heavier. With muscle failure setting in, my foot fails to clear the height of an oblong object sticking from the ground, forcing gravity to take me.

One of my knees slams on the ground as I fall sideways. I reach out to brace for impact, but don't hit the dirt as soon as I expected. My ankle screams in pain the instant my torso connects with the ground. Now oriented head down, I hang by my ankle against a steep slope, and whimper. A loud crack sounds before the rush of falling takes my breath away. Soil fills one boot, and my other foot grows rigid without the same protection. Freezing fire lashes over me, tearing pieces of clothes and skin away as I slide down over the steep, muddy slope.

I scream out when my shoulder connects with the ground. Pain crawls up my ankle and into my shin. I reach for it only to be met with a stabbing pain in my shoulder. I groan and lay there, the rain leaving no part of my person untouched, imposing a cold so deep it touches my bones. I bite my lower lip to stop the tears.

I'm so stupid. I sob in silence as the darkness whispers back, *'Should have groveled to your keeper for forgiveness.'*

I close my eyes, imagining the one place I long to be more than any other. *If I'm going to freeze to death, you're going to shut up and let me pretend I'm somewhere pleasant.*

A warm glass of milk keeps my tiny fingers limber, the steam tendrils filling the air in front of my face. The sun rises through the trees in the field behind my house. Papa and I sit at the kitchen table; he's pouring over schematic designs for a new engine. His eyes sparkle with each question I ask. The colors of sunlight change when passing through our stained glass windows. There's a knock on the door, and Mama opens it.

"Can Ayclee come play?"

"We're still eating breakfast, Rothe. Come in and join us," Mama says. Rothe joins us at the table for a pastry. A calm inches its way through my core when I enter this moment in my mind.

Hoarse voices speaking gibberish penetrate my peace. I twist my expression into one of repugnance. I clench my eyes tighter, refusing to let go of my short-lived journey back home. My throat grows tight, no longer silencing my whimpering. The heat of tears flooding from my eyes offer a surprising warmth I thought I'd never feel again.

I lay in the mud, motionless. Though all I want is to pull my knees to my chest and regain sanctuary, I can't move. My eyes jerk open with surprise when a weight lands over me and the rain ceases to fall. Agony crawls through every part of my body as something grabs my wrist and pulls, dragging me through the mud. My eyes roll into my head as I lose the fight against unconsciousness.

Unknown words spoken in different tones bring me back. My body is still, and I dare not try moving other than to open my eyes. Warmth engulfs my skin, threatening to take my consciousness again. I force myself to blink a few times. With blurry vision, I make out only a bright, dancing light and rippled black figures towering overhead.

"Tiamet? Nin . . ." My throat is scratchy, the names coming out as nothing more than a whisper. My lips quiver with fear and weakness as I let out a deep breath. My eyelids grow heavy once more, guiding me back into the void.

Tiamet – 35

"*She's* been missing two days, Tiamet! You have to do something!" Nineveh's eyes are puffy from crying and lack of sleep.

"Nineveh, I've been examining options. We don't have the resources to get everyone tracking her down within our two hundred miles of perimeter." It's been the same conversation for the majority of Ayathesti's disappearance. The panic and desperation clawing at my insides have been showing through as unconcern in my responses.

Nineveh's disgust is consumed by anger. "How! How can you sit there so calm, knowing she's left us? And was sick when she did! You told me she was hallucinating! I can't be sure if it was from the medication I gave her or a residual symptom of her infection! Not to mention how strange she was act—"

"Nineveh, take a breath. " Latif places his hands on her shoulders to stop her from pacing.

Nineveh looks up at him before pushing her face into his shoulder, sobbing. Latif looks at me, eyebrows lifted, sadness drooping his lips, concern lingering in his eyes as he wraps his arms around her.

"Are you sure there's nothing to do?" Hana approaches me near the sink.

"Why are you so concerned about her? She was super mean to you." I use every moment as an attempt to hide my shame at the direct hand I had in causing this.

"Well, yes, she was. But she's still part of this team, and we need to find her. Nineveh is right. What if she's hurt or in trouble and needs help . . .?"

I slam my fist on the counter. *If only they could see my agony . . . yearning at every moment for Ayathesti to walk through the door.* "What am I to do? Scrape up a team to go look for her, only to find she's sitting in a tree, too stubborn to come back with us, so we end up leaving her there anyway? If you are so concerned, feel free to volunteer. But remember who we're talking about here." I shift my weight from the counter and fling the door open, letting it slam behind me.

"*I* need you guys looking through everything you've got again. We have to find her." My voice is steady against the waves of distress crashing over me as I clench my hands into fists after entering the surveillance tent—again.

"Director, we—"

"I don't want excuses. Keep looking. At least find out which direction she started in. That may narrow things down." I pick up a tablet that holds some recorded footage and peel through it.

"Why did she leave again?" Jarem looks up from his table.

"We had an argument." I keep my focus on the screen.

"I guess I don't see why she'd leave over a petty argument."

"It was petty, but that's how she is. I know she's a control freak, but why she has to be . . ." My words slur to a stop.

"Be what?"

"Do you remember a few days ago when we had that perimeter breach?" I move my hand over the tablet to skip it backward. "Which quadrant was that?" I break my glance to look around. Everyone appears clueless. "Seriously? None of you know? Who was in here that day?"

"We rotate our shifts, and there ends up being about

four hours of overlap where there's only two of us here." Jarem looks at a chart on the wall. "Camera footage is large and, with limited data storage, it's recycled every few days unless otherwise specified."

"Sir, your attention is needed at Residence Four." Johi steps into the shade from outside, sliding her hands into fingerless gloves. "It sounded urgent."

I catch Jarem's eyes and nod for him to leave.

"What's going on?" Johi adjusts her hat to sit higher above her eyes than usual.

I step closer to her. "Which quadrant was the perimeter breach the other day?"

"Why does everybody want to know that?" She sighs. "West quadrant, I think."

"Why were you the only one here for that?"

She shrugs. "My partner had to use the facilities."

"What do you mean by 'why does everyone want to know that?' " I narrow my eyes, waiting on her response. *I'll take care of the poor security coverage with Jarem later.*

"I mean, that nerdy chick asked me like two days ago. I wasn't in a place to argue. She was pretty demanding, even pulled a rank card on me."

"Where have you been the last two days?" My blood boils at her careless attitude toward the situation.

"I've been resting. That was the last day of my shift." Johi sits calmly. "Am I missing something?"

"Nobody has seen her since then. I guess you aren't aware of who she is, but she's the key to this mission. Which west quadrant did you tell her to go to?" I scan through the different quadrant options in the west.

"I didn't tell her to go anywhere!" Johi says, getting defensive.

"Excuses will not get you far with me. Which quadrant?" Steady small breaths keep my voice robust. *Keep yourself together.*

"Next to the cliffs, where the perimeter beacon alarmed. Section Thirty-Seven." She seems to have adopted a sudden respectful tone.

I turn and exit as Jarem returns. Pushing the tablet against his chest, I look him in the eye. "Fix the security problem you've got here. Then get yourself prepared with a few of your people who can keep up with a three-day hike."

Dust kicks up from my feet as I dismiss myself from the tent without allowing room for argument. I walk back to my residence tent, crack the door open, and holler in, "If you want to find her, we're leaving in five."

I turn, letting the door slam behind me again while I stand there. Determination is on my mind as unstable anguish in my heart morphs into hope.

She has to be alive . . . We'll find her.

Ayathesti - 36

The pounding of a thousand hammers smashing into my skull pulls me back to consciousness. I try swallowing, but the lack of moisture simply causes my saliva to stick. With my lips glued shut, I press my tongue against them, peeling them apart. The throbbing of my injuries engulfs me, sucking away the strength I need to move.

I take a deep breath, bringing on an entirely separate pain. My lungs capture dust in the air, and I erupt in a raspy cough. Stabbing pressure shoots through my stomach and into my lower back, forcing me to coddle my abdomen in hope of relief. Faint mumbling captures my attention through the agony. I pry my eyes open and look at my surroundings.

Directly ahead is an opening to the outside world, trees within the foreground of blue sky. I follow the height of the opening to the ceiling, where light shines through a small hole. The walls are smooth stone, rich with orange, tan, and brown colors dancing with one another.

I muster up all the energy I have, bracing one hand against the ground. With a slow push and a grunt that catches in my throat, I roll over to lie on my back, removing the covering that lay atop me. I clench my eyes shut, the moisture refocusing my sight. My stomach lurches, and my breath catches when I see a nearly hairless figure crouching in the corner, rummaging through my bag.

"Hey! That's my stuff!" Concern for the glass vials I'd packed overcomes any logic in a cautious approach. I strain, hoisting myself to sit while struggling for air. The creature whips around to look at me, startled, before scurrying out the entrance.

Agony pulses through my shoulder, digging into my spine. "Ohhh . . . shit." I clench my teeth and hold my breath. Scooting myself across the ground to my bag, I wince with every move. Coming to rest against the cave wall, a chill sinks into my skull, and a shiver crawls over my skin. *At least it's reducing the pounding in my head.*

Gripping the strap of my bag, I drag it toward me. A wave of relief washes over me when I realize all my belongings are accounted for, unscathed. I sigh, releasing the panic and adrenaline that allowed me to move this far. I look at my feet sprawled before me, hopeless as the pulsing and radiating heat sink back in with the diminishing adrenaline in my system.

Look at me. Lost, broken, and stranded but only thinking about my supplies. I chuckle at my own thoughts.

'You're pathetic.'

I lean my head against the wall again and shrug. *I don't care.*

My amusement at the situation is interrupted when more creatures return. The grunts startle me, throwing me back into panic as I watch them make slow progress toward me.

"Stop!" I put my hand up, hugging my back against the wall. "Stay back!"

Surprised that I have any fight left in me, I look at my surroundings before looking back at them. My chest grows heavy and tight when they don't stop.

'Oh goody. This is the end. Should have listened to me and turned back.'

I reach into my bag and grab the first hard object I feel: a freezer canister. Hopefully, it looks dangerous enough to stop them. I pull it out and point it at them.

"I can defend myself!" My frantic voice echoes against

the walls and bounces into the tower of the cave. They stop in unison. With my vision going fuzzy, lightheadedness begs me to steady my breathing. I force my chest to move slower, deeper, and I examine the six creatures before me.

They have long thick hair sagging from their heads in different shades ranging from dusty blond to black. It's thick on some of their faces and underarms. It also makes a lighter appearance on their arms, torso, and legs. They stand erect as our kind does, rather than all fours like the many other animals on this planet, but their posture is slightly hunched over. Beady black eyes are close together in the center of their heads and above rather large protruding jaws. Between their eyes are prominent noses, some hooked, others flat. They move and wrinkle as these creatures grumble amongst themselves. The little clothing they do wear is almost as dirty as their faces and somehow clings to their bodies like magic. Their fur coverings are smaller than the one that covered me but are undeniably similar.

I put the hand of my strong arm on the wall behind me and attempt to use it and my good leg to stand. I clench my teeth in pain and effort before my hand slips. My shoulder slams into the wall, and I'm thrown to the ground. Reaching for the wall, I clench my eyes and pinch my lips together, begging the pain to dissipate. *Breathe . . .*

One creature steps forward and moves toward me. I stare at it as it sniffs the air, inching closer with curious eyes. Holding my breath, I pull back and turn my head with anticipation. A warm grip lifts my hand from the ground, and I peek one eye open. The creature pulls my hand upward, gripping my arm with its other hand to help me stand. I'm surprised at the gentleness of the touch.

Holding my weight against the wall, I inch down and grip the strap of my bag. I struggle to lift it, but weakness overtakes my body. The creature steps back, startled, when I grunt through clenched teeth and hoist the strap over my shoulder. I hobble against the wall, discovering the extent of my movement limitations as I go. When I near the cave entrance, the creatures scurry past me. I wouldn't want to feel trapped inside with me at the entrance either. Taking a deep breath, I prepare myself to endure the last few steps.

The warm air hits me as I lean my shoulder against the wall. The tension in my shoulders washes away within moments, rendering me motionless. My gaze goes to the sky, and I close my eyes as I absorb the sun. Each breath warms me from the inside out. *How long ago did I leave?* Licking my lips, I look over my shoulder to where I woke inside the cave before examining more of the landscape around me. After spotting a rock, I make my way over to it and ease myself to sit, my back resting against the tall cliff face that conceals the home of these beings.

Time to assess the damage. I bend forward, reaching to fold my pant leg up to examine my injuries. Heat crawls through my foot, up my leg, and rests in my lower back. My calf is black and blue from bruising. A large gash from my ankle to knee has formed a crusty scab. But as painful as it looks, I can't say it's the main source of pain. I exhale, clearing my lungs, and lean forward to unknot the crusted laces of my boot. Taking shallow breaths, I slip my foot out. *That explains it.* My ankle is swollen to twice its normal size. I pinch my lips together and close my eyes, leaning my head back against the cliff wall. I whimper a sigh of defeat. *Even if I knew where I was, there's no way I'd even make it halfway back to camp.*

Startled from my pity party by a grunt, I snap my eyes open and look at the creature before me. Squatting, it holds my boot in its hands, examining it by bringing it right up to its nose and taking a whiff.

"He said you were dangerous . . ." The boot thuds to

the ground, and it pulls away when I speak, switching its attention to my movements. "Oh no . . . I won't hurt you," I whisper, putting my hand up. It stands erect, reaching about five feet tall, lean and muscular.

I pull my bag onto my lap and flip the top open. The being watches as I remove a spare shirt and tear pieces of it off with my teeth. I wrap one long piece around my ankle, hoping it will help with the swelling. I struggle to make a sling for my dislocated arm, but after a few minutes of focused attempts, I manage something suitable.

After my best efforts at piecing myself back together, I stand and look around. There is a small wash by a path next to the cave. The creature urges me to follow as it walks down the path. I limp toward the edge and stop, staring down the decline. *Will I be able to make it all the way down without ending up flat on my face again?*

'Of course you won't. You're too feeble to do anything that demanding.'

The trickling sound of water beckons me, my dried lips, and my sandpaper tongue toward the base of the hill. With trees lining the path, I'm able to hobble between them and regain support at each one.

It's a slow descent to the bottom, but I eventually make it to the stream. The cool water washes over my hand when I dip it under the surface. I peer at my reflection—face dirty and eyes tired—before splashing water onto my hot skin. I run my wet fingers through my hair to calm the crazy ends, attempting to separate the clumps that have formed thanks to the mud.

I rummage through my bag and remove a canteen. I submerge the mouth into the water, and bubbles spew from the opening. Once it's filled, I hold my canteen upright, waiting for the internal filter to purify bacteria out.

I look across the stream to see smaller beings playing

cheerfully with each other in the water. Nearby are older ones wearing different coverings than those in the cave. Cloths adorned both their chests and groins.

"Those must be females," I whisper to myself. I look back at the one who had helped me stand in the cave and urged me to come to the stream. "I'm guessing that one is a male, probably the leader."

With my back against a tree, I watch the beings as they go on with their day. "They're not dangerous at all . . ."

I look up at the reddening sky as it warns us of nightfall.

Tiamet - 37

"**Could** she have made it this far? She didn't have many supplies," Nineveh says as the setting sun beat down on us.

"I think I could use a rest," Latif complains. "It's hot, I'm thirsty, and my feet hurt."

"I told you to stay if you couldn't keep up." I don't bother to hide my condescension.

"When I jumped on this rescue wagon, I didn't realize we'd be walking for seven hours straight!"

"We have seen no signs to indicate her path, so we need to keep a straight one until we find clues." *I can't believe I have to explain to him why we're walking in a straight line—again.*

"But sitting down for a few minutes won't stop us from doing that." Latif's sighs with exhaustion.

My step falters, and I look over my shoulder. Latif and Nineveh, along with three others, are sweaty and weary, their eyes pleading for rest. I look at the surroundings and let my backpack slide off my shoulders.

"Alright. Per your request, we can take a break here. With the sun going down, it will be more difficult looking for clues. We'll pick back up as soon as sunlight breaks the horizon again." I turn to the group as they collectively sigh, dropping their supplies where they stand.

We sit in a circle around a small lantern, eating protein bars. *They need to know what we might potentially face in the next few days.* Regardless of how understanding they can be, anxiety twists a knife through my stomach.

"You cool, dude?" Latif asks.

I let out a small sigh and reach for my bag. "There's something I need to tell you guys. And it's of utmost importance." I grip the printout of the creature and pull it out. Anger trickles into my heart the more I stare at it. I glance at Latif and Nineveh, who look at each other in confusion before looking back at me

"This is why Ayathesti left." I pass the paper to them face down and wait for their reaction.

Nineveh gasps, eyes growing wide but without fear. "Oh my!"

"That's incredible!" Latif hollers. "They look just like us! Well, not *just* like us, but look at that stature and the head shape! What the hell?" He passes the image to the volunteer next to him.

"This guy breached our perimeter a few days ago. Aya saw the security footage, and in a fit of rage from me not telling her about them . . . she took off." I avert my gaze to the ground.

"Well, why didn't you just tell her? I mean . . . these things are why we're here!" Latif says. "We were supposed to find a compatible species. Why even keep looking past them?"

"It's not that simple." My hair ruffles along my forehead when I shake it, as though I can shake off the weight of truth to his words.

"You know how she gets, Tiamet . . ." Nineveh's quiet voice adds.

"Yes, Nin. I am aware."

"Oh . . . I hope she's okay." Nineveh hugs her arms to her chest.

"I need you prepared for anything. This information is classified, and the only reason you're being informed is for the safety of everybody here." I look over my shoulder at the unhindered darkness of night.

"Are they dangerous?" Nineveh rubs her arms with her hands.

"From what we know? Yes, they are aggressive and very dangerous." They pass the image back to me, and I tuck it into my bag.

"Why the hell are we risking our lives if they're so dangerous?" Latif starts. "I respect Ayathesti, I do, but this hot head of hers is gonna get me killed! Or worse—"

"Oh, shut up!" Nineveh shouts at him, tears welling in her eyes.

I rub my hands together. "I tried to explain the dangers to her, but she didn't take that as a reason to why she wasn't informed of their existence."

"With all due respect, Director, I agree with her." Pimly, a security team member, speaks in a hushed voice, his head refusing to look away from the ground with his statement. "Part of my job is to ensure the safety of those in this mission party. How can I fight an enemy I don't know exists?" His shoulders sag in shame.

"The security team was issued instructions to come down and check for threats before setting up the perimeter." I motion toward Pimly, Stans, and Jarem. "Unless these beings are smarter than initially thought, they're still outside of our safe zone. We just need to find Aya and get back." I try hiding the concern from my voice.

"They must be right on the edge of our perimeter." Jarem gives Pimly's shoulder a comforting pat. "I'd like to know how they avoided our sweep team when setting it up. The system should notify us before even small critters cross the boundary."

"How does the system even work?" Nineveh's gaze meets Jarem's.

"It uses a nonlethal deterrent. It's designed to send a beam of radio waves at such a high frequency that the subject feels extreme heat and discomfort if it gets too close to the beam." Jarem lifts his hands as if to mimic the procedure and gives Nineveh a gentle smile. "The beam travels from one pole to another placed every hundred meters or so."

I look at Latif as he tries to comprehend the method of barrier. *Or is that confused look because of the smile Jarem just gave Nineveh?* "The system isn't flawless," I say, "which is why we set it up to alert us of any full crossings. Sure, it's designed to deter things from crossing its path, but that doesn't mean things can't or won't."

Jarem's focus moves from Nineveh to me. "Correct, Director. Our tests had a near a hundred percent successful deterrent rate. But who's to say they wouldn't go through it if desperate enough. If their lives were in danger, they may risk it. If they're smart enough, they may notice there are no lasting effects after they move away from the beam."

"Have you seen these things!" Latif's voice is loud, even without walls to reverberate it back at us. "They certainly look smart enough to notice that, if you ask me."

"They may look smart, but they're primitive beings nonetheless. If it's something they don't understand and can cause them harm, they're more likely to stay away. Like a rodent that gets shocked every time it's fed: given the choice, it'll starve itself." Jarem looks at Nineveh, who is biting a smile from her lips, before glancing back at Latif.

"Are you a specimen expert now? Or just security?" Latif's narrows his eyes at Jarem, failing at keeping his tone and expression neutral.

"I am whatever it takes to do my job protecting my people." Jarem says with confidence.

"Well, we're all here because you didn't do that job." I snap, unable to tolerate the petty, jealous banter between the two. "Not well enough."

"I've corrected the coverage issue at camp. This situation should have been reported immediately. Thus, you would have been notified." Jarem straightens his posture. "We did our best to screen for the most responsible and level-headed security members, but the long flight took a toll on plenty of passengers. And the lack of daily action and alertness training allowed some of us to grow complacent. I apologize that we're here for the reason we are." Jarem's short black hair sticks up, stiff from sweat. His rippling muscles can be seen under his uniform. *No wonder Latif feels threatened.*

"This is all your fault?" Latif grows red in the face.

"Stop." I stand, fists clenched. "It's my fault. Ayathesti ran off because of the tension our conversations inevitably come to. Jarem, I'm sorry I sounded accusatory. This mission's success is life or death for our people, Latif." I sigh. "You're aware that, unfortunately, it's pretty much all on Ayathesti's shoulders after we're done here. My acting orders of hiding this knowledge from her was an attempt to keep everyone on this mission safe, including those in security. And it backfired." I turn from them. "What's done is done. Let's rest, and we'll pick back up on searching in the morning."

"We'll find her, Tiamet." Nineveh's voice is gentle, pulling me from my fear that all is hopeless.

"I'm on first watch." I hear the rustling noises of everyone settling in behind me as I walk to collect myself, small pebbles of hardened dirt crunching as I do.

Ayathesti - 38

The faint trickle of the stream is the first thing I notice upon waking. The water in the air is sweet. I blink repeatedly, squinting as fire from the sun rushes to my brain. I lift my hand and rub my eyes to carry the sleep away. It's been a long time since I've slept under the stars with no walls around me. A soft smile finds my lips as I lie there, staring up at the pink clouds in the sky.

I sit up, inch toward a tree just behind me, and lean my back against it. Grasping my canteen, I ease myself to stand. Preparing for pain, I take a deep breath and begin my hobble toward the stream, finding that the pain in my foot has diminished compared to last night. *Still, it's probably best to keep pressure off of it.*

At the water's edge, I crouch down as low as I can before gravity takes over. I fill my canteen again, watching the bubbles escape.

Spending the last two mornings outside by the stream has been rather pleasant. The pain in my leg has eased significantly. I don't even clench anymore when I move around on it. My shoulder, however, is a different story. Each twist of my torso proves difficult from the damage of landing on it.

'It's broken. You'll have to rebreak it when you get back so Nineveh can set it correctly.' Her dark whisper has grown weak in my mind over the past few days as well.

But there's no swelling, so maybe it's not broken. The hope in my counter thought makes me feel lighter.

The past two days, sitting in the shade by the river, observing the beings, seemed like an eternity. I've come to discover they are not aggressive, as Tiamet made them out to be. They're actually rather playful. They see me as no threat, even bring me food. And a few of the mothers would allow their children to come close. Their language is something of another sort, consisting mainly of grunts and moans. But I did notice a slight speech pattern. Often when the leader, whom I call Reki, comes by to offer food, he tries to mimic the sounds I make when I talk to him. I've determined he's quite intelligent and curious.

"Speak of the devil!" Excitement leaps through me as Reki walks my direction. Screwing the lid onto my canteen, I battle to a stand without a tree for support. Reki's hand clasps my arm firmly, assisting me the rest of the way. "I was thinking about how I'm to get back to my camp. I should head out soon. Nineveh must have managed to lose all her hair at this point."

Reki returns conversation with some garble that I obviously don't understand. I look at the horizon, unsure of which direction to go. I guess that is the first thing to figure out before trying to get back. Aside from that, my foot needs maybe another day. Reki also looks at the horizon and grunts before looking back at me.

"I do miss being with my people . . . but it is very peaceful here." I smile at him a genuine smile, but my eyes hold longing. Longing for a cup of oojo. To use a water closet. To wash my hair. *It's amazing how the things I've taken for granted for so long are now the things I long for most.*

I turn away from the concern on Reki's face and make my way back to the tree before inching my way back to the ground and looking up to the sun rising in the sky. Reki takes a place next to me, with his legs crossed over themselves. He presents me with a tree bark plate full of berries.

"Thanks, Reki." I grasp a handful of berries, providing a kind smile as payment. As I pop one in my mouth, he nods, satisfied, before standing. I watch him as he makes his way to others gathering by the stream and offers the rest to them.

Tiamet - 39

"*If* you can't keep going, then pitch up a camp and stay here. I can go forward on my own." I'm having a hard time pressing Latif, Stans, and Pimly to go further.

"That's a swell idea! I'll do that." Latif returns to sit on his sleeping mat.

"Well, I *don't* think that's a good idea, Latif," Nineveh argues.

"Why the hell not?"

"What if we get lost and can't get back to you? Do you really want to be out here alone?"

"I won't be alone. These guys will stay with me!" He slaps Pimly on the shoulder and smiles ear to ear in Stans's direction.

"I think it's best if we stay localized for a few days," I interject, wanting to end the argument, "just in case she's on the move back to the compound. If someone stays put, maybe she'll bump into them on her way back." *We don't have time for this.*

Nineveh adopts a pout, folding her arms. "Okay . . . Just make sure you do a good job with that tent. I don't want to sleep crooked, Latif!"

Latif chuckles. "It was one night! Besides, that's the only way I can get you to come close." He gives her a wink.

"I'm just quite particular about my sleeping habits! One night was enough."

"Yeah, yeah. I'll make it extra straight for you," he mutters.

"We'll be back later. How late, I can't say at this point." The sun blazes down on us, burning my skin as I hoist a bag onto my shoulders. "Whoever doesn't want to stay here, let's move." The lack of sleep has me irritable, and my voice is hoarse because of it.

Nineveh looks at me with concerned eyes, as though she can hear the growing sadness in my words as the days go on. After checking the contents of her pack and removing some medical supplies for those staying, she secures it around her shoulders and torso.

I'm uncertain how long we've been walking when Jarem needs a restroom break. Nineveh and I watch him make his way to a tree.

Nineveh's head hangs as she looks for something to sit on. "Thanks for getting this set up, Tiamet."

"I think three days was enough time for her to cool off." I attempt to hide my worry by crunching a pebble with my foot.

"It'll be another day past by this evening, though. I hope she's okay." Nineveh pulls at a string on the strap of her pack.

"I wouldn't put it past her to have been on her way back when she spotted us and went around to get back to the compound, avoiding us all together."

"I don't think she would do that! She likes to be alone, but out here for five days?"

My heart thumps against my chest. "Yeah, I know. I can't shake the feeling she's in trouble. Otherwise, I may have turned around yesterday." I tuck my lips into an emotionless smile.

Nineveh nestles upon a fallen tree and stares at her knees. "Do you think . . ." Her shoulders droop, her voice cracking.

"No way, not Aya." I refuse to acknowledge the idea.

I stare out into the distance, scanning the horizon.

Nineveh clears her throat shakily.

I turn back to her. "It'll be alright. She's the toughest chick I know."

Nineveh nods, trying even harder to hold back her tears. "She's strong . . . but very fragile."

"Fragile?" *Fragile is one of the last words I'd ever use to describe her.*

"Yes. She acts tough, especially around you, but I've found most of the time, she's just trying to impress you." Nineveh looks at me with lusterless eyes and muted lips. It's a far cry from her usual dolled-up self.

"Why would she need to impress me? I believe I've made my interest clear enough."

"It's not that you haven't. She's unsure of herself. Being wrapped in self-doubt makes her question others' actions as well."

"I don't know. She seems pretty wrapped up in herself to me."

"She doesn't know how to cope. And not knowing what to say . . . well, ending conversations helps her avoid embarrassment." Nineveh takes a small sip from her canteen. "The standards she has of herself are pretty high, and she isolates herself to avoid not meeting those standards."

I sigh and shake my head. "That woman, so complicated. Is that why she—"

"Look what I found." Jarem trots back to us, holding his hand out.

I eye the object, trying to make out what it is as I walk toward him. "What is it?"

"I can't be sure. It looks like some sort of jewelry." He extends his palm toward me.

Nineveh composes herself and walks over. "This is her earpiece." Her voice sparkles with hope.

"Ah. Yep, I recall seeing it . . . on her ear?" I smirk, watching Nineveh examine it before handing it to me. "Where'd you find it?"

Jarem motions for us to follow him. "Back this way near a ditch."

My stomach flutters with anticipation. Hope holds hands with fear as they twirl inside me. *What else, if anything, will we find when we get there? Will we stumble across her lifeless corpse?* I catch myself needing to hold my pace back to not pass Jarem on the way.

After what seems like the longest part of the walk yet, we reach the location where Jarem had found the earpiece. I look around for other items that may have fallen from Ayathesti's person.

A small sigh slips from my chest when I see nothing. Hopelessness washes over me again, dragging me to the ground. I sit with my knees raised, elbows resting on top of them. My head droops, staring down the gully before me in defeat.

Nineveh kneels beside me, placing a gentle hand on my shoulder. "She needs us, Tiamet."

"Are you sure she even wants to be found?"

"Why would she leave it here?"

I look at her, resting my chin on my arm. "I can't think of a reason other than it fell off without her noticing, or she took it off because she's done with us . . . and our mission."

Nineveh scratches her cheek, shaking her head. "No. Her father was too invested in saving us for her to quit like that."

I twist my body to stand, but I'm tripped back down by a tug on my boot. Pulling at my foot again, I peer under myself to see what it's caught on. Scooting to the edge for a better look, I see a broken tree root jutting from the side of the gully.

"Ughh, damn thing," I mutter, pulling my laces from the serrated root's crooked fingertips.

After freeing my boot, I stand and scowl, kicking a stone down the steep slope. As I turn away from it tumbling down, a flash of white catches my peripherals. My breath stumbles in my throat, choking me. I'm unable to move while processing what I just saw. *Don't get your hopes up.*

With a shaky breath, I look over my shoulder and slowly turn back to face the gully once more. *Why didn't I notice those plants looking out of sorts before?* I follow the trail with my eyes all the way to the bottom, landing on a bush that looks particularly damaged. I scan the surrounding area to see it again, a small white . . . something. *Whatever it is, it's out of place. With the earpiece we found, along with the plants . . . This could be our only lead.*

"What's wrong? Let's look for more clues and pick a direction," Nineveh says, standing next to Jarem, taking cover in the shade of the tree.

Without a word, I jump over the edge of the gully. My feet sink into the sand, sliding when I walk down as I attempt to keep my balance. I examine the bush when I reach the bottom. The white object I'd seen is a piece of fabric stuck to one of the snapped branches. My heart leaps. *We have a lead.*

I grip the fabric and examine it. Then it hits me. *Ayathesti's in real trouble. This fall couldn't have left her in any condition to get far*. A frenzy kidnaps my logic, and I turn in circles, scouring the ground for more damaged plants nearby.

"What are you doing?" Nineveh peers over the ledge, her voice laced with distress.

My throat is too tight to answer immediately. I spot another broken bush and another following it, trailing down the base of the gulley. "Get down here!"

A wave of adrenaline-induced dizziness knocks me off keel, my breath coming out in short gasps. As I try to steady myself, I rummage through the terrain, trying to keep track of the direction her trail leads. The gully begins to level out as we approach the end. My heart sinks when the plants spread out and the clusters dwindle. *We can't lose her trail.* Standing at the end of the trench, I stare out across an open plain. Despair slams into me, dragging my spirit to the ground as it's crushed beneath.

Struggling to keep up, Nineveh makes her way to the end and stops beside me with her hands on her knees, panting to catch her breath. She looks up at me. "You seemed a bit excited there for a minute."

"I was. I thought for sure she'd be around that hill."

"But there was a sign of her and a direction for us to follow?"

"Yeah . . . Now we just need to search all that over there." I motion toward the land in front of us with a shallow nod. "I think I need a break."

I reach over my shoulder and pull on the handle on top of my bag, releasing it from my back. Plopping it down to the ground, I sit in the dirt. Nineveh follows suit as Jarem joins us. I shove my hand into one of the side compartments of my bag to grab a canteen. After a lazy twist of the top, I take a gulp. The cold fluid spills over the corners of my lips, dripping down my chin. I dab the moisture away with the back of my wrist.

Nineveh watches Jarem sit before turning to me. "You need to recollect yourself."

"I can't take much more of this." I shake my head and sigh.

A soft smile appears on her face.

"What?" I wipe away the beads of sweat trickling down my forehead.

With a soft shake of her head, her hair shuffling across her back, she says. "Nothing. I . . . I guess I've just come around to seeing what she's liked about you all this time."

I tilt my head, furrowing my brow. "What do you mean?"

Nineveh's cheeks flush. "Well, I always gave her grief when it came to her feelings about you. I thought you were full of yourself, sarcastic and rude to everybody around you. And quite jerk-like, actually . . ."

Letting out a chuckle, I place my canteen in the dirt and look at the sky.

"I'm sorry, I didn't mean to sound rude!" she says.

I shake my head and smile. "No, you're right. I can be a jerk. I have always been that way to get what I want."

"You're not *all* jerk."

I look over at her with a raised eyebrow and a smirk.

"Okay, you're mostly jerk, but a true jerk wouldn't be so concerned over somebody like Aya. She's not exactly the easiest person to get along with."

I chuckle again. "You think?"

"I know. But I appreciate you getting all of us out here to find her."

"We should have put a smaller barrier around the base camp to account for missed threats inside our perimeter," Jarem says, sifting sand through his fingers, looking out over the plains.

"Did we have enough supplies for that?" Nineveh asks.

"We could have if we'd planned for it." The dirt pile towers in his hand.

She smiles, eyeing his creation. "Was it not brought up before?"

I look over my shoulder at her. "The council didn't want to bother with additional security. Thought the outer border and the small number of bodies approved was already 'excessive,' actually."

"That seems a little ridiculous." She scoffs.

"That's politics." Jarem lets the sand fall and draws in it with his fingertips.

I avert my gaze to the dirt between my boots. "Even with that, this shit is all on me. I don't know what it is about her that makes me so crazy. If I could have just—"

"Tiamet, you couldn't have known . . ." Nineveh says softly, sitting with her hands neatly folded in her lap, her eyes staring through me.

I look back to the flat land ahead. "When we were attending TASA, she used to take the crackers from her lunch and feed them to the tree rodents." A soft smile creeps onto my lips, and I chuckle. "That's what she was doing the first time I saw her. There was a certain softness to her I'd only seen in one other person my whole life. She cared for something other than her own personal gain. Which, at TASA, that seemed impossible to find."

I pick up a small stone, turning it over in my fingers. "I wish I could talk to her."

Nineveh reaches into a pocket on her bag, pulls out a small container of nuts, and dumps a few into her hand. "Why don't you?"

"I try . . . I don't know what I do, but it always ends in a fight."

Nineveh shakes her head, offering me some nuts. "That's not your fault. She shuts people out."

Reaching over, I accept a few. "I know. She fears getting hurt. But I genuinely just want to hold an actual conversation with her that lasts longer than a few minutes and doesn't result in her storming out of the room."

"I don't know if you can say or do anything differently for that to happen. That part is on her." She turns and offers her snack to Jarem, who flashes a smile before accepting.

I let out a sigh, tipping the nuts into my mouth. I put my hands in the dirt beside me and hoist myself up. "Maybe I just need to keep working on it."

I clap the dust from my hands before brushing off my pants. When I turn to offer her a hand up, I see she's already accepted help from Jarem. After returning the container to her bag and smiling at him, she leans over and brushes the dirt from the side of her leg.

"It's hard," Nineveh says, placing a reassuring hand on my shoulder. "But let's just find her first."

I nod and pat her hand, looking out on the terrain before us. "Do either of you oppose us pressing forward? I think we should keep going, regardless of the sun setting soon."

Nineveh and Jarem shake their heads in tandem, agreeing to continue our search.

I nod toward the cliffs in the distance. "Let's head toward those cliffs. If it was raining when she was out here, she would have headed somewhere that looked dry." I reach down and grasp the handle of my canteen and slide it into its place in my pack.

"Maybe we can even get there before nightfall!" Nineveh's smile grows, her high pitch returning, even if just for a moment.

Ayathesti - 90

I laugh for the first time in what seems like ages as I sit around the evening fire with the tribe, gratefully eating the food they provided. The stars shine brightly in the dark sky. It's a moonless night, meaning a shroud of darkness surrounds us just outside the reach of the fire's light. Children hold hands and dance in circles around the flames, and others beat on the ground and trees to keep rhythm. Older women hymn and hum in harmony.

I had just finished eating my leafy greens when one child tugs at my hand, urging me to join them around the fire. My stomach bounces with laughter, and I throw my head back with a sigh of defeat before standing to join them. Taking care not to put too much pressure on my foot, I clap my hands and dance in circles around the fire, warmth piercing my clothes.

After a long while, they set me free from the dancing. I reach for my canteen when I sit and take an eager gulp as I watch everyone interact. Their numbers trickle down at a steady pace throughout the night until the fire begins to dwindle from a bright blaze to a calm ember. It casts a low light on the remaining members. I lean forward, placing my elbows on my knees, captivated by the dancing flames between embers.

"You know, Reki . . ." I say. Apparently he's learned my name for him, because he looks toward me when I say it. I smile at him, a hollow ache filling my chest. "I have had a great time getting to know your people."

He grunts an unintelligible response.

"It saddens me that I have to return, but it's where I belong. Honestly, I might go bonkers without you to talk to." My eyes sting, and I glance toward the sky, leaning back to rest my elbows in the dirt. "It's amazing, isn't it? That we come from so far away. And it seems like no time has passed at all. I still don't know if I can do this, even to save my people and my planet." I sigh, blinking away the moisture threatening to spill down my cheeks before looking back at him.

He smiles and reaches toward me in a reassuring gesture. *It's as though he knows what I've said and he's telling me everything will be alright.*

"Your people are so kind. You live happy . . . and free. I have to leave before they come for me and take one of you hostage for tests." I lay down and look back at the stars, getting lost in their sparkle. "Tonight was the best goodbye I could have ever hoped for. I can't imagine it any other way."

Reki grunts a few times more before standing up to leave, offering his hand to help me up. With a shake of my head, I pat the ground. "No, I'd like to sleep out here again tonight."

I smile, watching him walk up the path to the cave. Letting out a deep breath, I close my eyes, relaxation taking over me while the trickling stream and chirping bugs lull me into what will be the last slumber in this part of my reality.

My eyes shoot open at a loud cracking sound. I lay motionless, listening for more noises; my breath grows heavy and slow with anticipation. Stars are the only things visible, but even they are shrouded by parts of the darkened tree canopy. My heart races, and I clench my eyes shut, trying to think of what to do. I can try to find the path back up to the cave. *No, I won't risk putting them in danger.*

I sit up and reach into my bag for something that could serve as a weapon. My fingertips graze the handle of a dagger made from a stick, twine, and a sharpened rock. Reki had given it to me to help cut the rest of my jacket for additional bandages. *At least I have a means of self-defense.*

The rustling of leaves follows another loud crack before a faint light peeks through the brush. The pounding of my heart grows louder in my head and my stomach tightens. Every muscle in my body screams at me to move, but they refuse to at the same time. Footsteps emanate from the darkness, growing louder as the light grows brighter with each passing moment. A muffled voice comes with the light. I strain to hear what's being said. *I don't recognize that voice.*

I plunge my fingertips into the sand and maneuver myself to a stand, breathing slow and deep to stay quiet. A firm hand lands on my shoulder, keeping me in place. A yelp slips past my lips before a quiet grunt reaches my ear.

"Reki . . . oh—" I whisper as my tension melts away. Reki puts a finger against my lips, and I look toward the bushes. Bleeding silence. *They seem to have gone.*

"What do we do?" I whisper again, inviting Reki to drop his heavy hand over my mouth. Footsteps echo once more through the night, followed by the glow of light. Reki slips his hand under my arm and navigates me behind the trees just as the deceased fire pit is drowned in a bright artificial light. I squint, leaning my back against a tree, waiting for the pounding of my heart to die down. Sweat covers my skin, and my shallow breathing muffles the voices as I peel myself from the suffocating tendrils of anxiety.

Reki is crouched low, peering through leafy bushes next to the tree, watching the intruders. His brows furrow, and his lower jaw protrudes with his clenched teeth. *Angry. He's so angry.* His hands wring around the neck of a spear as he adjusts it, readying to charge.

I take a deep steadying breath, and the voices equalize as the panic dwindles. The sound of glass clanks together. *My extraction kit . . . They're going through my things.*

"This is definitely her stuff!" Nineveh's voice pierces through the deafening quiet of night.

A dagger plunges straight through my soul, threatening to knock me breathless to the ground as her voice echos deeper into me. I look at Reki, only moments away from charging.

"No, no, no!" I lunge, grabbing his shoulder, shaking my head furiously. My eyes plead with him as his round shoulder slips from my fingertips. *It's too late.* He pushes through the bushes, spear overhead as he rushes at the intruders.

"Reki! Nooo!" An ear-shattering scream bursts from my chest, taking my ability to breathe along with it. All I hear is a soft thud as I stumble out from behind the tree. I catch my balance, eyes falling to Reki's body on the ground. I scurry over, falling to my knees beside him, and struggle to roll him to his back.

"Reki . . . Reki wake up!" I tap his cheek lightly in desperation.

"Aya?" Nineveh says, her voice laced with confusion.

"Nineveh!" I look at her, then back to Reki, shaking his shoulders. "Nineveh, please. Make sure he's okay."

Nineveh looks to Tiamet with a questioning look. He shrugs and nods toward us. Nineveh walks over and takes a cautious knee beside him. "Aya, I don't know if I—"

"Damn it, Nineveh! *Please*! Just—please . . ." My voice chokes on a sob stuck in my throat. I clasp my hands together tightly next to my mouth, sitting back on my heels.

Nineveh hovers her hand in front of Reki's nose and mouth. Her lips pull to one side of her face with uncertainty before she tilts her head and jabs her fingers against the side of his neck. She nods, her soft voice penetrating the still night around us. "He's alive."

A river of tears flood down my cheeks when relief washes over me. "Thank you." The words spill through my lips over and over in a whisper as I tilt my head to the sky.

A strong hand under my arm lifts me to stand, and I'm engulfed in a familiar musk and a blanket of muscle before I can even open my eyes. Tiamet buries his face in my hair, a tear landing on my shoulder.

"Tiamet?" A smile tugs at my lips, and I melt into his embrace. A world of emotion I've never experienced before rips my soul into pieces.

Tiamet - 41

After what seems like an eternity with her in my arms, she pulls away and looks up at me before shifting her focus to Nineveh and Jarem. "What—how did you find me?" she asks.

I stare at her in awe, pulling her earpiece out of my pocket and holding it out for her to see. "We just got lucky."

She takes it, her eyes shifting from mine to Reki lying unconscious on the ground. "Why did you shoot him?" she asks as her fingers fumble in reattaching the piece to her ear.

"He attacked us." My heart races when I think back on it.

"But you didn't have to shoot him. He could have died!"

"It's an electric charge, Aya. Calm down, it's harmless."

Ayathesti's cheeks flush before she takes a knee next to Reki. "Don't tell me to calm down! He is the *only* reason I am alive."

"Now who's fault is that?" I raise an eyebrow, pursing my lips and folding my arms.

"You guys! Knock it off!" Nineveh steps forward. "Aya, it was an accident. He's fine, just unconscious, likely due to his fall after the jolt."

"Do you seriously expect us to be out here without some kind of self-defense?" I say.

"Nineveh, thank you for making sure he's okay." Ayathesti grabs her bag, ignoring my question. *That's okay, it was mostly rhetorical anyway.*

She reaches into her bag and pulls out a piece of cloth

and wraps it around a branch. She walks to the fire pit and pushes it around before it lights up. "Stay here." She turns and walks toward a path up the hillside.

"Hell no!" I start after her.

She turns. "I'll be right back."

"Bullshit."

"Tiamet!" The pitch of Nineveh's scolding rattles my eardrums. "Aya, we will wait here."

"Don't expect me to come after you again if you don't come back." I clench my teeth and watch her disappear up the path.

I pace, shaking my head and breathing heavily. "She's not coming back," I say through gritted teeth, clenching my fists under folded arms.

"She will." Nineveh taps Ayathesti's bag next to her in the dirt. "We have her stuff."

"On the bright side, I'll bet she got a good sample we can take back," Jarem says.

She pulls the case from the bag. "Actually, all the vials are empty."

"*What*?" I whip my gaze from the path and stare at her. "Make one of them *un*-empty, then!"

"No."

"Nineveh, now is not the time to take sides. This is the perfect compatible species, and I am *not* dragging this thing back with us!"

Nineveh shakes her head, folding her arms and turning away. "No."

Unclenching my fists, I yank the box from her hand. "Fine, I'll do it."

"Stop, Tiamet. Stop to think about why she didn't get a sample. There must be a reason." She sits there, staring at me, making no attempt to retrieve the vials.

I kneel by the still body on the ground and open the case. *I can do this. I've seen it done enough times to have the basic idea.* After examining the vials and body, I see a vein pulsing in Reki's arm. After tying it off, I prep the vial and insert the needle into the vein. Crimson blood bursts into the vial. After pulling it from the needle housing chamber, I tuck it back into the box and fill a second as backup before handing the container to Nineveh.

"We can't take the whole thing with us . . . so we'll take what we can."

Shame riddled on her face, Nineveh tucks the box into Ayathesti's bag just as she appears on the path with two more of the creatures behind her. One clutches a spear, and the other holds a bow in his hand, a sack of arrows strapped to his back. Nineveh scoots away from the body on the ground, and Jarem steps in front of her.

With furrowed brows, I turn to her. "What is this? More of them?"

Ayathesti stops. "Back away from him."

She's never talked to me with such strength and demand before.

"Back off, Tiamet." Her eyes pierce straight into me, her strength sending a shiver down my spine. I take a few steps back before she, and the other two, go toward Reki's body. She places the torch on the ground, kneeling beside him. With one man on each side he is lifted from the ground, and they make their way back up the path.

I share a glance with Nineveh before looking back to Ayathesti. "What was that all about?" Tiamet steps toward her.

"Like I said. He saved my life. I had to save his." She turns around, picks up her bag, and makes her way to the river. "You might want to refill while we're here."

She dunks her canteen into the water. Then she screws the lid on and walks toward where we arrived. "Let's go," she says, her voice void of emotion as she pushes through the bushes.

"Now wait one second." I screw the cap back onto my canteen and jog after her. "It's the middle of the night. It'd be best to rest and get an early start in the morning."

Nineveh nods, a tired rasp to her voice. "I actually must say, I agree with him, Aya."

"We've been up since the last sunrise to find you." Jarem holds his hand out to Nineveh's canteen. She hands it to him, and he tucks it into her bag.

"No. We leave now." Ayathesti pushes on.

Nineveh whimpers a sigh of exhaustion. Jarem holds out his hand to help her over a log blocking the path. She takes it, glowing at his sympathetic smile. I grunt in protest before following them, constantly looking over my shoulder to make sure we're not followed.

Nineveh bumps into Ayathesti's back when she stops abruptly. "Oh, do we get to sit down now?" she asks in a hopeful tone.

Ayathesti nods, letting her bag slide from her shoulder to the ground. "Not for long, though. We can get a few hours before we have to get up and keep going."

"We've been walking for almost two days, Aya. Nineveh needs more than a few hours." I'm already pulling blankets and pillows from my pack, and toss one to Nineveh with a teasing grin.

Ayathesti rolls her eyes as she sits on the ground. "I slept earlier tonight so I'll stay up and keep an eye on things. The sun will be up in a few hours."

Nineveh tucks the pillow under her arm and fumbles

with the clips cinching her pack around her torso. "I do not! I am perfectly capable of continuing!"

I grab a protein pack and raise a brow. "You're not fooling anyone. You were practically walking with your eyes closed back there."

"So?"

A chuckle rumbles in my chest. "So you need to rest. You're the doctor. Why do I have to tell you this? Jarem has been correcting your path for hours just to keep you going straight."

Her face goes pink. "I'm eager to get back! I don't enjoy sleeping in the dirt and weeds!" She gracefully swats Jarem's hand away from helping unclasp her pack.

"Nobody made you come along." I smirk to keep another chuckle at bay. *Though it was Nineveh who made a big fuss about getting a search party together.*

"Nobody asked you to come looking either," Ayathesti mutters under her breath.

"What was that?" I turn.

Ayathesti shakes her head. "Nothing . . ."

There's a writhing in my chest as my stomach turns over when I walk to her. "No, really. What did you say?"

Nineveh lets out a soft moan. "You guys, don't start. Let's just sleep so we can—"

"Hold on, Nin, I want to hear this." I stop, towering over Aya where she sits.

She looks up at me expressionless. "No, you don't."

"Now I'm even more intrigued." I cross my arms.

"Leave it alone." Ayathesti opens her canteen and presses the metal mouth to her lips.

Leaning down, I grip her forearm and pull her to meet my gaze. "I won't," I say through clenched teeth.

Nineveh sits on a blanket, pleading. "Tiamet, you're just as tired as the rest of us! Please, come rest before everybody says things they don't mean!"

I glance at Nineveh, her eyes tired and puffy, then at Jarem pinching his lips together and getting comfortable on another blanket. When my gaze comes back to Ayathesti, she's looking out over the plains, avoiding eye contact.

"Fine." I thrust her arm away and return to my blanket to lie down. "This isn't over." I link my hands together, resting them under my head.

"Thank you." Nineveh sighs and lays down, her hand finding Jarem's arm as everyone falls silent.

Tiamet - 42

A jolt to my feet yanks me from sleep with a snort and gibberish in my half-awakened state. “Para-babble dish!”

Nineveh’s giggle jitters her shoulders as she looks at Jarem.

“Okay . . .” Aya hoists her bag over her shoulder and stares down at me, eyebrows raised. “Nice dream?”

I sneer at her before scrambling up off the ground. After gathering all the blankets and pillows, I stuff them haphazardly into my pack and secure it to my torso. “So”—I turn to face the group—“the good news is we’re ready to get back to the others!”

“Oh no . . . what’s the bad news?” Nineveh moans in a high pitched sigh.

“Bad news is. . . I haven’t a clue which direction they’re in.”

Ayathesti steps down from a log she’s standing on. “They’re that way.” She points as she walks past us.

“How do you know? What if we get lost!” Nineveh’s eyes are still puffy from the lack of sleep.

“I saw the smoke from their fire this morning.” Ayathesti keeps walking toward the direction she pointed to, though the plume of smoke is no longer visible.

“But how do you know it wasn’t smoke from those things you were with? I don’t even think Latif knows how to make a fire!” Nineveh struggles getting her bag onto her back, and Jarem is quick to help her.

Ayathesti shouts over her shoulder at us. “Well, I know it’s not them because A: they are back that way. And B: they don’t do fires until late afternoon.”

"Wow . . ." When I'm comfortable with the distance between me and Ayathesti, I whisper to Nineveh, "Her taking control of situations is actually quite . . . annoying."

Nineveh elbows my ribs. "What is it supposed to be? Inspiring?"

I chuckle, rubbing where she just jabbed me. "Honestly, I always imagined it to be sexy."

"Oh, gross. Shut your mouth!" Nineveh snaps her attention toward Ayathesti. "She was out here by herself for over a week. She may need time to adjust back to how she normally works."

"Alright, alright. I'll give it some time." I start jogging toward Ayathesti, shouting over my shoulder at Nineveh, "Oh, and she wasn't alone."

I pocket my hands as I slow my pace from a jog to match Ayathesti's. "Seems like you're in a hurry."

She flicks her eyes in my direction but presses forward in silence.

"What, now you're not gonna talk to me?"

Again, not a word.

"Weird. Last night you seemed so eager to tell me what was on your mind." I can't keep my annoyance out of my tone.

"What do you want me to say?" she finally says, unenthused.

"I just want to see you with emotion other than"—I motion my hands sporadically in the air—"whatever this is!"

"I want to get as far from there as possible." Her words end sharply. To the point.

"I thought you never wanted to leave?"

Ayathesti drops her gaze to her feet. "What gave you that impression?"

"You never asked for us to come find you, remember?" My heart races, pushing blood to my head with anticipation of the argument about to ensue.

"I knew it." Ayathesti shakes her head, scoffing.

"Knew what?" A half smile hides beyond the corners of my lips.

"I knew you heard me!"

"Yes." I hook my hand under her arm, stopping her. "But I wanted you to say it to my face."

She looks at me with pinched lips as Nineveh and Jarem walk past us, absorbed in their own conversation. Her shoulders shrug with a sigh. "I didn't want to."

"Be found. Yeah, I gathered that." I keep my eyes locked on her, waiting.

She struggles maintaining eye contact. "No . . . I didn't want to say it to your face."

"Why? I'm not the one who loses my temper when we talk."

Ayathesti put her hand on top of my arm. "I know. I was just . . ."

This is hard for her. I know that. She brings her eyes to mine, and I stare into them, getting pulled so deep I could drown. "Just?"

"I was scared, that's all." With little effort, she pushes my hand from her arm, breaking eye contact, and starts walking again.

I grab her arm again. "Woah, wait a second. Scared of what?" I furrow my brow.

Sorrow fills her eyes when she looks at me.

"Of me!" I hold back a chuckle. "Am I scary?"

"No!" She sighs. "I was scared to disappoint you—to disappoint myself." The glassy finish in her eyes grows thicker, her chest and shoulders heaving.

My near smirk fades. All I can think to do is wrap my arms around her and pull her close. "You don't. I'm just glad you're okay."

"I wasn't."

I pull back from the embrace as she grins, a calm tear making a slow descent down her cheek. I lift my hand and swipe the tear from her chin.

"I couldn't even walk without limping until last night," she admits.

"What happened last night?"

"Can we not talk about this right now?" She glances toward Nineveh and Jarem, who had stopped walking but were still talking. "This is embarrassing . . ."

My hands slide down her arms and grip her hands briefly before letting go. My eyebrows furrow, a hammer smashing into my already fractured heart. "I embarrass you?"

"No, that—" She looks at me with a deep sigh. "That's not what I meant."

My confidence shatters. "Well, what did you mean?" *What is this feeling? There's a sudden distance between us.*

"I *mean* stop asking me all these questions!" She turns, using the back of her hand to wipe more tears away.

"My questions aren't embarrassing." I stand, motionless.

"No, they're not," she sniffs. "I'm embarrassed that Nineveh and that . . . guy . . ." She looks back over at them now sitting under a tree.

"Jarem, security lead. He was willing to come save you . . . because I made him." I look from them to her.

Ayathesti nods, clearing her throat. "Right, well they're waiting, and it's embarrassing me."

"Right . . ." I push past her, the longing I'd once had to speak with her again twisting into knots in my stomach. "Let's go, then."

Ayathesti - 43

The walk with Tiamet, saturated in tension from the previous words exchanged, reaches an unbearable silence.

"So! Did you two hash things out?" Nineveh's voice returns to its annoying level of optimism as she accepts Jarem's hand to help her up.

I look at her from the corner of my eye without a word and keep walking.

"I suppose you didn't, then . . ." She quickens her pace to catch up to me, her footsteps landing in tandem with mine.

"Can we just . . . not?" I say.

"Okay. Well . . . I'm glad you're alright!"

"Yeah, I know. But I wasn't."

"You weren't?" She gasps. "I knew you needed us!"

"Yeah, I needed you."

"What happened?"

"My ankle twisted up pretty badly, and my shoulder dislocated, I'm guessing. I could barely even move when I woke up four days ago." Though I've used my shoulder minimally since then, the pain lingers., and I rub it to ease the ache.

"Oh my goodness! Four days ago?" Nineveh eyes my shoulder. "We set out four days ago, and you disappeared at least two full days before we even left."

I sigh in disbelief. "Guess I was out for a few days then."

"Are you okay?" Nineveh places her hand on my shoulder.

I nod. *Please move your hand . . .*

"Thanks for coming back with us." There's a certain relief to her tone as her cheer returns.

"What do you mean? Why wouldn't I come back with you?"

"After last night, it seemed like you didn't want to leave."

"Not you too!" I move my shoulder from under her hand in annoyance.

"I'm sorry. I'm not trying to jump down your throat. You just seemed pretty upset when we left the river."

"I was."

"Why were you so upset?" I can sense Nineveh's eyes as we walk.

"Nin, can we not? Please? I'm tired, and I just want to get back."

Nineveh nods with a smile. After a few minutes with the only thing to break the silence being the voices of Tiamet and Jarem behind us, she giggles. "It was so cute!"

I look at her, raising an eyebrow. "What?"

"How worried he was about you." Nineveh looks back at Tiamet and Jarem, her nose scrunching and cheeks reddening.

"Worried?" I hesitate before looking back at them as well. I catch eyes with Jarem as he looks at Nineveh. *There's a secret hidden behind that smile.*

"Yes! He didn't quite know what to do with himself. I was begging him for a while to get a search party together. Finally he snapped out of it."

"He was *that* upset?"

"Are you kidding me?" Nineveh taps the back of her hand against my arm in a friendly, teasing manner. "He talked about the first time he saw you and everything! As if you were never coming back."

"Oh?"

"Yes! Saying how cute it was when you'd feed the tree rodents. How his favorite thing about you is how gentle and soft you are." Nineveh giggles a little more. "It was disgustingly cute!"

"He actually said that?" I glance over my shoulder, making eye contact with Tiamet. *I only ever fed those rodents a few times. I'm surprised he remembered it.*

Nineveh nods eagerly before her voice goes soft. "Why won't you talk to him?"

"I—"

"I know. You're scared! But he really puts himself out there. You could at least meet him halfway?"

I take in her words and give her a hesitant nod. "I know he does. But I've always been a private person, Nin. You know that."

"Yes, well . . . you should try."

"I thought you didn't even like him. 'He's so fake with everyone!' you would say." I do my best imitation of her.

"I do *not* sound like that!" She folds her arms in protest.

I chuckle. "You sure do."

Nineveh smiles. "Alright, maybe I do! But I guess I was being prejudgmental! He was worried about you."

"Yeah. I'm sure he doesn't want to take blame for me going missing."

Nineveh rolls her eyes, bowing her head in defeat.

I observe the sun's position against the horizon. "How far out did you guys leave the others?"

"I'm not sure, but the sun was about where it is now when we left them, and we found you in the middle of the night, so . . ." Nineveh looks around, slowing her pace.

"We should be a few hours out, then."

"How can you be sure?"

"We left right after you found me. We didn't make a

quick pace before resting but left when the sun came up, and it's now almost the middle of the day." *I didn't realize I was keeping track. I guess having nothing to do other than stare at the sky made me more aware of what mid-day looks like.*

"Oh! I guess that makes sense."

"We need to head to the left!" Jarem calls from behind us.

I look over my shoulder to Tiamet and Jarem jogging toward us.

"What makes you say that?" I stop, allowing them to catch up.

"Because that's where we found your earpiece." Jarem points to the mouth of the trench.

Staring at the opening sends shivers up my spine, anxiety digging her claws in deep. Pain radiates through my shoulder as I relive smashing into the ground, flashbacks of falling down the steep slope gluing my feet in place.

Tiamet turns and furrows his brow. "What's wrong?"

I shiver and shake my head. "Nothing, lets go."

After walking along the trench and after about two more hours of flat land, we reach the area where Latif, Pimly, and Stans made camp.

Latif laughs, slapping his knee before standing. "Wow . . . you guys look like shit!" Nineveh glares at him and gives him a playful slap on the shoulder when he engulfs her in his arms, planting his lips against her cheek.

Tiamet sits on a rock, sighing. "Well, if you weren't such a wimp, you'd have experienced all the excitement to get us looking like this!"

Latif picks up a pot with chunks of meat in boiling water and holds it out to us. "But then you'd all be super hungry!"

Nineveh unclasps her backpack, causing it to slip from her shoulders and fall onto Jarem's head as she walks around to set it down. She gasps, whipping around. "Oh Jare. I'm so sorry! That was an accident!"

He rubs the back of his head and chuckles, looking up at her. "I guess we're throwing stuff now."

I peer into the pot, grimacing through clenched teeth. "You should probably stick to what you do best."

"What's that, boss?" Latif says to me, as he looks at Nineveh with a raised eyebrow.

"Absolutely nothing." I smirk.

Tiamet lets out a deep, uncontrollable laugh. "There she is!"

"Harsh . . ." Latif pulls his attention back from Nineveh and Jarem and retracts the pot from my view. "You don't have to eat any, then!"

"It's appreciated, Latif." I lift my pack over my head and set it on the ground before kneeling in front of the fire. "It's good to see your face."

He scoops some of his stew into a tin cup and hands it to me. "Well that's something I never thought I'd hear you say."

I lift it to my lips and inhale. It's thick and smells savory. I sip the broth. *More pleasant than I expected.* Latif holds out a silver spoon, and I take it, seating myself.

When the contents of my cup are empty, I reach for my canteen and drink the remaining sweet water inside. Memories of the past few days flood my mind.

"I don't know about you guys, but I could use more sleep." Nineveh yawns and rests her head on Latif's shoulder. He reaches over and grips her hand.

"After the late night and full day of walking, I'm in the same boat as you, Miss Nineveh." Jarem's comment earns him a glare from Latif.

"Seeing as Aya has slept the least of all of us, and being the director, I concur it's best to get a full night of rest before continuing back." Tiamet looks around as though waiting for others to offer alternate suggestions.

"I'm fine," I say softly, expressionless. *Honestly, I'm exhausted. Surprised I kept pace all day to make it this far, really.*

"It's a long walk ahead. I need everyone better than fine." Tiamet holds a rolled-up blanket to my shoulder.

Is this some kind of peace offering? "Yeah, okay. Whatever you say, Director." I take the blanket, unwilling to argue with anyone, including myself. I lay down and stare up at the sky, watching as, one by one, the stars twinkle their way into existence.

I mouth the words to ensure secrecy. "Goodnight, Reki."

Ayathesti - 44

After what seems like an eternity of walking, the main camp pops into view on the horizon. The excitement shows on the others faces, and in their voices. At first sight of the tents, my stomach wretches, preventing me from breathing.

'Welcome back to everyone judging your every move.'

My heart pounds heavily. *I'm the only one not excited to be back.*

'Because you don't belong.'

Should I even continue on?

'Why should you?'

I can just turn around right now, walk back and live with that little community in simplicity by that stream.

'Why bother with that either. They didn't follow you out here or try to get you to stay. They don't want you either.'

My breath stutters as my throat tightens when her dark whispers start to reveal their logic. *Focus.*

'No, give in. You know I'm right.'

List the reasons to stay.

'There are no reasons.'

Latif, Nineveh, Tiamet . . . Mom, Papa . . . Rothe . . .

Hara is reading a book in the front room of our tent. The sweet, minty aroma of oojo in the air knocks my head back and pinches the back of my throat. My breath shakes. I stop just inside the door, closing it behind me but too scared to let go of the handle.

"Oh! You're back!" She beams.

Tiamet nods, lifting his pack from his shoulders as he heads toward the table. "Yeah, finally."

"And you found Aya!" Hana sets her book on the chair beneath her before walking to the kitchen. "You look famished! Are you hungry? Do you need a drink?"

Tiamet plops down in a chair at the table with a sigh, letting his pack fall to the floor. "I'd sure love a glass."

Hana pours a cup and places it on the table in front of him.

Nineveh has her hands in her hair, freeing it from the ponytail. "Oh, I'm quite alright without, thank you." She takes a seat at the table as well, tousling her hair.

Hana's gaze meets my own. She holds the pot up without a word. I look at it, then at the others before shaking my head. I slip my bag over my head and walk to my room, then close the door behind me.

The darkness is vast as I stand there. I close my eyes, letting out a sigh. With it comes relief and regret all in the same moment. Sitting on the edge of the bed, I slip my boots off and examine my ankle with my hand in the darkness, checking for tenderness. I slip my dusty pants off and plop them on the floor. I drop my shirt atop it. Lying on the bed, I pull the blanket up to my chin and listen to the rhythm of voices from the kitchen before they fade away.

My wiggling toes scrape against the blanket while I wake in the room's surrounding darkness. I dress in fresh clothes, feeling better after having undisturbed rest in total darkness. The hallway is dark when I come out of my room. I make my way to the empty lounging area. Even Hana hasn't started cooking yet. My feet guide me to the front door as I pull my hair from my neck, tying it into a messy bun.

Gold, orange, and yellow tones splash across the sky in a tequila sunrise. I absorb the sight for only a moment, breathing deeply before making my way to the research tent.

Upon entry I scoff. "Typical."

My assumptions of nothing being touched in my absence are confirmed. *Even so, I had hoped Latif may do something.* Shaking my head, I walk in and ready myself to clean up the mess I'd left before departing. *Oh well. At least he didn't mess anything up either.*

I set my bag on the metal counter in the middle of the small room. I remove the contents one by one, examining them for damage before placing them back in their places. First the gauze and syringes, all in acceptable condition. Next I pull out the box of sample vials. Considering the fall I had, the likelihood of them all being broken is high. I set the container on the cold surface, hearing broken pieces slide against one another. Opening the box, I count them. Numbers two, three, five, and eight.

"Not too bad I guess, only four broken." Talking to myself has certainly become habit at this point. After placing the majority of broken pieces in the trash, with gloves on, I reach for the first unbroken vial from the black cushion surrounding it. Fatigue blurs my focus as I look for cracks before I swipe the outside with a sanitation wipe and place it in the supply crate.

I continue with the next vial, and the next, the only disruption being the low rumble in my stomach. *I wonder if breakfast is ready yet.*

"Only two more. I'll finish up first." I pick up the next vial from the black cushion, my arms slowing with hesitation. Lifting the vial to my nose, I squint and blink, furrowing my brow. After placing it into a plastic tube, I put the sample on a rack in the freezer chest.

I place my hands on the countertop, scouring my memories for when I had extracted the sample. *Was it when I was unconscious? Was I going around jabbing people while unconscious? No . . . I could barely even move at that point.*

"No, I doubt they would have kept me unharmed if I were sticking needles into them." I shake my head. *Nineveh. . .* "No. There's no way." *But there's no other explanation. It happened when I wasn't there.*

Anger eats its way through my core. I turn on my heel, leaving the contents on the table. Snapping the gloves off and tossing them in the bin on my way out, I consider my options as I walk back to the residence tent. I swing the door open, exposing everyone at the table inside.

"Oh, thank goodness!" Nineveh's shoulders fall with a sigh. "I thought you left again."

"What the hell is going on?" I stand with arms folded, staring her down.

"What are you on about?" Tiamet cuts in.

"You know damn well what I'm talking about! Don't even try to pretend you don't."

"Aya, calm do—"

"Don't tell me to calm down, Tiamet." My throat is tight as I clench my teeth and my fists.

"Ayathesti!" Nineveh scolds. "Deep breath. Then tell us, what's got you so upset?"

I let out a heavy breath. "Oh, so you're pretending not to know too?"

"Know what?" she asks.

"How did he get you to do it? We all know he's incapable of doing it himself, so tell me. *What did he say* to get you to do it?"

She drops her gaze to her hands. *Shame.*

Tiamet closes his eyes and nods, letting out a sigh. "It wasn't her."

"Bullshit! Two full vials of blood, and she had absolutely nothing to do with it? I don't think so. How can you go so low to have her take blood from someone unconscious?"

Tiamet stands, walking toward me with his hands in front of him. "Aya, she refused. I did it all on my own." He grips the sides of my arms.

I shake them off while taking a step backward. "Seriously? Even if that was believable, why? Tell me why you did it. He deserved to at least know. Instead you violate his body while he's unconscious."

"Aya . . . I had no other choice." Tiamet steps toward me again.

"No choice?" I put my hand up, gesturing him to stop. "And don't put your hands on me. You had a choice!"

"What alternative? To bring him back with us? Scare everybody here? Not to mention keeping him under control!"

My jaw drops as I point at him, disgusted with the idea. "You wouldn't dare!"

"Please, Aya, calm down." Tiamet steps closer again.

"I can't believe you would even consider taking him hostage for testing!" I begin to pace, my hands on my head. "Of course, it's my own fault for even trusting you after you shot him!" My breathing increases.

"Aya—"

"What if it had been me? Would you have shot me too!"

"Shut up!" Tiamet shouts, capturing my wrists in a tight grip.

I snap my gaze to him. Silence hushes the anger surging through me when our eyes lock.

"Please . . . Aya . . . understand. A small vial of blood to save an entire civilization—*our* civilization. That seemed like a small sacrifice. We got the sample we need for you to do your work, and he will be okay. We can go home now."

I stare at him in silence, contemplating his words. I swallow hard, preparing myself. "Still. You should have told me."

"Would you have honestly let that fly?"

I study his face before shaking my head.

Tiamet drops his hands from my wrists. "I can't believe this. I'm the director, yet I'm doing things behind your back because you wouldn't approve. Why even take the vials if that's not what you were planning?"

My cheeks heat up, my fingertips tingling with nerves. "Honestly, that was my intention."

"What happened?"

"I thought they would be different from how they are. They have families and . . . habits and a language! That they use to communicate! They don't speak our language, but they somewhat understood me! I . . . I can't even exp—"

Tiamet presses a fingertip against my lips. "It's fine. It's done now, and you don't have to worry about it anymore. Come get some food."

I nod with a smile and walk to the table.

"So do we really get to go home now?" Nineveh's smiles so wide it almost looks unnatural.

Tiamet nods, filling his mouth with food.

A wave of sadness burrows into my chest. *This place is so foreign and distant, and I do miss home—my silence, my routine, my certainty in what each day holds.* I stare at the plate in front of me and listen to the surrounding conversation, contemplating my feelings of wanting to stay.

"Oh, thank goodness! This place is not good for my skin!" Nineveh giggles.

"Well, it's not home. That's for sure." Tiamet licks crumbs from his lower lip. "Can't wait to get back to civilized living."

"I want to sleep in my own bed again!" Hana says.

"Well, these beds aren't too bad, but I definitely miss my own!" Tiamet returns.

"The sunrise is another thing. And the day is so hot here!" Nineveh looks at me. "What do you miss most, Aya?"

With my mouth full of food, I chew slowly. Their eyes are trained on me, expecting a response. "Well . . . I miss the stars."

"There are stars here. Doesn't count." Tiamet's voice is light, taking on a teasing quality.

"Okay, fine."

"Special nightgown?" he asks.

I shake my head, remaining silent.

"The news?" Hana offers.

"Your glass stained windows?" Nineveh adds.

Once again, I only shake my head.

Tiamet sits back in his chair, fingers interlaced behind his head, one foot propped up on his other knee. "Well there's got to be something other than the stars."

"If you must know . . ." I sigh.

He nods, tousling his hair across his forehead. "I must."

"Alone."

He shakes his head. "I won't leave it alone."

"No!" My fork makes a loud clang against my tin plate when I drop it. "I *miss* being alone!" I drop my head into my hands, letting out a deep sigh.

Silence falls over the room before Nineveh and Hana excuse themselves from the table. When I glance up at him, Tiamet is still seated, looking at me with concern.

"Stop looking at me like that. I'm fine."

He leans forward. "Aya, I'm worried about you."

"I already said I'm fine."

"You just yelled at us that you want to be alone, yet

you've been alone for the last week. And every moment since we've been back."

I take a deep breath in and blow it out steadily. "I didn't mean it like that."

"Well, then, elaborate. How did you mean it?"

I shake my head, unsure of what to say next. Pieces of hair fall from my bun, tickling my nose. With the way he stares at me, I'm unable to ignore it, and move a hand to my nose, swishing the itch away. "I . . . I'm a person of predictability, routines. I have things the way I want them at home, and I feel out of place here."

"You could have opted out."

I nod, looking up at him. "I know."

"But you came anyway. Why?"

"Part of me wanted to come."

Tiamet nods, pinching his lips together. "A bigger part than the one that wanted to stay."

I hesitate. "No."

"I think that may be the case."

"I can't let anyone down. I wanted to be here, to see this planet, and to take part in writing history."

"Nobody would have been let down by you staying back, Aya."

"That's a lie."

He shrugs, sitting back in his chair, folding his arms. "Name one person."

My eyes meet his, my fingers trembling with nervousness. Accepting the realization of what I'm about to say makes my breath quiver. "Me."

He reaches for my hands and takes them in his. "I think we're nearly there."

I shake my head.

"Aya, you need to stop. Stop doing this to yourself."

"I . . ." My breath is heavy and trembles with the

threat of a sob pushing up in my throat.

"I know it's hard, but, really, can't you see what everybody else sees in you? What happened to the woman who managed to get classified information from my security team to go find those . . . things—"

"People," I correct.

"Okay, fine, yes. *People* to get a sample."

Pride, hidden behind shame, tugs at the corners of my lips. "That wasn't me. I was mad at you for not telling me what was going on."

Tiamet playfully pushes my hands from his. "Yeah? Doing it to spite me."

I chuckle unexpectedly. "Not to spite you!"

"Riiight . . ." His eyebrow quirks upward.

"I just wanted to make you as upset as you'd made me." My cheeks flush when I admit it.

"Whatever your motivation, you have had that same confidence inside of you all this time. You just need to find it again. Hold on to that."

"I don't know if that's a person I want to be yet."

Tiamet leans back in his chair, hands behind his head again, beaming ear to ear. "What happened?"

My brows furrow. "What do you mean 'what happened?' "

"Don't get me wrong . . ."

"Wrong about what?" My shoulders tense up.

"I'm not sure how to say this subtly. Aya, you've changed," he says. I look away. "I like it! This is likely the longest conversation we've ever had without you running away."

"I do not run away!"

"Like hell you don't!" His chest shakes with his chuckle.

"I don't!" I can't help but smile. *Apparently, he's been*

keeping track.

"But really . . . what happened?"

I sigh. "I was stranded . . . for a good amount of time. Nobody to talk to, other than myself, of course. I guess I never realized how nice it is to have somebody there to listen."

"Curious."

"With two days of walking, talking to myself, I got annoyed at myself!" Tiamet smiles as I continue. "Then I wake up in this cave with Reki and his people. Scared as shit at first, I tried to keep my distance. But his curiosity kept bringing him close . . . and he was helpful! I messed my leg up big time, and my shoulder had so much pain I couldn't even use my hand! Tiamet . . . he saved my life."

"As you said before. Pretty adamantly too, if I remember."

"It was raining, and I tripped on something. I fell. Far and hard. It was the most pain I've ever felt in my entire life. Physical pain at least. I couldn't even move. I had accepted death as my fate before I passed out, soaking in mud. I woke up in their cave."

Tiamet shakes his head. "Were you scared?"

"That's an understatement!" I say. He sits forward again. The previous smile fades as I relive the moments. "I eventually stopped talking to myself and talked to Reki instead. It was like he could understand me even though our languages differed."

"Wow . . ."

"I know! No matter how badly I wanted to, I couldn't run away." I place my hand on my shoulder, where some of the pain is still present. "I had to adapt. It feels nice . . ." My voice trails off as my eyes glaze over in thought.

"Being back?" he asks.

I shake my head, grinning. "No—well, yes. But I

mean, it feels nice to not be holding on to so much after talking with somebody. To get it all out and off your shoulders right there." I thrust my hands forward. I pick up a playful tone, redirecting my gaze toward him. "But you!"

He points at himself. "Me?"

"Yes!" I poke his chest. "You make me want to pull my hair out sometimes!"

"That's just part of my charm!"

"Charm?" I laugh. "Yeah right."

"You don't think I'm charming?" He tucks a few strands of loose hair behind my ear.

"In your own ways . . ." My breath stutters at the proximity of his face to mine. I look at him from the corner of my eye.

"What ways?" The heat from his breath grazes my skin. His gaze flickers to my lips, then to my eyes. I grow weak at their deep purple draw.

"Oh, you don't get to know," I whisper.

"What? Not fair! Tell me." He smiles, taking my hand in his.

"Nope!" I return his smile and stand up slowly. His hand slides away from me, his fingertips sparking shocks of static across my skin.

"C'mon, Aya!"

I stand and pass him, walking toward my room.

Tiamet - 45

"*Well*, how did that go?" Nineveh asks, waiting for me outside the tent.

"It was fine," I say, an unshakable smile on my lips.

"Hold on, you guys actually talked?"

"Yeah, she's come a long way."

"I guess . . . It's not like her to speak so openly about how she's feeling."

"You're not joking. I've never heard her talk so much in the entire time I've known her." I look at the sky, leaning my weight against a tent support post.

"I'm thrilled you two can be in the same room together, but when are we leaving?" Latif runs his fingers through his hair.

"We'll leave soon enough. Don't worry."

"I am worried. I want to go home!" Latif sighs, leaning his head on Nineveh's shoulder.

"Give it a few days. Let's make sure everything is good with the sample before we head back." I look over my shoulder at the tent.

Latif perks up. "Fantastic!"

Nineveh pokes his shoulder, giggling. "I can't see why you're so excited to get back! This is practically a permanent vacation for you."

"Latif." I look at him with both eyebrows raised. "Do everybody a favor and *do not touch* that sample!"

"I resent that, buddy." He puts his hand to his chin, smirking.

"I'm serious. Aya nearly took my head off when she found out I snuck it from her precious friend when he was unconscious."

"I don't understand." Nineveh furrows her brows. "It's not like her to stand up for herself, let alone someone else."

I shake my head, the tips of my hair sticking to the sweat on my forehead. "Like I said, she's done some growing up. I actually like it. Kind of sexy."

"Oh, gross!" Latif sticks his tongue out, grimacing.

Nineveh walks her fingers up the side of his arm. "What, you don't like romance?"

I sigh. "I liked her before, but now that we can hold a conversation? Stop! It may be too much."

Latif scrunches his shoulders up, shuddering. "Stop! It *is* too much!"

"What's too much?" Ayathesti closes the door behind her as she exits the tent.

I cross my arms and chuckle. "Nothin' . . ."

She glares playfully. "You were talking about me, weren't you?"

I shrug and tease her with a smirk. "Maybe. Or maybe we were just teasing Latif."

Ayathesti shakes her head, rolling her eyes. "Well, you know where to find me." The corners of her eyes smile at me when she walks by. She pulls her hair into a bun as she makes her way toward the lab tent.

Latif watches her from over his shoulder. "That was… weird."

"Told ya. Sexy." The smile on my face refuses to leave.

Nineveh gently slaps the back of Latif's neck.

"Ow . . . What did I do?" he asks, rubbing his neck

Nineveh folds her arms. "I've been here the whole time, remember?"

"I didn't forget! I just meant that she normally wouldn't take to us talking about her so well!"

Nineveh glowers at him "Nice save."

I chuckle and shift my weight from the tent support. "I better catch up on neglected reports. You two play nice now." I turn to enter the tent.

"Director!"

I stop, peering over my shoulder to see Stans and Jarem jogging toward us. Latif scowls when Nineveh beams at Jarem, who smiles and nods at her in acknowledgment.

I turn to face them. "Jarem, Stans, what's going on?"

Stans is struggling for air. Jarem stands with his hands on his utility belt. "There's been another perimeter breach."

Nineveh covers her mouth. Latif throws his head back, arms falling in protest at his side. I look each person in the eye before glancing behind them to the lab tent, my heart sinking. "Shit."

Ayathesti - 96

After hours of working in the lab, I clean up and make my way back to the residency tent. Pushing the door open, I sigh. With eyes closed, I stand there for a moment, bowing my head. *My clothes feel limp . . . and heavy. Gross.*

"Rough day?" Tiamet asks from the corner chair in the lounge area.

"Something like that."

He nods his head toward the chair next to his, inviting me to join him. I turn to the kitchen and grab a glass of oojo first.

"That's been out for a while," he warns while I rummage through the food cabinets, pulling out spices to sprinkle into the fermented liquid.

"That's exactly what I need." I stir the mixture with my finger and proceed to the chair next to him. Slumping into it, I hold the glass against my chest right under my nose, inhaling deeply in an attempt to let go of the latest arguments I've had with myself.

"How's it going?"

"Decently, I'd say." I lift the glass to my lips, and a small amount of tea slips through them. I hold the fluid in my mouth, closing my eyes and resting my head back against the chair before swallowing.

"Why don't I believe you?"

Eyes still closed, I release a small smile. "Because I'm lying."

"So it's not going well?"

I shake my head and extend my feet outward so they

rest lazily on the floor. "Not at all. I can't seem to get the DNA isolated."

"Why not?" Tiamet sits forward.

"Hell if I know. You probably extracted the sample incorrectly. Every time I try, the DNA is completely destroyed and useless." I take a large gulp from the glass.

"You sure it's not your chemical extraction combination that's the problem?"

"I've been trying things all day, and nothing is working. If I can't get a strand or two out of what's left . . . I don't know what to do."

"We will just have to go back for more."

I snap upright. "Don't you even consider it!"

"Realistically, Aya, I have to consider it." His fingertips drum the side of his chair.

"Like hell you do." I empty half the cup's contents into my mouth, gulping down heavily.

"What would you have me do, then?"

A shiver crawls down my spine, making me shudder. A smile follows. "Mm, that's good."

"Aya?"

"Hm?" I look back at him.

"What would you have me do?"

"Right. What would I have you do? Let me go—alone—to get more samples."

He shakes his head. "No."

"What the hell, T?"

"I'm sorry, but I won't allow that." His tone is unyielding.

"Why not?"

"So, sooo many reasons, Aya."

"Oh yeah? Like what? Please, tell me why you can't let me go save our entire species!" I tip the cup upward, draining the contents from it. I walk to the kitchen and place the cup on the countertop next to the sink. My stomach reminds me I haven't eaten anything all day. Pulling the cabinets open, I look for something to munch on.

"It's not safe to go alone."

"I won't be alone!" My stomach tightens and forces a hiccup to my throat. "Reki will be there!"

"What did you put in that?" He makes his way to the kitchen, picks up the glass, and sniffs it before rinsing it in the sink.

"Besides, I went alone last time, and everything was fine!" I lean my back against the counter, tapping my shoes in an upbeat rhythm on the floor.

"Aya."

"Relax, Tiamet." The muscles in my stomach force up another hiccup.

"Are you okay?" He leans against the counter, folding his arms across his chest. "You spiked your drink, didn't you?"

"I'm fine. It was just someth"—I hiccup—"thing to take my mind off the entire day." I step forward and rainbow my hands through the air, chuckling.

"Oookay, you need rest." Tiamet offers me his hand.

I swat at it and place my other hand on my abdomen, attempting to curb the hunger pains. "I'm fine! Just *super* hungry!" I throw the doors to another cabinet open and move things around for a better look.

"Seriously? Aya, I've known you since the academy, and you just smiled more in the last two minutes than you have in all the time I've known you. You need some rest." He grips me under the upper arm and drags me away from the lower cabinet.

"Stop it!" My attempts to free myself from his grasp are lazy. "I am quite capable of keeping myself standing."

"If you want me to stay away from the idea of getting

another sample from your friend, you need to get this right tomorrow." He escorts me down the hallway with one hand under my arm, the other on my lower back. He reaches for the door, twists the knob, and pushes it open with his foot.

"Come on!" I giggle.

Tiamet walks me through the doorway. "Good night, Aya."

I fall back onto the bed, reaching for him, excitement racing through my chest. "Nooo! Come on, come talk with me!"

Tiamet towers over me, looking at my outstretched hand. I see hesitation growing in his eyes. He looks away, taking a deep breath as though to solidify his decision. "I'd best not," he says in a softened voice.

"Fine. Your loss." I extend my foot and tap the door closed behind him with the tip of my boot.

My head is swallowed by a thunderous rapping outside of my door. My head pulses, and I cover my ears with my hands to stop the ringing.

"Ahh! Go away." My voice scratches against my throat as I peel myself from the bed. My vision spirals into darkness, and the pressure in my head intensifies like a vice pressing against my skull. The pounding continues.

"I'm coming." My feet drag beneath me as I leave my room and mosey down the seemingly endless hallway, tucking loose strands of hair behind my ears.

"Good morning, starshine." Tiamet smirks at me from his usual place in the corner.

"Aya, you look dreadful! Are you okay?" Nineveh's high pitch is like needles pressing into my skin.

"Yes, Ayathesti, are you okay?" Tiamet raises a condescending eyebrow.

I look at him and roll my eyes. "Don't even open your mouth."

He chuckles. "Was it worth it?"

The corners of my mouth curl upward as I hold back my smile, turning away from him.

"Was what worth it?" Nineveh asks as Hana hands me a cup of oojo.

"Working late." Tiamet taps his fingers against the side of the chair.

"Mmmm." I bow my head toward the glass, inhaling deeply. "It's always worth it to work late."

"You should let me check your throat. It sounds raspy. Is it tender?" Nineveh watches me as I seat myself next to her, shaking my head.

Tiamet turns a page of what he's reading. "She'll be fine. Haven't you ever stayed up late?"

Nineveh stares at him. "Sure, but she always stays up, and this isn't what she looks like!"

"Nin, I'm fine." After taking a sip, I rest my forehead on the table, closing my eyes.

"See, she's fine." Tiamet closes the folder in his hands. "Maybe today will be less stressful."

"Stressful?" Nineveh looks at me.

"Apparently, Ayathesti is having trouble with that sample we acquired." Tiamet walks over, placing his hand on the back of my chair.

"What's wrong?" Nineveh asks.

Tiamet shrugs. "I wasn't the one out there working on it all night."

"Even if you wanted to, I wouldn't let you," I mumble.

"Well now, I just want to help." He shakes my chair teasingly.

"You're too incompetent." I lift my head and rest my

cheek in my hand, lifting my cup to smell the oojo inside.

"Well, I'm not so sure you're so competent yourself! Not as far as last night goes, anyway."

"I resent that." The saliva in my cheek has crept its way to the corner of my lip, and I slurp it back into my mouth. "I was fine until about . . . ten minutes after I cleaned up for the night."

"Sorry, not buying that. You went out of control a little too fast." He drags a chair from under the table and sits next to me.

"What can I say? I know what makes me tick." I smirk at him from behind my glass. "Not to mention I had nothing to eat yesterday."

"What is going on!" Nineveh looks between us. "I know you're not telling me something."

I straighten and let out a deep breath, placing a hand on her forearm. "Don't worry, Nineveh. It's just a stupid inside joke."

Nineveh looks at Tiamet, who shrugs and shakes his head. "You expect me to believe that you two have an inside joke? Oh please, Ayathesti, you can't even be in the same room as him for over five minutes without going ballistic!"

I purse my lips begrudgingly. "That's not true."

"Ha!" Tiamet raises a brow. "Not true since two nights ago."

"Yes. You've been acting different since we found you." Nineveh places her hand on top of mine. "What happened out there?"

I lose myself inside the darkness of the liquid as I stare into my glass. "I guess I just found myself. With nobody else to talk to, I had to learn to accept what I was saying and actually hear myself." I place the cup back on the table and stretch my arms behind my back. "It was . . . therapeutic."

Tiamet hides a smile, shaking his head.

"I could never do it. You're lucky to be alive, Aya! Promise me you'll never run off like that again." Nineveh moves her hand to my shoulder.

I put my hand on Nineveh's shoulder opposite to mine, and look at her mockingly. "If you can promise Tiamet will stop acting like an egotistical maniac and not get under my skin, then I can promise you I won't get mad and run away to confront his lies."

"Well that's not fair! It's Tiamet. There's no chance of that happening." Nineveh's bottom lip pouts forward.

"People change."

"Not people like him," she says.

"Ouch . . . I'm right here, Nin." Tiamet slumps in his chair, arms folded.

"I was like him. I changed." I push against the back of the chair to balance it on its hind legs. Something pulls on my boot, and it begins to slip off my foot. I let go of the table, and the chair falls forward to rest on the floor again.

I glare at Tiamet in annoyance. "Seriously?

"What?" He smiles, lifting his hands up with a shrug.

"It's early, and you're gonna play games with me?" I lean forward, slipping my boot back on. Darkness dominates my vision when I sit up, my head swimming in a whirlpool. Flattening my palms on the table, I clench my eyes. *Please stop spinning . . .*

"It's not early . . ." He straightens.

"Are you okay, Aya?" Nineveh puts her hand on my arm.

I nod, taking a deep breath before opening my eyes. "Well." I slap my palms against my thighs and push against them to stand. "I better get back to work so everyone can leave."

Tiamet's expression turns serious, dropping any previous signs of banter. "Are you in any condition to work?"

"Rarely have I seen her like this!" Nineveh lowers her voice to a whisper. "And she's usually really drunk the night before in those cases."

"I heard that!" I grip the back of the chair to regain balance.

Tiamet snaps up as though to catch me.

"I'm fine." I pull my arm away and correct my posture. "Haven't you ever stood up too fast?"

Then I turn and walk out the door.

Tiamet - 47

I look up as the door opens and Jarem enters, looking around as though he's lost something important.

"Jarem?"

He looks at me, shoulders heaving. "Director, where's Nineveh?"

I shrug. "Last I saw she was at the table. She could be in her room or in the med tent."

"She's not in the med tent. I checked there already."

"Is something wrong?"

He starts back toward the rooms. "It's about the latest perimeter breach."

I stand up and follow him down the hallway. "You found something?"

Nineveh opens her door as his large fist pounds on it. "What's going on?"

"Miss Nineveh, I need you to come look at this."

"Jarem, what's going on?" I ask.

"It's that creature from the river. We've taken him to the med tent."

"Oh no . . ." The words slip from Nineveh's mouth as she rushes past him.

Ayathesti - 98

It seems like only a few hours have gone by when a bright orange light shines through the entryway of the tent. Looking over my shoulder, I see Tiamet enter.

"Checking in on me, are you?"

Tiamet shoves his hands in his pockets and leans against a tall cabinet, watching in silence.

I push a button to start the centrifuge cycle, then reach to my left and push another button on a small white timer attached to the cabinet. To follow it up, I grab a sanitation cloth next to the timer and wipe the surface of the table, cleaning up loose items as I go along.

Tiamet clears his throat.

I shake my head. "My work is quite boring to most people. I don't know why you want to watch."

"Are you about finished?" His voice carries a hint of something. *Is that sadness? Desire? I can't quite make it out.*

I look at him, shifting my weight to one foot, and shrug. "I think so, but I'll know for sure soon. What's wrong?"

Tiamet crosses his ankles, looking at the ground.

"T?" My eyebrows furrow, and my jaw clenches. *What's wrong? Why won't he look at me? Something must be affecting our ability to go home.*

"How much longer do you expect to be in here?"

"About an hour. Why?" I turn from the bin and stare at him.

"Come find me once you've finished up. We need to talk." He exits the tent without making eye contact even once.

After a few more wipe downs of several surfaces the timer beeps incessantly. I rush to the centrifuge and click it off, then stop the timer. Once the spinning stops I open the lid to pick up a small vial and hold it up to the light. The fluid appears to have filtered from the sample completely with this second round of being put through the centrifuge.

After donning a fresh pair of gloves, I use the buffer solution on the spectrophotometer and follow it up with a minuscule amount of solution from the DNA microtube. I take a deep breath. This is it—the final moment to determine the concentration and purity, and see if I wasted another entire day of work. I push the button till it snaps, and then the machine evaluates the sample.

A smile crawls across my lips after the grueling wait. After closing the lids on the microtubes firmly, I walk them to the freezer box and pack them into the coldest section. A flutter rages in my stomach. I clean up the remaining contents on the counter and rush from the tent.

The table sits empty, the lights dim. I peer at the time. *It's early enough. Everyone should still be eating*. Looking around, my eyes fall on Tiamet in the corner chair, twiddling his thumbs.

He looks up as my eyes land on him. "Aya."

"Whaaat's going on?"

He nods to the chair next to him. "Have a seat."

"Right, I forgot you wanted to talk." I make my way to the chair with a skip in my step and sit down, watching him. "What's up?"

Tiamet raises his tented hands to his chin. "How did it go?"

My blank expression twists into a smile. "I got it."

Tiamet raises his brow as a half smile finds his lips.

"That's great news."

"Yes, it is!" I lean back in the chair. "I thought you would be more excited, though."

"I'm excited. Now we can start the procedure to go home."

I'm smiling so wide that my cheeks begin to ache. "So what did you want to talk about?"

Letting out a sigh, he looks at me. "You won't like what I have to say."

I bite my lip, my smile fading. "What is it?"

Tiamet stands, putting his hands in his pockets, pacing in front of me.

"Tiamet . . . tell me." I uncross my ankles, intending to stand.

He puts his hands up, signaling me to stay seated. "I don't know how to tell you this."

"Not telling me isn't any better. Tiamet, you're freaking me out. Just spill it would you?" A wave of panic drowns me when he turns away.

"Our patrol picked something up . . . someone." He turns toward me, folding his arms.

"Someone? Did someone else get lost? I di—"

"Not one of us." His arms heave with the sigh.

My heart sinks into the ocean of panic it was treading before. I can't even get a word out. *Talk. Say something. Why can't I do anything but stare at him.*

'There, there. I'm still here for you. Come back to me,' the dark mistress of my mind taunts as I stare at Tiamet, waiting for him to keep talking.

"There was another perimeter breach."

"Who?" My eyes grow hot, my throat tightening.

"Reki." He casts his gaze upon me, dropping his arms to his sides.

Lost for words again, I try to swallow. The tears waste

no time as they crawl down my cheeks.

"I know this is hard to hear."

"Is he . . . okay?" My voice cracks.

Tiamet looks away. "We thought he would make it, but he—"

"Oh my . . ." I plunge my face into my hands to conceal the agony, a sob on my shoulders.

"I'm sorry." He steps toward me.

"No. I don't believe you."

"Aya, look at me." Another step toward me.

I snap to a stand. "This better be a sick joke, Tiamet. And it's *not* funny." I turn away, wiping my hands on my pants.

I hear his feet shuffle toward me moments before I'm engulfed in the warmth of his arms, his muscles gently holding all my anxieties inside me.

His breath carries over my neck with a whisper to my ear. "Aya . . . he's gone."

My knees give way, my body falling against his as we sink to the floor together.

"You're a liar."

"Aya."

"You said you would leave them alone." My head rests against his shoulder, tears falling onto his arm.

"We did. We don't know what happened. There was another perimeter breach, and when Jarem and his team got there, they—"

I shoot forward, whipping around to face him. "So they shot him? Why is it always shoot first, ask questions later?" My throat is still too tight to scream as loudly as I want to.

'You're his. He wanted to keep you for himself.'

Tiamet's soft palm rubs my shoulder. "I wasn't there. I don't know what happened. I don't think—"

"One person breaches our perimeter and he gets shot?" My cheeks are soaked with tears that refuse to stop flowing.

His shoulders fall in a sigh before he stands. "Look, I didn't have to even tell you about this. Only a few people know. But we didn't even bri—"

"You're keeping it a secret too? That's so low! He can't hurt anybody now, so why are you keeping him a secret!" The agony surges into uncontrollable anger—an anger I've felt in his presence many times before. *Why does he always make the fire inside me burn so hot?*

"We're not keeping him a secret. It's unnecessary information for everybody to know."

"Because you know it's wrong for it to have happened at all! I can't—" I close my eyes and hug my knees to my chest.

"We tried to save him, Aya. Nineveh saw to it herself." He comes back to the floor, kneeling next to me. "What would you have me do, Aya? I can't turn back time."

I scoff. "Nothing. Not like you would have done anything, even if I asked." I stand up and walk to the door. I reach to open it, but his hand takes a firm grip on my wrist. I whip around and glare at him. "Let me go!"

Tiamet shakes his head. "I can't let you leave."

I yank it from his grasp before walking out the door, sending a glare at him over my shoulder. The door slams behind me as I walk toward the medical tent. *What can I even do?*

'You can do nothing. You're worthless.'

What's done is done, and nothing can change that.

'If you had just stayed behind, he'd be alive.'

It's my fault? He can't be dead . . . But why would Tiamet make that up?

'To keep you for himself.'

I have to see for myself.

Nineveh stands from her chair. "Aya . . ."

"Where is he?"

Nineveh looks behind me, hesitating.

"I said where is he? Nineveh . . ." Hopelessness squeezes my chest.

Tiamet pushes the door to the side. Nineveh looks at him, then back to me before moving to a cloth-covered table and places her hand on the side of it. "I'm so sor—"

"Save it!" I snap, walking over to the table. I lift the top of the cloth to expose Reki's face. My eyes burn, and my breathing shallows when I see the long gashes in his cheek, running down his neck, and ending behind his shoulder. I fall onto his body in a sob.

Tiamet walks over and stops next to me, placing his hand on my shoulder.

"What—how . . ." I peel myself away and slowly lower the cloth back over the lifeless body. "I find myself hating you once more, wishing it had been me."

Tiamet lets his hand slide off of my back. "I'm sorry."

"I don't care. This was it. I'm done." Exiting the tent, I walk back to my room. I close the door behind me, determined not to come out until we leave.

The smell of oojo renders me conscious as it wafts under the door to my room. I peel my eyes open and blink. They're dry and swollen from crying. I sit up and look around, hoping it was all a dream. After slipping my boots on, I pull the door open and exit my room. I pace myself when walking down the hallway to find everyone in various places around the room. When I emerge from the darkness, they all seem to stop what they're doing, looking at me with concern. Avoiding eye contact with all but Tiamet, I walk to the oojo pot and pour a cup before seating myself at the table.

"Good morning," Hana says cheerfully.

I glare at her, then stare into my glass. "I have to leave."

Slapping the file in his hand onto the table, Tiamet takes a seat next to me. "Absolutely not." His voice is firm, definitive.

"His family needs to know!"

He shakes his head. "They have plenty of people there to look after them."

"He was their leader!" I stare at him. *Please . . .*

"I'm sorry, Aya. You can't leave."

I stand up, knocking my chair to the floor behind me. "Stop me!"

Just as quick as I can turn around, his hand is secured around my wrist. "This time, I intend to."

"Let go." I plant my feet into the ground to pull away.

Tiamet shakes his head. "You're not leaving. Not this time."

"What are you going to do? Lock me in my room?" I speak through gritted teeth, nearly causing me to spit at him when his hand constricts tighter around my wrist.

"If I must." His eye contact is unwavering. *How is he so calm, so collected?*

"Fine." I pick my chair back up and sit. His hand slides from my wrist as my heart pounds with fury against my chest. "When did you grow a set?"

"You'll want to watch it, Aya."

"Or what?"

"Or I'll report your little incident to the council. You're lucky I haven't already written it up." He takes his cup and sips from it.

"Why are you being such a hard ass suddenly?" I fold my arms, my shattered respect for him coming through clearly in my tone.

His face is like stone. "I'm not even going to answer that insubordination." He stands up and walks to the front door but hesitates with his fingers clasped around the handle. "If she tries to leave, notify me immediately." He yanks the door open and slams it shut behind him.

"House arrest?" I say out loud to nobody in particular while Nineveh and Hana avoid eye contact. "House arrest and isolation. Great! This will be fun. Screw both of you." I empty the contents of the cup into my mouth and slam it onto the table, glaring at them before walking down the hall to my room, locking the door shut behind me.

Tiamet - 49

I find myself in the lavatory with my hands on the sides of the sink, engaged in a staring contest with the mirror. My black hair has grown quite a bit since we arrived, the ends brushing near the top of my tired eyes. My skin appears to have grown darker too, or maybe my face is just dirty.

I fill my cupped hands with water and splash it onto my face before rubbing it in and pushing it into my hair. *The stress of everything lately hasn't been kind to me, and it shows.* And it wasn't just Ayathesti running off. The stress started setting in before then. *How did I think I was cut out for this?*

I sigh, staring at the sink and considering how much to include in my final version of the report. With Jarem as the lead of the security team, he'll have his own report compared against my own. Any attempt at hiding information to protect Ayathesti may result badly for me.

"Why am I protecting her from this?" I halfway hope for someone to answer. "Just do your job. Lead the people. Take charge. That's all you have to do. Get everyone back in one piece. With the sample . . ."

I pinch my lips together, nodding. "She'll hate you forever. Deal with it. You have a job to do. Damned if she gets hurt by it in the end. She only cared about herself when she took off." I return my focus to the mirror, straightening my posture. The tips of my hair brush the side of my forehead when I shake my head. With a nod and another deep breath, I leave the lavatory.

I poke my head into the security tent. "Who knows Jarem's

most recent location?"

There are three people in the back of the tent wrapping cords around nonvital monitors, and one person sitting in a chair observing the security feed. All eyes look toward me when I speak.

"Director, sir." The girl in the chair shoots to her feet. "Jarem left this tent about fifteen minutes ago, sir."

I nod a few times. "Did you see which direction he went?"

"Sorry, sir, I-I was watching the monitors . . . I—" Her cheeks flush pink over her marigold skin as she blinks a few times to avoid looking away.

"Oh, relax." I put my hand up, her shoulders visibly dropping with relief. "It's fine, I'll find him. Thank you. Keep up the good work." I step away from the tent and look around. It's hard to believe equipment is already being prepared for launch.

Even though I made the order, I hadn't expected things to move so quickly. Crates are stacking higher and thicker in various locations. People are bustling around with preparations to go home. *My job here is nearly done. The mission was a success, and not even by my doing.* I sigh as weights slough off my shoulders. *It's all thanks to the one person who couldn't care less about succeeding.*

Jarem's voice carries commands over the shuffle of people working. Night has fallen, making it harder to see without flood lights. I follow his voice, eventually spotting him through the crowd.

"Jarem," I holler over moving bodies.

He turns to face me. "Director. What can I do for you, sir?"

I nod, looking around in approval. "Nice work here. I didn't expect things to be attended to so quickly."

"You gave the order. Everyone is eager to get out of

here tomorrow. Hate the heat, they say. I figured nonessentials could be packed up to give us an easier morning."

"That is a good observation."

"Did you need something else, Director?"

"Jarem, I'd like to know what's been put in your report." No sense in beating around it.

"What do you mean, sir?" He points toward a stack of crates by a big boulder to someone holding a crate before redirecting his gaze toward me.

"I mean, what extent of detail are you including about the perimeter breach, search, and unfortunate death of that native man?"

"Oh. Well, all of it."

"All of it." I repeat with an expressionless nod.

"Yes. I didn't have it all recorded, so conversations are not verbatim, sir, but the search operation is vital to how we received the sample from those things." He folds his arms, squaring off with me. "That the very thing we retrieved the sample from passed through our perimeter. When we went to check on him, he was in a near death state, and we couldn't save him."

"Yes, you're correct Jarem. I believe it is best to keep that death as quiet as possible for now. At least until we understand what happened. Nineveh has agreed to examine the body upon our return." I mimic his posture.

"Miss Nineveh, in her sweetness, would offer to uncover that truth." His sepia cheekbones adopt a splash of rose.

"Our understanding about them is invaluable. However, too many details could result in backlash from others about how things carried out here." I glance over to the security tent. "I don't want to jeopardize anyone's career over something that happened during this mission. Some of your patrol party could see that backlash if this ever got out."

Jarem rubs the back of his neck. "Director, with all due respe—"

"I'm not threatening anyone, Jarem. I'm simply asking we take care with the information that's available in this matter."

He nods. "I understand, sir. I won't alter my report, but I'll enforce confidential information."

I smile, the weight on my shoulders reducing a bit. "How about you get everyone here to call it a night? We can work more efficiently in full light. Looks like it shouldn't take long to finish up at this point."

"Whatever you say, Director." Jarem excuses himself to spread the word.

With my hands in my pockets, I look up at the sky and breathe deeply. It's time to start mentally outlining my report to the council. Sorrow creeps in as I accept the likelihood of losing my position in future missions as a result of the events that unfolded. *Maybe I wasn't cut out for this anyway, seeing as I couldn't even separate my feelings for Aya from my responsibilities.*

Ayathesti - 50

The ball rises and falls in a rhythmic pattern as I toss it into the air above me, my eyes unwavering from its motion as I lie on my bed. *How did it happen? Could I have really prevented it? What caused the severity of his wounds? Was that him breaching the perimeter? Maybe he was just running from some local predator . . .*

My eyes well up with guilt—and anger—the more I think about his cold, lifeless body on that table. Squeezing the ball after it lands in my hand, I clench my teeth. My heart pounds, and my breathing grows shallow before I chuck the ball against the door, causing it to rattle. It's all I can do to hold back my scream. *All I want to do is scream. Scream at Tiamet. Scream at Reki. And most importantly, scream at myself.*

I force myself off the bed and pace the small footpath beside it. A light tapping echoes from the other side of the door. Unsure if I'm ready to talk to anybody yet, I ignore it. The *tap-tap-tap* echoes once more, pushing me to grab the door handle and fling it open.

"What?"

Nineveh is standing there, bearing a plate of dried and broken bread pieces. "I thought you might be getting hungry. It's been nearly ten hours."

"No, thanks." I close the door in her face and turn around, folding my arms.

"You need to eat," she says, her voice muffled.

"I'm not hungry."

"Okay, but if you get hungry, you can come out, you know."

I stand there with my back against the door. *Should I keep my emotions inside or let them out? Will anything lift this pain?* Only a moment passes before more muffled voices speak. I slide my back down the door till I'm sitting on the ground and turn my head to press my ear against it.

"How's she doing?" Tiamet's voice is easy to make out.

"Not so well, I'm afraid." Nineveh's high pitch is equally noticeable. "She refuses to even eat."

"Let me try!" The annoying teenage-boy trait to Latif's voice makes my insides cringe.

"Latif, stop! If she won't talk to me, I'm doubtful she'll talk to you," Nineveh says.

"I could always give it a shot." I roll my eyes, even though my stomach flutters at Tiamet's offer.

"Perhaps we should give her more time . . ." Resentment tingles in my fingertips when Nineveh makes this suggestion.

I pull my ear from the door. *If I'm not allowed to talk to anyone, I'll talk to myself instead. If I just pretend like someone's listening, maybe it will help, just like it did by the river.*

"I'm sorry, Reki . . . If I hadn't shown up, none of this would have happened." A lump crawls into my throat before nestling there, making it hard to swallow. My voice cracks. "I feel so awful for this happening to you, Reki. If I had just isolated the DNA one day sooner, we would have left. Why would you come here? Honesty . . . I just want somebody to take this pain away. I don't think I have the strength to try on my own. You were there to help me before, even though you didn't know a damn thing I—"

My heart panics when another knock rattles the door. I hesitate and clear my throat before raising my voice to answer. "What?"

"Aya, it's Tiamet. Open up."

Just hearing his voice shows how difficult it may be for me to stay upset with him. A small smile crawls onto my lips though my throat is still tight from the emotions threatening to burst from me. "Is that a request or a direct order?"

"No games. I just want to talk."

With a slow hesitant lick to my lower lip, I stand up, crack the door open and look at him. In one hand, he holds the same plate Nineveh presented earlier and holds a cup in the other. His eyes drown in sorrow when he looks at me. It's an expression I've only seen on his face one other time: the night he chased me home from the Zeyo and stood outside my door—the night I broke him.

"May I come in?" His voice matches the gentleness of his eyes.

I step away from the door, pushing it open for him to enter while simultaneously picking up the ball that had ricocheted into the corner.

He motions toward the bed. "May I?"

I raise my brow and shrug, biting the inside of my cheek and motioning for him to sit.

"You've been in here a while." He taps the door with his foot to shut it behind him.

"Yes, I'm under house arrest, remember?" I can't help my response being snappy.

"Telling you to stay here was not an implication that you're restricted to this tiny room."

"Sure made it seem that way."

"How so?" He sits. "I said not—"

"Oh, shut it, Tiamet. Specifically telling them to come get you if I tried to leave? Yeah, that's not an implication at all, now is it." I take a deep breath and close my eyes, attempting to calm down. "What was I supposed to do otherwise? Sit there at the table and put up with everyone staring and tiptoeing around me? Ergo, room."

"Come on, Aya. Sit. Have some food."

I look from the plate to the cup, then at his face. Somehow, somewhere, a sudden likeness of Reki emits from him, a likeness that makes my stomach constrict with the threat of tears. With a shaky breath to prevent a breakdown, I turn away and bounce the ball against the floor, catching it when it comes back up. I hang my head. The tears are unstoppable. They roll down my cheeks like a silent river.

A hand brushes the side of my arm in a caring touch. His proximity closes in behind me. "It's okay."

The tears seem to flow with more ease after hearing his words. I shake my head, disagreeing.

"Talk to me, Aya." He raises his other hand to my other arm. The warmth in his palms soaks through the ice barrier that has been surrounding me for the past day.

I bury my face in my hands, a sob shaking my shoulders. "It's all my fault . . ." The words spill out as a muffled sob into my hands.

"How could you know?" He rubs the sides of my arms.

"If I had just stayed here, he . . . he would . . ." My knees give way, gravity taking me.

Tiamet follows me down, stroking my arms from behind. "You did nothing wrong. This is not your fault. I'm the one in charge. I take full blame for this. You should blame me for this."

The warmth spreads when he wraps his arms around me. I lean my face against his arm, hugging him closer. "I'm sorry." My breath is still shaky, but the sobbing waters calm.

Tiamet holds me in silence, his breath brushing my hair against my skin in a steady rhythm.

A shiver runs down my spine. "You have always kept true to your word. I should not have accused you of . . ." The lump in my throat returns. "Of . . ."

"Aya, you were in shock. I've taken the brunt of your anger before. I can handle it." His nose weaves into my hair, his chest pressing against my back as he breathes in. My shoulders relax as I lean into him.

My heart thuds furiously against my ribcage, and I bury my eyes into the crook of his arm, conceding to the sorrow. *Dare I embrace this moment? It's hardly a gesture of romance. But then why do I feel like it could possibly last forever? I could stay here, wrapped in his comfort.* The option seems real until a tap sounds from the door.

"Aya, it's Nineveh . . ." *As if she doesn't know I can recognize her voice.*

"Yes?"

"Is Tiamet still in there? Jare—er—someone in security is looking for him."

Tiamet breathes in another breath of my hair before pulling away, looking at me with longing. "Yes, Nin, let him know I'll be one moment."

I look at him before closing my eyes and rest my head against his shoulder.

"I told him already. He insists it can't wait!"

He sighs, loosening his embrace and making his way to stand. "Maybe he just wants a reason to talk to her." He smiles and walks over to the door before looking back.

I stare at him, watching the battle between me and the responsibility of others in his eyes. "Go," I whisper, nodding my head at the door.

Hand on the knob, he looks at me. "I'd love a smile."

I force a smile to the corners of my lips. "Just go." I break eye contact and look at my hands tangled with each other in my lap.

He sighs again before the door opens. "What's the deal? Why is he being so impatient?"

"I wish he would tell me! But he wouldn't. I didn't know what else to do. I mean, after all, you are . . ." Nineveh's voice trails off as they walk away.

I scoot back to lean against my bed and rest my head upon it. The cup tips over, depositing the fluid onto my blouse. Pinching my lips together, I close my eyes and sigh.

Tiamet - 51

"After all, you are the director." Nineveh walks with me down the hallway as I fight every urge to look back at Ayathesti's door.

"Yes, yes. I know I'm the director. It's just getting late. I don't know what could be so important it can't wait till morning."

Nineveh shrugs as we exit the tent.

We approach Jarem, who's waiting outside with his arms crossed.

"What's going on, Jarem?" I look around. Save for a few security members wandering about, there's nobody else in sight.

He straightens his posture as we approach him. "Director, sir . . . We have a big problem."

"Big problem? We don't need big problems right now. What's happened?"

He looks at Nineveh and then back to me, as though waiting for approval before continuing on. I fold my arms, realizing how serious it is. "Nineveh . . . would you excuse us?"

She huffs, pouting her lower lip.

"Sorry, Miss Nineveh," Jarem says. "It was a pleasure to see you again, but this is a matter of top security clearance. With approval, I can catch you up later over a cup of oojo or something."

Really? A "top security clearance matter" and he's finding time to flirt? I clear my throat. Nineveh's eyebrows go upward, and a soft smile graces her lips before she turns and walks away.

"Sir, our camera streams picked up something I think you should look at."

"Shit, more of them crossing the perimeter?"

His expression is ice cold as he shakes his head. "No, this couldn't be them. It's impossible."

My curiosity is piqued as he motions for me to follow him into the security tent.

"Go ahead and play the recording for the director," he says to the same girl that was monitoring the feed earlier. She presses a few buttons, and the footage plays.

I stand there. There's a flash of light and movement. It's so quick I struggle picking up on what it is. I furrow my brows. "What was that?"

Jarem shakes his head. "I couldn't pick it up on normal speed either. I had her slow it down. Go ahead, Serli."

I step closer to the screen, watching closely. The light flashes over the entire image. As the exposure equalizes, my stomach wretches. An elongated cranium and a body propelled by two legs, it bolts across the screen. This is nothing like the people in the village we visited. It moved at a great speed and jumped over the fifteen-foot perimeter pole.

My throat finally loosens enough to speak. "Do we have another view of this incident? I want to see where it's coming from and where it's going."

Jarem nods to Serli, who pushes a few more buttons. I watch as the creature emerges from a beam of light in the middle of the terrain. It looks around and approaches the perimeter. Then it stops, exposing its teeth in a snarl, and jumps backward. It looks around and crouches before jumping over the perimeter beam, launching itself at something out of the frame.

"Is that it?" I'm at a loss for words.

Arms folded, Jarem nods. "We checked other feeds, but this was it."

"What the fuck."

"Sir?" Jarem places a hand on the back of Serli's chair.

"Can we get those clips saved? This . . ."

"Before, we didn't have that option if we wanted to keep all the feeds going at once. Since tonight is our last night, most of the monitors are now only online if triggered, so we have a few seconds we can use to save this."

I nod. "Yes . . . we'll need to show this to the council. I… I may have learned about this type of being in my academy days, but it's been so long . . . "

"Sir?" Jarem rests his hands on his belt.

I look at him, wide-eyed and lightheaded. "This could be what killed Reki."

"We're ill equipped to protect ourselves from a violent being such as this. What do we do?" He stares at me. Serli looks up, also awaiting the answer.

"Keep it quiet. Inform only security members. Set them up however necessary for optimal use throughout the night. I'll load the launch capsules so we can get out of here as early as possible."

"Director, you're looking at pulling an all-nighter. Is that wise?"

"Jarem, I have no other choice. I can't cause panic. I trust the team you've selected, and that thing is at the perimeter. That's a decent distance, so we should be okay." I sigh and clasp my hands together. "But I don't want to risk sticking around longer than we have to. At first light, we'll finish packing so we can leave."

He nods and moves to walk past me. I place my hand on his shoulder to stop him. "Oh, and, Jarem . . . bring it to Nineveh in a gentle manner. We need to figure out if this thing could be responsible for Reki's death."

A sympathetic smile tugs at his cheek. I stand there frozen in place.

Serli clears her throat. “Um . . . sir?” she says in her mousy voice.

I stare at the monitor. “Yeah?”

“You should sit down. You’re as white as the clouds.” She stands up, offering her chair. I nod, still staring at the screen before sitting.

Ayathesti - 52

After hours of being holed up in my room, dreading the thought of leaving, I move from the spot on my floor. It's time to make an appearance. I can't even be sure how long I've been sitting in the same spot, staring at the wall after Tiamet left, thinking of all the things needing attention once we arrive home. *Have I allowed myself enough time to be hidden away? Maybe not, but I'm feeling claustrophobic.*

I wipe my hands on my pants and walk to the door, pushing through a wave of hesitation before turning the knob. With my dirty shirt in hand, along with the cup and plate, I step into the hallway. *It's dark. Everyone must still be sleeping.* I make my way to the kitchen and set the dishes next to the sink before heading out the door.

The tendrils of crisp air brush my skin and play with my hair. I take a breath. The cold fills my lungs, making me feel lighter. *And free.* I look around the base. There were stacks of crates and boxes everywhere. It's evident that people are eager to get home.

The sun is still moments away from rising on the horizon. Even the stars are still visible and glistening beyond the setting moon. *I could just float away.* I feel so large yet so insignificant. *This is it. We did it.* My heart races with the desire to move forward at full throttle. The heavy weight of leaving is replaced with the anticipation of returning, to look upon this land again with a fresh pair of eyes. How much will change while we're away?

Well, at least they haven't packed the water closets yet. I smile and beeline for the lav.

"Aya!" Nineveh's voice cries out.

"Oh god, no." I mutter and walk faster.

"Aya, wait up!" Her voice grows louder as she catches up.

"What is it, Nineveh? I'm not really in the mood to talk." *The sun isn't even up yet. Why is she?*

"Aya! We're going home!"

I stop at the lavatory door and turn to face her, a look of vacancy on my face.

"Isn't that exciting?" Nineveh looks me up and down.

"Do you need something? I'm on a mission." I toss my shirt over my shoulder and shift my weight to one foot.

"Why are you so . . . I don't know if I've ever seen you so clean." Nineveh eyes the shirt.

"Gee . . . thanks, Nin." I purse my lips, raising an eyebrow. "I had a beverage accident on my shirt, and I need to rinse it out. Do you mind?"

"Oh, not at all!" Nineveh stands there with a bright smile planted on her face, like a robot on pause.

I stare at her, blinking slowly.

"Oh, you mean alone?" She puts her hand to her mouth, stifling a giggle. "Well, do you mind if I wait here for you?"

Looking around, I get a glimpse of Tiamet speaking with Jarem, delegating work to those emerging from the tents.

"Did he tell you to keep an eye on me?" I scoff. "Honestly, Nineveh, I'm too exhausted to even bother right now. Do whatever you want."

I turn on my heel and enter the lav. I scrub my shirt vigorously to take out some of the harbored frustration from the past day. At least five minutes had to have passed before I could no longer avoid eye contact with myself. I look into the mirror, locking eyes with my reflection. The stress and sadness of the events leading to this moment have sunken into my eyes. *At least I look just as exhausted as I feel. How can anyone stand to look at me in this state?* My skin has lightened at least two shades, and my hair has fallen from its restraint. My lower lip is split and scabbed over from dehydration. I grip my blouse and ring the water from it.

"I matter. I made a difference. Nothing that happened here was a mistake, for it shaped me into the person I never had the strength to be on my own. You are worthy of everything you desire to be." I stare at myself in the mirror while saying these words. A rush of fulfillment surges through me, sending chills over my entire body, dissolving the darkness crouching in the shadows of my mind. I close my eyes and wipe the tears away in acceptance. Tossing the shirt back over my shoulder, I exit the lavatory and smile at Nineveh.

"So how are you doing?" Nineveh follows me as I walk back toward our tent.

"I'm fine."

"Did you get the stain out?"

"Yes, Nineveh, I did." My step is determined, confident.

"So we're expecting to have everyth—"

"Nin, I'm just going to stop you there." I stop outside the tent door and look at her. "I'm not exactly in the mood to entertain lengthy discussions."

She sighs. "Yes, that's fine."

"I'm sorry, but . . . I'm exhausted. I didn't sleep at all last night. I didn't even realize it was morning until I came out here." I take a deep breath. "I just want to close my eyes for a bit, but I'll be up shortly."

My eyelids grow heavier with each step toward my bed. They weigh down enough for me to slip away effortlessly when my head hits the pillow.

Ayathesti - 53

I sit up in a state of confusion when a loud clanking reverberates through the walls. I catch my bearings as I enter the hallway now flooded with light. The front canvas of the tent is now completely open to the outside world. A rush of excitement holds hands with the drag of sadness. They're disassembling the tents. *We're going home . . . and parts of me are still torn up about it.*

Nineveh is standing at the front of the hallway. "Oh, good, you're awake!"

"It looks like everybody's been busy."

"And you look rested. Are you feeling better?" she asks. I nod as she walks over. "Good. Now you can pack your room! I have extra boxes if you need them."

I look toward my bedroom door as an eerie sense of dread rains over me, as though something scary lives in that room.

"Unless you're not up for it . . ." Nineveh adds.

"No, I'm up for it. The sooner we can get back to normal life, the better."

I push my door open and step inside. *Where to start?* I look around. *It's not like I have much to pack.* I grab loose items around the room and stuff them carelessly into the chest at the base of my bed. The green ball I'd spent the past day with. The blouse that was now dry and stiff. Extra clothes. My spare, now dirty shoes. Crinkled up papers I'd stuffed into my pockets while working. Without paying much attention to what I grab, I keep tossing items inside.

Finally I reach down and pick up the bag I'd taken

with me to Reki's village. Grasping it in both hands, my heart swells with that unwelcome, familiar ache. I bring it to my nose and inhale deeply. It still smells of burning wood, throwing me back to that spot under the big tree by the river. My eyes grow hot, and I plonk it into the chest. I let out a deep breath and swallow the tears away.

"She's already awake and packing," I hear Nineveh say outside.

Tiamet. He's the only person who would ask if I'm awake and what I'm doing. I shake my arms, tossing away emotions. After closing the lid to the chest, I walk to the door.

"Oh!" I gasp and let out a chuckle, a hand on my chest. "You scared me."

Tiamet lowers his hand from its knocking position and stares at me. "Morning."

"Good morning!"

"So . . ."

"So . . ." I look past him with a shy smile. "Can I get by you real quick?"

"Oh, right." He steps back, allowing me to pass.

Nineveh looks at me when I approach. "That was fast!"

"Yes, I didn't have much. Just some crumpled up papers and extra clothes."

"That's fabulous! We'll get your chest to the module soon." Nineveh buries her nose back into her clipboard and walks away.

"Perfect." Looking back down the hallway, I see Tiamet standing in the same spot, a perplexed look on his face. I smile and walk out of what used to be the entrance of the tent, hoping he'll follow.

I count the seconds in my head as I walk through the morning heat to the lab tent. My smile fades with each moment I don't hear his voice behind me. "Stop it. You're being selfish. He's busy." I mumble as I walk into the tent.

"Who's busy?" Latif nearly drops a crate on the ground.

"Woah! Careful, Latif, you'll break something!" Panic drives me forward, and I grab the crate from his hand and set it on the table.

"C'mon, boss. I'm not completely incompetent. I did everything else while you were . . . indisposed."

I glare at him. "Excellent word choice. So what you're telling me is that I need to check on the sample?"

Tiamet laughs from the entrance of the tent. "Seriously, Aya? You think we'd let him pack something that important?"

I look over my shoulder at him. "Well . . . who else?"

"Pft. They asked me," Latif interjects. "I told them to forget it!"

"Yes, he saved the day. Wasn't confident he'd do it to your expectations and refused." Tiamet stops at the corner of the table. "So it's all yours. We're ready to get it up to the module as soon as you're ready for us to."

With eyes sparkling at Tiamet, I turn to Latif. "I can give credit where it's due. Nice job, Latif."

Latif and Tiamet furrow their brows in unison, looking at each other, then back at me.

"You feeling okay, boss?"

I sigh. "Yes, Latif, I'm alright. Why?"

"You're being a bit . . . how do I put this . . . happy?"

"What do you mean? I'm always like this."

Laughter shakes his shoulders.

"What's so funny!" I turn to Tiamet. "What's so funny?"

Tiamet grins widely. "In all the time I've known you, I think I may have seen you like this only once before."

"Well, I always feel like this."

"It certainly doesn't show, then." Tiamet folds his arms. "What's got you so elated?"

I flash him a shy, flirtatious smile before looking away. "Oh . . . We're going home!"

"Weird. Yesterday you wanted to stay."

"Who said I wanted to stay?"

"It was all over your face, Aya." Tiamet tilts his head.

"Wait a second, I didn't even see her yesterday," Latif says.

"I still exist even if you don't see me, Latif." My words drown in sarcasm.

He sneers his nose at me. "I'm not a complete idiot, despite what you think!"

"It's not necessarily what I think that makes you an idiot, Latif."

"Okay, children, calm down," Tiamet says.

I take a deep breath to anchor myself. "Sorry . . . Let's just get this stuff packed and get out of here."

Tiamet watches me moving about the tent before I stop and turn to him. *The smile on his face . . . what is that? Hurt? Confusion?*

"We don't need a babysitter. We can handle this." Hopefully, my attempt at sounding confident doesn't come off as rude.

Tiamet's smile grows bigger, and he puts his hands up, backing away toward the exit. "Yes, ma'am. You know where to find me."

I let out an exasperated breath. *That whole thing was more frustrating than I intended . . .* I check the freezer chest to secure the sample for the journey. Once it is ready to go, I pack the remaining supplies into crates and stack them outside the door where Latif had begun piling them. What I'm really doing is trying to quiet my mind. It seems to be working . . . for the most part. At least I feel less sadness about Reki.

Crate by crate, I witness my temporary life on Earth being placed in pieces on top of one another outside. We have the door tacked open and the generator off, preventing the room's temperature to regulate. A bead of sweat slithers down my temple, and I wipe it away with the back of my wrist.

Setting the final box down, I push the hair stuck to my forehead off to the side. I turn for one last look. Only the walls, cabinets, and table remain. A breeze blows, chilling the perspiration on my skin, sending a shiver down my spine. I force myself to swallow the lump forming in my throat as I stare at the barren room.

"Aya!" Nineveh shatters my world from afar.

I clear my throat and turn, placing a hand atop the final crate before walking away, refusing to look back.

"The last of the bedrooms are being taken down. I suggest you do a sweep of your room." She taps on her clipboard. "You should probably change into your launch suit while you're at it."

I nod and smile at her. "Thanks, Nin. I'll do just that."

I walk to the small area that was once my room and stand there. Closing my eyes, I scour my memories, looking for something I may have missed earlier. I unroll the suit and rub the cloth between my fingers before putting it on. The fabric is light, and it breathes, but I leave it open partway for more airflow. I sit on the bed and place my hand on top of the pillow before reaching underneath, then pinch a small, hard, round piece of stone. I retract my hand from the pillow and look at the item in my hand: a rust-colored stone with a hole through the center—a bead from his hair. I had taken it as I was crying over his body on that table.

"Reki . . ." Closing my hand around it, I hold it to my chest. "I won't let your death be a waste. I'll be the strength you showed me I have."

I stand, zip my suit up the rest of the way, tuck the bead into the waistband, and check that Rothe's gift is still there before I enter the hallway. Tiamet appears from his room just down the hall, also changed. I smile at him and walk by in silence. I stop when he places a hand on my shoulder. Frozen with hope, I slowly turn to him. His face hosts a smile of indescribable softness.

"You look quite happy," I whisper.

He nods. "I am. You also look happy."

Averting my gaze to the floor, I nod. "It will be nice to get home."

As though sensing my hesitation, Tiamet tucks a finger under my chin and tilts my gaze up. "What's wrong?"

I shake my head. "Nothing. Things are changing, and I'm just trying to keep up. I'm petrified of being left behind…"

His eyebrows jump as he slides his hands down my arms to grasp my hands. "I would never leave you here, or anyone else for that matter." He holds my hands against his chest.

I chuckle. "That's not what I mean."

"Oh . . . Care to elaborate?"

"With everything that's happened, I just . . . want to be as happy to go home as everybody else is."

"You're not?"

I sigh. "I am. Just—I'm saying goodbye to this place in my own way. It won't affect me later if I do it right the first time."

Tiamet nods slowly. "I think I get it. Process it all you need. Think of all the positive things taking place once we arrive home."

"Yes . . . I love to work, but something about this place has changed a piece—"

"I'm not talking about work." Tiamet's smile dances with hidden meaning.

I smirk in response. "C'mon, T, the cots weren't *that* bad!"

One of his hands finds the small of my back. He pulls me closer, his voice growing more hushed. "It's not about the beds either . . ."

My face grows warm as I'm drawn into his stare. My knees weaken, and my chest heaves while my heart pounds in my ears. *Why can't I stop thinking of the relief that no one is around to witness me melting?*

"What, then?" My voice is but a whisper.

He moves in, his face growing closer to mine, when he presses our cheeks together. "We'll be equals." He pulls away, pressing his fingertips into my lower back.

"Aren't we already?" I know what he's implying, but I want him to say it directly.

"Well . . . yes."

I feign confusion with a raised eyebrow. "Then what do you mean?"

"I won't be your mission director anymore."

"And?" My heart feels as though it's leaping from one side of my chest to the other. I feel the smooth fabric of his suit beneath my fingertips.

"You know, maybe I'll just let you sit on that." His hand slides off my back, his fingertips brushing against my waist as he pulls away. "Maybe I'll let you find out once we get there."

Tiamet - 54

Leaving her on the edge like that was almost too much to bear. I walk away, dreaming of the day I get to kiss those lips again. But now is not the time to get swept away by those gold-laden ocean eyes of hers. I make my way across the compound to Jarem, the feel of her fingers lingering on my chest.

"Jarem."

He turns from his conversation with two others and straightens his already perfect posture. "Sir."

I glance toward his team members. "Anything new to report on our potential visitor?"

"No. I have my people watching around the clock with no sign of anything unusual."

I nod, slapping him on the shoulder. "Great news, my friend. And that other bit of cargo we're taking home with us… It's secured with a sign off-from medical?"

He shifts his gaze to Nineveh across the once courtyard, clearing his throat. "We . . . eh . . . It's almost ready, sir. Miss Nineveh and I worked on a new rig to keep it in good condition until we reach the ship." I look toward Nineveh hauling pieces of pipes and wiring into the medical tent. His cheeks flush. "I was checking in with my personnel before assisting her to finish it."

"That's the last tent to get packed up before we can launch," I tell him. "I'd like to get out of here without any chance of that thing paying us a visit. If it's a night creature, I don't want to be anywhere near this place when darkness falls."

He nods again. "I understand, sir. I'll get right to it."

I smile at him, letting out a breath. "Great! You've done an amazing job here, Jarem. I'm glad they selected you for this."

Jarem clears his throat. "Director, um . . . There's something we neglected to acquire before our return."

"Oh?"

He looks out to the distance. "With that potential threat, I ordered my people to leave the perimeter posts where they are."

"Jarem."

He puts his hands up. "I know, I know. I was unwilling to risk losing anyone, and I also delegated all manpower here to keep watch over the compound."

"Jare—"

"I know you'll get shit from The Council for that. So I'm requesting our team hold back after other pods have launched so we can pick them up."

"Jarem!" I say again. He rubs his neck, looking at me with a smudge of shame on his face. "It's okay. You made the right choice for everyone's safety."

His shoulders visibly loosen as I continue. "It's not ideal to leave them where they are. Leaving our tech could alter the natural evolution of this planet's inhabitants. We'll be back, but too much time will have passed between now and then. We need them picked up before we go, so thank you for volunteering. Too bad we didn't think to bring one of those unused buggies from home, eh?"

He chuckles. "I appreciate your understanding, sir. I'd better not keep Miss Nineveh waiting if we're to leave before sundown. Excuse me."

I nod, turning to the two he was just speaking with. Their sunken-in eyes send a pang of guilt through me. "How are you guys holding up?"

Serli nods. "Not a worry, sir. I am still up for

retrieving the perimeter posts."

Pimly smiles at Serli. "I won't claim I'm not excited to sleep on the trip home, but I, too, am capable of finishing our tasks before then."

"Great. If there's anything you guys need, find me. Jarem should focus on helping Nineveh get our new cargo secured before launch."

They nod in unison.

"Does anyone know where Nineveh is hiding?" Latif says, approaching from behind. "I've seen her head popping in and out of groups all day, but I can't seem to pin her down." He stops, hands on his hips, looking at all three of us with a squint. "This looks exciting. What are we talking about?"

"Miss Nineveh is in the med tent"—Serli nods her head to the side, toward the last tent standing—"with Jarem."

His eyes widen as he looks toward the tent. "She what?"

With an unconcerned smile, I tell him, "I've asked them to get something ready for me before we go."

"What the hell could a moronic meathead like him help a brilliant mind like Nineveh with?"

Serli glares at him, and Pimly clears his throat.

"You guys can resume your security duties. Thanks," I say, dismissing them. They turn and walk away, Pimly pushing Serli away by the shoulder while she continues to glare at Latif.

"He's the muscle required for the stuff she'll need help with." I turn back to Latif, his face growing red.

"They've been working on it all day?"

I bobble my head left to right. "On and off, yeah. It's vital—" He opens his mouth to speak. "And no, you can't help or even know what it is. It's classified."

"Pft. Classified. I've seen how you handle 'classified'

with Ayathesti."

"This is one thing Ayathesti must not discover. There are five people who know about it, and that's already too many."

"So those security people get to know about it, but I don't? Dude, she's my girlfriend. I'm gonna find out anyway."

I shake my head. "No, I don't think she'll tell you no matter how hard you press her."

"I'll find out. I have my ways." He refuses to look away from the tent.

"Latif, this is something not even your father would tell you."

His chest roars with laughter. "My father? My father would tell me anything to get me in his successor's seat."

I smirk. "But I know you really don't want that."

"Yeah . . . well, I've been thinking more about that. Might be worth looking into when we get back." He stops laughing, a hand against his thigh, as if tucked into an invisible pocket.

"Trust me. What's going on in that tent isn't anything you're gonna want to see."

"You're not helping my decision to not walk in there, bud."

I put a hand on his shoulder. "Your inability to not blab to Aya is too risky."

"I don't blab!" He furrows his brow.

I pat his shoulder, laughing. "Yeah, okay. If you say so. Just stay out of there, would you?"

He rolls his eyes. "Fine. But only since you asked *so* nicely."

"Let's finish packing the pods and get off this rock!" I turn and walk with him toward the pods.

"Oh, man. I'm so done with sweating!"

"What do you mean? You look so much prettier with a shine to your skin!"

He punches my shoulder, sending us both into laughter.

Ayathesti - 55

I soak in the sun's beauty saddled on the horizon. The rest of my group stands around me near our launch capsule, their voices lost in the dull roar of other conversations saturating the air.

I want to remember this view forever. Something to grasp onto when I get overwhelmed. The area where we'd set up our camp looks so different as a barren land, it's rather inviting. *How fortunate am I to be part of the first team to come here? Lucky? No, I earned this.*

One by one, each person enters the module, eventually leaving me to stand outside alone. I'm not quite ready to let go of the view yet, but with one final breath, I force myself away from the sky and step inside, refusing to look back. I place myself in the final empty seat. Closing my eyes, I bow my head.

Tiamet stands at the panel opposite to the door. With a sequence of buttons, the hydraulics hiss and hum while pulling the door closed. My stomach wretches, screaming at me to acknowledge the sadness of this ending. The door latches shut with a clank. Another sequence of beeps prompts me to open my eyes. I watch Tiamet walk back to his seat across from mine. The lights dim as a series of bells ring out with increasing speed. Finally one long beep sounds, and a low rumble echoes beneath us. The force of liftoff drags every inch of my body into the chair. As I maintain eye contact with Tiamet, one final tear crawls down my cheek.

The force of our ascension subsides as we break free from the atmosphere. With a small shudder, our module docks. I sit in my chair, listening to the locking mechanisms creating an airtight seal. The lights in the cabin grow brighter, and one above the door pulses green. Even after the chair releases its grasp of my suit, I remain seated for a good few minutes until everyone else has vacated the compartment.

I stand. The lack of weight is bewildering. I flash back to when we first landed on the Earth's surface, when I'd felt like my movements were weighted down by boulders. It's no wonder the native people are so much smaller. The amount of gravity is crushing.

I'm consumed by a wave of familiarity yet remain disconnected from my surroundings upon re-entering the main room with the big window. I can't help but look out to see her surface glowing in the darkness. The shiny blue marble looks so small from this distance. Clouds are forming storms over the surface. The lands next to the deep oceans host shades of green and orange. The entire collection of terrain is tucked neatly inside the glow of a healthy atmosphere.

As I lean against the steel beam framing the window, pride and acceptance replace sadness and longing. Triumph and hope grip my soul, sending me to a place of contentment as I hold the image of the planet in my gaze. I lean against the glass, the corners up my lips turning up in a toothy smile. With my forehead pressing against the clear surface, I close my eyes and sigh—a silent promise to return. A hand radiates heat into my shoulder.

"Isn't it magnificent?" My heart feels like it could float away when I speak. Tiamet's smell engulfs me as I turn and look at him, my head still resting on the window. "Tiamet . . . I . . ." I take a deep breath, convincing myself to maintain this new habit of speaking openly with him.

"It's okay, Aya. We don't need to live inside any regrets we adopted while we were here."

I smile and look back to the sphere suspended in darkness. "I was just going to say thank you. If you hadn't put in a good word for me, I never would have received this opportunity."

Tiamet's eyebrows twist as he shakes his head. "I didn't."

"You didn't?"

He presses his lips together. "You were their number one candidate. Didn't even have to fight for it like I did."

"You're being modest. I'm sure you didn't have to fight, Director." I bump my elbow against his teasingly. "You're clearly the best person for it."

He shrugs, folding his arms. "The council had four others in consideration ahead of me."

My eyes jump back to him, perplexed. "That makes no sense. How'd you convince them?"

He smiles. "I took a lesson from the smartest person here. Made a big fuss about how important being on point and thorough is. Once the others saw that I wasn't giving up, they ducked out."

"I'm glad they picked you. Obviously, it was the right choice."

"You're just saying that because you know I let you get away with so much more than others would have." Tiamet smirks and pokes at my side.

I click my tongue and chuckle. "I resent that!"

"Because you know I'm right!"

"Actually it's because I got the chance to know you better. I've been avoiding that for a long time . . ."

"Wait, why have you been avoiding that?" His smile fades like waves washing away the shoreline.

Embarrassment slaps pink onto my cheeks. "I'm sure you've heard the saying 'Never meet your heroes.' Well, it's kind of similar. I've just felt something for so long, I was terrified for anything to change. I didn't want it to go away…"

"Did it?" He steps closer, wafting his smell through me once again.

Shaking my head, I look up at him.

Tiamet's content smile returns as he strokes my arm with his fingertips. "That's a relief."

"Oh! *You're* relieved?" I chuckle.

He nods, refusing to break eye contact. "I am. You're not the only one who's scared of things changing."

"Oh, would you two come on!" Nineveh breaks our staring contest as we look at her simultaneously. "We're all eager to get home and you two are just standing over there babbling about who knows what!"

"Relax, Nineveh." Tiamet shifts his weight, letting his fingertips slip from my arm before starting toward her. "We were just chatting."

I watch them walk away, Nineveh's voice echoing off the walls as they pass through the doorway into the next room. "You can chat when we get home! Oh, also Jarem needs to see you. He said it's urgent."

I turn once more to stare out the window, placing a gentle hand on the glass. "Until next time . . ." I whisper my farewell before turning to join everyone in the sleeping room.

Nineveh stands at the console in the center of the room again. I step into my pod and strap in. The experience is as I remember from before, though this time I feel different. My heart and mind are at peace, rather than rattling around inside me with fear and anxiety. I lay my head back and look at Nineveh, who proceeds with initiating the sleep sequence for the flight. I look up toward the nozzles as they disperse purple fog into the chamber.

I look around the other pods and gaze upon everyone's faces before locking on to Nineveh, who looks to

Tiamet in the entryway. With my mind attached to her as an anchor, my eyelids grow heavy, and I'm consumed in the darkness of sleep while the pod coddles me in a gelatin cocoon.

Tiamet - 56

"Jarem is in cargo, waiting for you," Nineveh says as we walk to one of the pod chambers. I nod and continue on to cargo as she takes a place at the console in the center of the room.

"Sir." Jarem stops pacing and faces me, one hand covering his other arm.

"Jarem. Nineveh said it's urgent?" I puff my chest out in an attempt to feel as big as him.

"Director . . ."

"Yes, Jarem?"

"I—it—they—" His face is pale, his eyes wide.

"Woah, hey. What happened. Are you okay?" I step toward him and place my hand on his shoulder.

"That thing . . ." His chest heaves under his torn shirt, trying to catch his breath.

My throat tightens. "Did anyone get hurt?"

He shakes his head, lifting his hand and showing me the wound. "Just me."

Three slashes stretch across his forearm. Although covered by his makeshift bandage, blood saturates it entirely.

I wince at the sight. "Did you not get medical from Nineveh?"

He shakes his head. "I didn't want to drag her into anything."

"Jarem. She's medical director and perfectly cap—"

"Tiamet."

I stop and look at him. *Is the lack of color in his face because of the cut or from what he witnessed?* His skin gleams with sweat.

"Sorry, Director . . . sir." His eyes are wide, captive to an empty look. "We . . . It's on board."

My eyebrows sink. "What do you mean it's on board?"

"Shit!" He pushes past me to the room's entrance. With the pull of a lever in the wall, the thick steel door to the main decks of the ship slam shut.

"Jarem. What do you mean it's on board?" I turn to him, my heart slamming against my chest as I hang on the edge of his words.

"We were putting the last of the perimeter posts inside when it showed up. It almost . . . " His eyes narrow, as though reliving the memory over again. "I pulled Serli in right from under its . . . whatever weapon it had. Tiamet—er—sir. It's locked in the capsule."

"The hell you say?" I whip around to look at the door to the capsule. "How?"

"I managed to knock it out . . . somehow. It was all so fast, I don't—" Blood seeps through his fingers.

"Are you sure it's contained in there?" I ask. He nods, struggling again to catch his breath. I direct him over to a short stack of crates and sit him down. "Okay, wait here."

I open the door back to the main deck of the ship and walk through. I walk in to see Ayathesti's pod nearly filled with fog. "Nineveh . . ." My voice is shaky.

She whips around to look at me, concern on her face. *I must really sound freaked out to give her that look.*

"We need you in cargo. Now." I don't wait for an answer and pass back through the doorway. My hand shakes weakly on the metal lever as I wait for her to enter before closing it again.

"What's so worrisome that you've lost your tan, Tiamet?" she asks.

I nod toward the crates. Jarem is leaning forward,

head bowed. A small pool of thick blood is gathering at his feet. She gasps, rushes over, and kneels beside him.

"What happened?" She touches the hand covering the wound.

"He says a creature with a weapon of some sort attacked them." I walk closer to them.

"How long has he been like this?" She peels the sticky bandage wraps from his arm one by one.

"I can't say how long exactly. It was before they left the surface."

"That's at least twenty minutes!" She rushes to a locker in the wall and flips the door open. After digging around for a minute, she returns with a new roll of bandages, gauze, a syringe, a small glass bottle of fluid, and a larger bottle of fluid. She kneels beside Jarem again and pours some of the liquid from the large bottle over his arm. He jolts, clenching his fist, and makes a hissing noise through gritted teeth.

"Oh, Jare, I'm sorry. I have to clean it to see what's going on."

I hover over her as she works. "Is it supposed to still be bleeding like that? I've never seen an injury bleed that long."

Her ponytail shimmies as she shakes her head. "No, most injuries would have clotted by now."

I lean closer before the smell hits me. It's sharp and sour, forcing me upright again.

She places a bloody hand on the side of Jarem's face, making him look at her. "Jare, this is going to hurt . . . a lot."

He nods. Nineveh takes a gauze piece and wipes around the lacerations.

"That wasn't so bad." He chuckles before she puts the gauze directly on the openings in his flesh. A growl erupts in his throat, eyes rolling back, as he slams a fist against the crate closest to him.

"I know. Just a few more minutes." Her eyes grow wide, and she licks her lips, pinching them between her teeth. "Tiamet, I need you to go back to the locker and get the bottle of saline."

"What does it look like?" My heartbeat pulses in my ears.

She sighs and motions me closer. "Here." She grabs my hand and places it over the gauze. "Press, but not too hard."

I reposition myself closer to the floor and do as instructed while she rummages through the locker again. When she comes back she's got a small white glass bottle and a pine-green one in her newly gloved hands. My eyes plead for her to relieve me of wound-pressure duty before I hurl. She sticks the needle in through the top of the small white bottle and extracts fluid.

After dismissing me, she kneels in front of Jarem, one knee in the deep green puddle on the floor. Peeling away the gauze, she presses the tip of the needle around each gash, spacing them out to get good coverage. "That should help with the pain during this next part."

He's leaning his head back against the crate behind him, his eyes closed. His free hand is still balled in a fist. Grasping the saline, she floods the channels in his arm. Jarem winces, pounding his fist against the wood next to him.

"Almost done," Nineveh says, reaching for the pine-green bottle. She drenches a final gauze pad and places it over the three wounds. Lifting the wrap, she looks to me. "I need you to hold this spool off the ground so it doesn't get in the blood."

I loop my finger through the center of the spool so it can unwind as she wraps it around his arm. Resting the freshly bound arm against his torso, she places a hand on the exposed, undamaged skin of his chest. "There you go, Jarem. Not as good as new, but it should hold you over for a while."

With his head still leaning against the crate behind him, he peers at her, returning her gaze with a weak smile. He places his other hand on hers. "Sweet Miss Nineveh . . . I thank you."

Her cheeks flush, and she looks to the floor.

"He'll be okay now, right?" My fingers are tingling from the stress of the situation and my inability to do anything.

Nineveh nods, sliding her hand away from Jarem's arm to mop up the mess on the floor. "Yes, he'll be alright. Thank you for coming to get me . . . but, Tiamet, how did he receive that kind of wound? I've never seen anything like it. Not outside of history books, anyway."

I shake my head and watch her, pressing my thumb to my lower lip. "We had another perimeter breach last night. A freaky reptile-looking creature. Huge. It attacked them while retrieving the perimeter posts."

"Do you think those were from the claws of the creature?" She disposes of the blood-soiled items and snaps her gloves off before tossing them in the bin as well.

"He said it had a weapon, but that's all I got out of him. He was hysteric."

She puts the back of her wrist to her forehead and dabs at a bead of sweat. "Based on the cauterization of the epidermal layer and the lack of it in the lower tissues, it was most likely caused by a weapon of some kind."

I stare at her, expressionless.

"What?" She sighs, looking at her blood-stained hands.

"He also said it was on board their capsule. Locked inside. Unconscious." My stomach lurches with the idea of that thing being on the ship.

"Eject it." Jarem's voice is raspy and low.

I look over Nineveh's shoulder to him as he adjusts his posture. She turns to him as well and walks over. "Just relax," she says as she places a hand on his shoulder before looking at me. "Can you do that? Eject the contents of the capsule?"

Jarem coughs. "No . . . Eject the entire pod."

"We'll lose all cargo on that container if we eject the whole thing." I tap my foot as I think through the options. "We should depressurize it. Suffocate the creature while allowing it to remain attached to the ship. We lose no cargo, and we also get the chance to examine the creature once we get back."

"It's a threat to—" He sits forward, chest thrown into a coughing fit.

Nineveh sits on the crate next to him, rubbing her hand across his upper back in a soothing motion. "Shh . . . Let's get you to sleep." She lifts his good hand as she stands to pull him up.

Nineveh presses a few buttons at the center console, prompting his sleep cycle.

"I think you should eject the capsule . . . " Her voice is quiet, almost shameful, as she stares at him in his pod.

"If there are more of those things here, we need to know more about them. Our probes didn't pick up on them before we came. Otherwise they would have been on our list and we would have brought more lethal forces to manage it properly." I shake my head. "No, I think it's better for us to be well prepared for our return."

Her face drowns in sadness as she nods. "I understand, but whatever it was . . . nearly killed him. Whatever caused that wound . . ." Her chest lets out a shuddered breath, and she turns to me, glassy-eyed. "Tiamet, he—he could have died from that injury if he had kept bleeding like that. Can we really risk taking something like that home with us?"

I place a hand on her shoulder. "If we release all the air, it won't be alive when we get home."

"But can you be sure?"

"We'll take precautions when opening the capsule. We can't risk not knowing what we're up against when we return. We can't allow our entire species to perish on a 'what if.'"

She sniffles and nods. "Yes, you're right. We should get to sleep too. I'll get cleaned up."

I pat her shoulder, trying to offer some reassurance before leaving the room to depressurize the capsule.

Ayathesti - 57

I squint as light shines through the lid of my pod, and the gelatin fog around me evaporates. The clear lid opens and speeds the process, draining the fluid portion by my feet. Disoriented after releasing myself, I stumble around before making my way to the large door across the room.

It slides open, and I'm surprised when there is no one on the other side. Half hoping the door will open to that little blue planet in the darkness, I'm instead greeted by the stone walls of the KRUL. We are home.

My eyes well up with relief as I walk closer to the window, as though years of stress are floating from my shoulders.

"There you are!" Nineveh says, emerging from the pod room. "One moment you were there, and the next you disappeared! Come, sit. I need to check your vitals. Otherwise you can't go home alone tonight."

It feels good to sit. Though the gravity of Earth is greater than ours, and I had built up a nice muscle tone, the trip back left my body achy and weak once more. Nineveh places a mechanized cuff over my arm. After it beeps, she pulls out a tablet and hovers it over my face before dragging it down my body. With a nod and a smile, she clicks it off.

"You appear to be fine. But, Aya, call me *immediately* if you feel unwell." She squeezes my shoulder gently. "Promise me." Her tone matches that of a scolding mother.

I nod and chuckle. "I promise, Nineveh. You'll be the first one I call."

"Good! Now, let's get out of here, shall we?" I take the

hand she offers.

We pass through the pod room and stop at a small door. As it opens, she holds her hand up for me to enter first. After stepping into the room, the door slides closed. A dark purple light flickers on the same time a white mist seeps from nozzles lining the side walls from top to bottom. The mist is thick and trickles in through my suit, leaving static on my skin. *I don't know if I'll ever get used to this process.* The thickness of the fog is suffocating even though the clean room to the labs is similar. The lights dim as the fog disappears through a grate in the floor, and the door in front of me crawls open.

I'm greeted by the towering walls of the work deck, along with echoes of cheers and applause from the crowd gathered inside. The only thing keeping me from panicking is seeing those walls soaring into the high ceiling above me. I cringe at the ear-shattering volume of the group, which leaves my ears ringing.

I step down, attempting to disappear into the mass of people. *How could I forget how overwhelming so many people in one place is?*

Looking around, I quickly find an escape and maneuver my way through every gap I can find until I reach a door. I burst into the lobby, the loud voices safely closed in the room behind me. *It's surreal to be here again.* I glide over the dark floors and look at the high ceilings and smooth walls. Habit is already guiding my feet toward the entrance, where I'm determined to leave unnoticed. *Just like that, I'm back to my old self, counting down the steps till I'm outside and away from possible conversation.*

"Aya!"

I stop as though my shoes have melted into the floor. I turn and see Tiamet running across the lobby.

"Oh, good, it's you." I let out my breath when he gets

closer.

"Where are you going?"

"Home."

"Ahh. We're all going to the Zeyo to celebrate. You're not coming with us?"

"I never received that invitation. I just woke up, and then there were like three million people and loud noises and . . . I had to flee." My gaze meets his with a shy smile.

He chuckles, looking over his shoulder to the work deck. "Well?"

I bite my lower lip. "Well, what?"

"Will you join us?"

I look over at the setting sun. *It's so easy to fall back into my old habits of being isolated and alone, of avoiding uncomfortable situations.* "Well, I'm kind of tired . . ."

"Give me a break," he says, shaking his head.

"What?"

He rubs the back of his neck nervously. "You should come." He smiles.

"I don't know if I want to . . ." I drop my gaze in embarrassment.

"Well, I'd like for you to be there." He steps closer. "And I think there are some things we should talk about. You know, clear the air a little?" I look back at him before peering around his shoulder at the groups of people gathering. "Are you afraid?" he asks.

"Afraid?" I roll my eyes. "Please."

"Your hesitation is reassuring . . ." He sighs, sarcasm lingering on his breath. "If you really don't want to go . . ."

"I . . ." I look at my hands, picking at my fingernails.

He stands there in silence, taking my hands in his. It stops my nervous fidgeting, but his waiting eyes don't help calm the rest of me.

"I'm sorry," I finally say.

"You're going to make me kidnap you . . . aren't you?"

A smile touches the corners of my lips. "No, I just—"

"It's okay," he cuts me off, shaking his head. "I get it. Social status and everything."

Avoiding eye contact, I speak in a hushed and soft voice. "Tiamet, it's not like that."

He drops my hands before stuffing his own into his pockets, shrugging nonchalantly. "Yeah, I understand. Don't worry about it." He turns away and walks toward the large group of people getting ready to leave.

"Rain check?" I say as I watch him walk away.

He turns to look back at me, his eyes drowning in sadness. "I'll just see ya around?"

I nod slowly before turning to leave. "I wish I could show you what it feels like to be me." I speak so softly only I could possibly hear the words.

A surge of regret washes over me as I stand at the top of the steps outside the building. The low hue of purple city lights flicker into existence on the horizon. As the cool breeze dances around me, I stand strong, feeling a newfound sense of hope for the planet and our people.

I stare at the ground at the bottom of the steps. Once more, I can't help but feel this is just the beginning. *I have put so much time and effort into my journey so far, yet moments like this leave me empty. It's as though I've made no progress at all.* I look over my shoulder, through the glass, and hesitate with a new set of inner conflicts. I close my eyes and let out a deep breath before shifting my weight.

To take that first step back on home soil . . . alone . . . am I ready for that? That first step will, once again, mark the beginning of a long journey—short lived life for many, but an eternity for our future. I turn and walk back into the building.

Tiamet is still standing in the lobby when he looks

over his shoulder at me. His eyes beam when they meet mine. *If I'm going to start this new adventure, I don't want to be taking that first step alone.*

Melody Kepler is an Architectural Drafter by day, Mom by evening, and writer by night. After seven years of working on the same project, she's ready to debut with Extension.

As someone who enjoys learning about new things, one consistent area of interest is psychology. This has helped her create dynamic characters in her writing and aides in their authenticity. Creativity is a motivator, and Mel expresses this in more than just writing—she enjoys sketching portraits from still images.

Also, being one of an analytical mind, she is taking control of the college education reins and working toward acquiring her Landscape Architecture degree. The goal she has in mind for this is urban planning. With it, she hopes to bring more nature and flow into the every day lives of those within the community.

Suffering from work-related anxiety makes life difficult, but what if your job involved a mission to rescue your entire world from extinction? Meet Ayathesti—compassionate, perfectionist, loner—the geneticist undergoing this stressful plight.

With planet Naratu dying, the only thing keeping the Mujai people from extinction is aerosolizing gold into the atmosphere. The Council has identified a planet abundant in the metal and has selected a team to gather preliminary information. Ayathesti accompanies the team on the eighty-seven-year flight. Her task? To isolate and collect DNA from an indigenous species to gene splice with their own. To create a hybrid species. The purpose? To establish a localized colony to supply gold as needed. But having a compassionate heart leaves Ayathesti with an inner conflict: show mercy and prevent the enslavement of a new species or ensure her people's survival?

Things grow even more complicated with Tiamet as mission leader. His intelligence, confidence, and drive are exactly what make him perfect for the position. But they are also why he's a perfect distraction for Ayathesti. Being in charge has challenges of its own, including making sure everyone is moving toward the same goal. And keeping up with changes as they arise has him juggling priorities. Given his history with Ayathesti, he's confident he can get her on board to do her part.

If Naratu is to survive, they both need to fill the demands of their roles. While Ayathesti wrestles with her sense of right and wrong, Tiamet faces the pressure of leading a successful mission, and both struggle to fight the pull drawing them together. Will Ayathesti compromise her morals and go through with her duties? Can Tiamet stay focused and return everyone home safely? Will there be enough time on the brief visit of this foreign land—a planet they call Earth?

www.ingramcontent.com/pod-product-compliance
Lightning Source LLC
Chambersburg PA
CBHW020241030826
48979CB00030B/2404/J

* 9 7 8 1 7 3 4 7 1 3 0 2 2 *